THE QUICKSANDS

By Jude Njoku

New and urgent creative voices are being heard from Africa these days, and Jude Njoku proves to be a lusty member of the chorus. He unfolds his story against a richly varied background of violence and tenderness, love and hatred, passion and remorse. What this intricate story demonstrates in full measure is the subtlety of African culture and the confidence Africans have developed in their heritage. There is no longer any need to take guidance from western values now that the sleeping wisdom of Africa has been reawakened. African fiction is by far the most powerful medium in which to reveal this reawakening to the rest of the world, and Jude Njoku deserves to join the ranks of African writers who are being heard beyond the boundaries of their homelands. African literature is taking the place of African political theory, a sure sign of cultural rebirth. This author has demonstrated that he is part of this vital renaissance.

Robin Saikia
UK

Jude Njoku in his novel entitled 'The Quick Sands', recognizes his obligation to his society and wants to participate in the task of re-education. He creates a sensation of the life of the society and as such forms part of the total cultural recreation of the society. He is in the formulation of the social cultural philosophy and values of the society which he casts in the most effective and convincing form that he can command. The author helps to establish values and often assists a generality of people in making a single choice from the many choices open to them. His quest has been to find in the aspiration of his contemporary society new ways of reaching understanding in the light of traditional values as they are confronted with the impact of modern ideas. Njoku offers a vision of life which is essentially tragic, compounded of success and failure, informed by knowledge and understanding relieved by humour and tempered by sympathy, imbued with awareness of human suffering and the human capacity to endure. I strongly recommend 'The Quick Sands' for wider society.

Ajaelu V.A (Mrs.)
Nigeria

Jude Njoku, combined historic experience and romantic creation to give his themes the polishing they require to fascinate his audience. The book is stimulating and rewarding to those who have read it. I recommend it for use in schools and colleges.

Ohanu F.O
(Senior English Master)
Holy Ghost College,
Owerri, Nigeria.

THERE WERE CRIES AND MOANINGS; SNIFFING AND GNASHING OF TEETH.

Eringa's eyes were open and unblinking.
Blood gushed out her open mouth. The other half lay some metres away. The forests and farms had been turned into slaughter houses.

As a mother you should have educated your daughter on the process of growing up as soon as you noticed she had reached puberty.

Superintendent Yusuf shook his head.
The mystery was getting deeper. Lizzy certainly has more skeletons in her cupboard. The DPO was worried. He thought he had all the cards. But the mortuary scene revealed that Lizzy still held the joker.

All rights reserved. The text of this publication or any part thereof may not be reproduced or transmitted in any form or by any means, electronic or mechanical, including photocopying, recording, storage in an information retrieval system, or otherwise, without the written permission of the publisher.

Published in Nigeria 2005
By
New Generation Publishers,
13, Akinyele Street,
Aguda, Surulere,
Lagos – Nigeria.
ISBN: 978-978-37207-0-1
Tel: 234-1-8034094666
E-mail:newgeninworld@yahoo.com

DEDICATION

I DEDICATE THIS BOOK TO ALL PARENTS, ESPECIALLY WOMEN AND MOTHERS WHO REGARD THE SOUND UPBRINGING OF CHILDREN AS THE VERY ROOTS OF A DECENT SOCIETY.

ACKNOWLEDGEMENT

I remember and cherish memories of my late father, Mr. Herbert Njoku. I also acknowledge the invaluable contribution from my mother, Mrs. Christiana Njoku. I hereby acknowledge the wise counsel of Mrs. Mary Theresa Mbanulusi who always came to my rescue when all hope appeared dim on the crystallisation of this book. I must not forget to mention the innumerable array of my benevolent benefactors who always ensured with pleasant smiles that my baskets of needs were always filled to the brim.

I cannot forget my editor Mr. Ifemesia Iferenta whose literary imputs were always frank, free and fruitful.

Chika Onukwufor tremendously assisted towards the making of this book. He spent sleepless nights to ensure that The Quick Sands sees the light of the day.

Most importantly, I owe my greatest gratitude to God Almighty for the inspiration.

PREFATORY NOTE

The metallic din that emanated from the hovel of an eccentric blacksmith seemed to steadily magnify with resounding intensity in my ears. I had read "The Quick Sands" with an air of detachment and a feeling of the ever-pervading adventurous arena that hosted a civil uprising in the sixties.

As I progressed, the thick film that tainted my belligerent eyes gradually dissolved and assumed a more discernable negative. Soon the negative metamorphosed into a beautiful and highly blooming spectacle of reality. I was actually reading a work of art; a fictional feat and I could not wait to see its demise. Having completed this self-imposed assignment, I heaved a sign of relief, or rather of satisfaction, and then proceeded to do this little write up. This task I eventually undertook as a debtor's obligation.

If you want a candid answer, I would not hesitate to surmise that "The Quick Sands" is a moral tale, which carries with it, motley characters whose professional inclination keeps rocking them like a tempest. As they floated, glided and sank, their fate hung on the balance. Their innards churned and ached. Justice was staring and waiting to be met while nemesis stood still ready to strike.

One may say that Jude Njoku's story is devoid of a plot in an obsolete conventional literary sense. This paradoxical assumption can aptly be likened to the seeds of the sower that fell among thorns hence were choked to death. Indeed the environment within which the characters find themselves provides the plot in the novel. This discovery was a self-actualisation and provided the fuel that held on to my automotive mind until I finally grounded to a halt in my literary journey.

The ululations that often herald the emergence of a new life is not forgotten in "The Quick Sands", despite the lurking adversities. The conventional seed of child upbringing, which discourages the maxim of sparing the rod and spoiling the child, is not allowed to sprout.

Experience is given a free rein as the participants find themselves savouring in their various environmental pools. Yes, there is the pastoral tinge of the rural as humanity fled amidst an impending holocaust. There is also the siege within the urban setting as the same humanity flee for their dear lives. Humorously, however, some of these flights were cowardly for the sophisticated crowd cannot defend themselves from the ravages of mere female lunatics. These cowardly acts however assume a rather significant stance in the novel for one creates a reunion and generates the major conflict on which "The Quick Sands" thrives. This is the incidental meeting between Lizzy and Oguaa.

As soon as any young girl attains puberty, her mind is fraught with multiple ideas. She basks in the glory of womanhood and floats within a whirlpool of fantasies, illusions, dreams and realities. Marriage becomes an obsession and with good breeding and luck, she may achieve her ultimate desire. With "The Quick Sands", the environment conspires to make such lofty marital ideals an utopia. Oguaa, is caught in a quagmire of the fast lanes of city life, hence her existence becomes precarious and tragic. The supportive casts of friends, foes, neighbours with sometimes good intentions invariably lend credence to Oguaa's 'Seeming' revolt.

Before the advent of "The Quick Sands", the agrarian policy has undergone drastic changes. The extended family system is slowly disintegrating since it has been decapitated by the death of its commander-in-chief, old Pa Anselem.

Dotun, Jimmy, Lizzy, Nnenna, Majek are already numbed by the craze for sophistication and the trauma of the inordinate ambition to get rich quick. If this pronouncement is a truism, have our actors in "The Quick Sands" been found guilty?

Read this small book as a parable, and you will discover man's bestiality towards his fellow man! Read "The Quick Sands" and discover how the divine power of providence stretches out its invisible hands of rescue!

Chika C. Onukwufor

AUTHOR'S NOTE

Dear Reader,

The idea of writing books came to me as an inspiration. I remember one night, as I was holding communion with myself a voice spoke saying, "You can write."

I experienced and saw the fortunes of the Nigerian Civil war as a little boy. The war planes which hovered and unleashed their deadly arsenal seemed to me like kites and hawks. Through the eye of an adult I then saw the attendant forces that accompany the inevitable quest for survival in the city. The seamy side of life was vivid. The attainment of affluence, which characterized the privileged minority, looked unattainable.

"The Quick Sands" is the blend of my two eyes - the eye of childhood, which accounts for the youthful experiences explored in this little book - mainly acts as a springboard for my adult eye to leap from. The blend of my eyes has been simplistically orchestrated to prove a point. Our world is a cipher. We can only change if we understand the circumstances surrounding our existence.

Oguaa's story is a living testimony. Her precarious world is a moral tale. Her gullible character is an enigma and the intricate web woven around her can be any individual's potential stigma; a social vice, which all mankind should fight and destroy.

JUDE NJOKU

ANYAMBA

I can recall vividly the state of panic that engulfed the entire staff of the Community Bakery at Obubra. I do remember the waves of uncertainties that hung menacingly like the dangling sword of Damocles over our heads. There was a pervasive feeling of hope that this imminent danger would pass. However the danger rather assumed a garb of frightening reality. In offices, there was mass resignation. Most people had sent their baggage and families home.

Mary was reluctant to leave. We had just been married for one year and she was in the early stages of her first pregnancy. My uncle Anselem had written series of letters asking that I resign my appointment with the Bakery and return home with my wife. I could not comply with my uncle's demands for Mary has responded unfavourably to the charged atmosphere. She had suffered a miscarriage and was just recuperating.

Eringa, my uncle's second wife had entrusted her two sons Nneji and Udoka to Nwayieze and arrived Obubra to find out why I had refused to return in spite of the prevailing uncanny atmosphere. However after much persuasion, pleading and heart-rendering cries and appeals, I let Mary pick a few of our belongings and accompany Eringa back to Umuayalu.

Mary's departure created a vacuum in my existence. My mind was now a reeling pool of blankness as it shuttled between fantasy, delusion and the terrifying realities I daily observed from my office window at the Bakery site at Obubra.

The sun blazed down on the scurrying mortals, most of whom were either dead, or pining away in agony. The cloud was playing a romancing game of hide and seek within the furious glare of the sun. When scorched by such fierce smiles, the cloud would scuttle away, becoming tiny fleeing fingers pointing accusingly at the unfriendly sun.

The thought of my sister Nnenna and her husband Uko crossed my mind. They should be safe in Lagos but I would rather wish they returned home.

I could hardly taste a morsel after my wife left in company of Eringa. For me the world was now fraught with difficulties.

I will travel home. Yes, tomorrow I must leave Obubra and its Bakery for a short visit to Umuayalu.

1

It was about 4 O'clock in the morning. The harmattan wind was heavy in the air. The thick grey cloud blanketed the atmosphere making visibility almost impossible. The cold was so biting that the heavy woollen army blanket reminiscent of the Hitler war, could not prevent the sharp cutting edges of the cold from having their toll on Anselem. The crickets could not sing their noctural hymns. The few middle-aged men who had earlier defied the sharp eyes of the conscriptors could not venture outside for fear of the chilling cold. The amorous nuptial flights to the hovels of women who had either been widowed by the civil war, or become grass windows due to the long absence of their husbands, were halted.

Mary had several worries. Her husband had been forced to join other able-bodied men in the war in defence of their fatherland. Is he alive or is he dead? Mary did not know and could not tell. In addition she had suddenly been woken up by contractions which kept recurring every eighteen minutes or so. These contractions which lasted for some seconds each time affected her backside. She did not know what it was all about so she kept pondering over many possibilities as the contractions moved from one side of her abdomen to the other.

She was startled when Anselem banged three consecutive times on her wooden door. The old man's banging coincided with the distant din of cannon fire. Mary's heart had an instant jump. She quickly tied her loose wrapper firmly across her round and firm breasts and frantically searched in the dark for her headtie. She felt under the pillow. Again she ran her fingers on a six-foot rope, which extended from one wall to the other. Each end of the rope had been knotted at the head of a six-inch nail stuck to the wall of the house. On this long rope she hung old clothings. On it also she temporarily hung new dresses worn on social occasions. Such dresses are usually withdrawn, stretched with her bare hand and neatly stacked into a large portmanteau box.

After more groping, she felt the faded headtie, retrieved it from the line, and tied it securely round her waist, more to hold the wrapper than for anything else.

Anselem cleared his voice and asked.

"Is somebody sleeping in this house?"

She did not dare ask who it was because Anselem's voice was familiar, clear and loud.

"My daughter", he said, "don't be carried by fear. It's your father asking to have a word with you over.."

Before he could finish Mary had drawn the latch to the right of the wooden door which had no padlock. She could not fathom why the old man had woken her up at that unholy hour of the night.

Suddenly the second cockcrow was heard in the villages around. As soon as one cock crew the others took up the refrain and chorused from their owner's huts. The sharp piercing shrill of the cocks drowned the 'boom' of the cannon fire in the distance.

"Good morning Papa", she said trying to genuflect. Mary had learnt to call Anselem Papa, the way she addressed her father, as a mark of respect.

"My daughter, our people say that a toad does not run in broad daylight for nothing. Either it is after something or something is after its life". As he spoke the darkness shielded his shrivelled face, but Mary could discern the position of his mouth.

"The 'dum' of the large gun is like the noice of the locomotive train. No one hears it on behalf of the other. It's not a question of what we shall do. It's a question of courage. We shall leave our home-steads before daylight announces its presence. No matter your state of well being, we shall not leave you behind. To be fore-warned is to be fore-armed".

Before Mary could mutter a few words, Anselem struck the carved walking stick with which he had been supporting his grey moustache and wrinkled face and rose to go. Mary did not know whether it was the awe of the old man or the thought of the foreboding conveyed by his words that caused her an instant loss of speech.

Anselem had come to play multifarious roles in the village especially during this period of uncertainty. As the oldest man in Umuayalu, he had become the repository of the people's love and history. Through his three wives he had become the provider for the motherless children in the village. He had helped restrain many young men who were bent on thrashing their refractory spouses. Many young men have also sought his advice on varied issues ranging from matrimony to farming. He seldom visited people. Rather people carried their problems to his hut. So when he knocked on Mary's door, she received it with mixed feelings. The old man did not just visit her. His visit portends danger. What would she do?

As soon as Anselem left Mary's doorpost, she knew that she had to act fast. She rummaged under her bed to locate a large coloured basin which was one of the items of dowry provided her by her parents. Before now she had only used it to store tits and bits. It could only come handy when one thought of bathing a baby. All the same she drew it out of its quiet corner and emptied its contents on the bare floor. She began to fold some of her wrappers and place them one after the other into basin.

Her contractions continued and seemed to spread over her whole body. She stopped her packing to adjust the wrapper she had tied when Anselem first came into her hut.

Another knock, this time gentle on her door, disrupted the trend of her thought. However she was bold enough to grope blindly for the box of matches she kept just under her pillow. She found and struck it the first time. It caught fire. She made an arc over the flame and her left hand and lit the hurricane lamp which stood near her bed.

"Mary", Eringa called as soon as she noticed the light rays piercing through the crack in the door panel.

"Who's calling?" she answered.

"It's Eringa. How was the night?"

"Good morning, ma. Thank you," Mary said.

"How are the children, Nneji, Udoka and Martina?"

"They are alright, but they are still sleeping," answered Eringa with a wry smile on her face.

She looked through Mary as if measuring the extent of her well being. Then she ran her eyes through the dimly lit room. She sighed and instinctively sat on the lowly wooden bench. She noticed a twitch of fear in Mary's face.

"Our husband said that he came to you about an hour earlier," she said more of a statement than a question.

"Yes, Papa did".

"And he revealed to you the unspoken fear in the minds of other villagers".

"It's true. Since then I have managed to pack a few things. What should I include? Can you imagine packing one's whole belonging into a basin! It's incredible."

"Yes, it is," Eringa consoled. "But what can we do? We have heard stories of refugees abandoning their homes without any form of preparation".

"But, but what can I do without my man around and with this load?" She pointed at her bulging abdomen as she said it.

"I have been having movements and kicks inside me. I can't say what is happening. Mama Martina, I'm just confused. Where are we running to? How long can we leave our homes to sojourn elsewhere? What food can last for a week, or a month?"

As she asked these questions partly to Eringa and partly to herself, the story her paternal uncle told them about a year ago became vivid in her mind. Paulinus, for that was her uncle's name, lived and worked in Enugu for several years before the coal city was overrun by the vandals. It was a hot afternoon. Shelling and mortar fires were everywhere in the northeastern part of the town. But the city dwellers thought it was not real. Some of them had hoped that the vandals would not penetrate the rough terrain of the rocky city surrounded by hills. But they were mistaken. Christopher, a chief clerk in one of the parastatal had sweated as he ran from the office at the secretariat to his house in Ogui.

He pushed his key into the key hole and turned the door knob. Before he could wipe the sweat from his brow, bullets landed on the roof top of his house like a bolt from the blue. He searched his house for what to pick and run for his dear life. He detached his radiogram from the plug adaptor on the wall, found it heavy and dropped it. He then lifted his 18 inch black and white television set. Again he found it heavy and dropped. Christopher opened his large metallic box. That was also too heavy to lift. He felt his pockets for money. He did not have much because he had planned going to the bank the next day. Indecision and another array of bullets hit the outside walls of the house, made holes, but could not penetrate. Soon he heard groans in the distance. The steel song of machine guns was near. In a hurry he was able to retrieve a bundle of broom as the only possession with which he left Enugu that hot afternoon.

Eringa left after patting Mary on the head and body as gently as a mother caressing her baby.

Eringa is the second wife of Anselem. Of the three wives of the sage, she is the only one who asks regularly after Mary. Her care for Mary had intensified since the latter started undergoing metamorphosis. Not that the other women did not care. But Eringa was exceptional, perhaps because she came from Ogugu the same town as Mary. She also had a lot of regard for Anyamba's intelligence as a young boy.

When the first daylight struck, the entire community of Umuayalu had been deserted. Grey-haired men, women and children poured out of their huts to the bush path. It was as if a whistle had been blown to start a race. The women carried their basins and baskets on their heads. Some of them securely strapped sucklings to their backs. Most of them had loosened their hair removing the plaits to enable them balance their loads securely. They had carried household effects and foodstuffs. Some tied two or three wrappers around their waists to economize space in the basins and baskets. The children carried their school boxes and bags stuffed with few dresses. Some boys led goats and sheep along while the women also carried livestock.

At first they wore heavy sullen faces. The harmattan was severe. The cold wind blew and raised dust which poured on their faces. Some quickly turned round and used their backside to receive the millions of sand grains. Others with heavier loads accepted their fate and allowed the sand to splash into their eyes and nostrils.

Anselem was trailing the group of his extended family. He was initially reluctant to embark on this exodus. The untold hardship, the suffering and the disruption of social bonds were too much for his greying hair. The demolition of carefully constructed values and concepts attendant on the war had battered his belief in humanity. Occasionally he muttered a few words only meaningful to his mind. The picture of events since the crisis began became vivid. To him, man has become a victim of a force unleashed by himself and now rampaging freely while others watched in helpless despair. An angel of death now wrecks carnage on a people but there is no commanding voice to cry "Hold! Enough".

He has seen wars but the magnitude of this destruction, of this indiscriminate slaughter and the general breakdown of sanity were beyond his imagination. His trend of thoughts was interrupted by three consecutive 'dum' 'dum' of cannon fire. This time the vibration was shattering to the young and feeble. They quickened their steps.

"Papa, take it easy," encouraged one of his grown-up daughters, Agnes. She was groaning under the weight of her own load but she mustered enough vigour to prop up the old man.

"Thank you, Agnes, I can see that your load is beginning to weigh you down. Difficulty is a test of maturity."

Mary had her own load resting on a pad formed from two of her wrappers folded into a concentric circle. It was soft. Although she had put in a few things in her basin, the weight of the load seemed to increase as more fluidish trickle travelled unsteadily down her right leg. She unconsciously stopped to allow it fall on the ground. She then continued her journey though she was now slipping backwards, walking at the same pace with the younger children.

"Chei, I've forgotten my catapault", said Udoka as a tiny bird chirruped past him. I must run back for it".

"Run back to the village? Do you know how much distance we have covered? You must be mad to think of running back home", Nneji said.

"But I left it on top of my mud bed. It won't take me time to collect. I shall be fast," he said trying to…

"If mama hears this she will flog you. I'm not waiting for anyone".

"Please, Ndaa, just stand on the path while I run home. Afterall, we haven't travelled far".

"This boy wants to die… Don't you hear the noise of the guns? By the time you come back we would have passed the next village".

"Yes, but I can still meet her. I can walk faster than her," he said pointing at Mary with his protruding mouth.

"Do you think you'll walk faster if you are carrying her load? Udo, there's nothing your sharp mouth can't say. She could hear you and report to Mama."

"If she reports me to Mama, I'll no longer run errands for her. Look at her walking like a girl with shit in her anus. I must go for my catapault. There'll be many birds to kill".

But Udoka could not carry out his threat.

* * * * * * * *

Eringa was slightly unnerved when she noticed that Mary was no longer keeping pace with the rest. Soon, the convoy reached a small body of water. The bush around it was greener and leafy unlike the shrivelled grasses and trees they had passed along the bush paths.

The women teased one another while the children chatted and joked.

Everyone seemed to have slowed down around the brook

ostensibly to drink water, but actually to rest after trekking for over several hours. The unmistakable 'dum' 'dum' of the guns accompanied by bursting grenades abruptly silenced them. This time the deadly music was preceded by the more aggressive and deadly solo of "Kwapu" resulting into what the refugees regarded as an urgent message to flee – "Kwapu, Kwapu unu dum" – meaning "pack out and flee, all of you."

The joyous voices of the children quietened and the whole forest became a graveyard. Even the domestic animals seemed to have caught this message of death and destruction. The intermittment bleating and crowing were momentarily withheld.

Their struggles as refugees had just begun. The faces of the children were dotted with scratches inflicted by dried twigs. Their abdomen were drawn in and famished and this was accentuated by the fact that they had not breakfasted. The children yawned regularly, their unspoken language told a lot. They were hungry and tired.

Suddenly a kite fluttered above the air. The children's eyes followed it as it swirled round and threw its gaze on the seated company. Perhaps it was a regular visitor to the water where it preyed on smaller birds. Or perhaps it had seen the chickens which had squeaked and propped up their heads from the baskets shielding them.

Then, as if propelled by the keen interest of its spectators, the bird began to fly faster. It released droppings on Eringa's basin. They merely fell on the wrapper with which she covered her own basin.

As soon as she noticed it she cursed. "If it's a bad omen may it follow you the kite."

As if it heard the curse on its head, the kite flapped it wings steered backwards and quickly coursed its way skywards.

Eringa quickly picked up two dried leaves from the ground. She held each in one hand, brought their margins together and scooping up the droopings, she threw them away together with the leaves. She looked carefully to find out if it was entirely cleared off. Not satisfied with her first attempt, she picked another dried leaf, bent it into two and scrubbed the spot clear. After that she drew near Mary and said: "I was worried when I saw you trailing with the children."

"Well I can still manage to walk some distance but the pain is burning at my heart region and at my loins."

"Sorry, Mary, bear it like an adult. I shall now keep by your side as we walk along".

While they rested, the women broke slice of yam and cocoyam into smaller slices and distributed to the children.

The latter touched each slice on the red palm oil placed in an enamel bowl and ate them with relish oblivious of the dangers ahead.

"You have soaked too much of the red oil", complained Martina to Udoka.

"No, I only took a little to cover the thin slice of my cocoyam".

"It's not true, look at it, the oil is already finished." She slanted the enamel bow to buttress her accusation.

"Can you two not eat without quarrelling? They don't even realise that this place isn't home".

"Mama leave them alone. They are merely trying to be noisesome. I'm eating my own slices without even using red oil", stated their brother Nneji as he widened his large eyes to frighten Martina into silence.

"Okay, okay, Marti, eat, I'll give another oil if that one finishes. But Udoka, be careful before I flog the daylight out of your eyes", warned Anselem.

Other children prattled in their own familiar way as they ate their food. The food was not tasty since little or no salt was added to the yam or the red oil. Such things as salt and sugar had become exotic that people worried not about them any longer.

After the breakfast during which the adults ate little, the party hurried to their feet and started another round of the journey. It was a journey whose end no one knew. It seemed they were only running away from the 'dum dum'.

A few kilometers to Ezeukwu, they met another large group of aged men, women and children who were going in the same direction. Their own villages were also under siege like Umuayalu. They passed bunkers built by the people to conceal themselves from the menacing air raids. They saw more bunkers carefully camouflaged to protect their owners from the ravages of the incessant air raids which had claimed untold number of lives.

After a few more hours of laborious trekking, the wearied travellers came to another brook right inside the forest. They decided camping there for the night. Anselem and a few other old men threw their long walking sticks aside and spread themselves on the bare forest floor. The luxuriant giant trees whose leaves had refused to yield to the ravages of the dry harmattan wind, gave good cover to the refugees.

At least they felt covered from the eagle-eyes of the deadly hawks. The latter had always left wailings and groanings of wreckages and mass death on their trail any time they flew across these areas to empty their entrails.

The men conversed on such topics as the fertility of soil in virgin forests; the possible effects of harmattan on next year's cropping. They were however afraid to mention the carnage of the war. The war itself was like an albatross tied round their necks.

Soon Mary shouted. Her screams attracted Eringa who tried in vain to cover her mouth.

She was afraid of the outcome of such loud noise. She offered a few encouraging words and patted Mary on the back. Simultaneously Mary felt some fluid exude between her thighs.

Calling her husband's third wife, Adaugo to the scene, Eringa instructed her to sweep a portion of the ground. Mary's basin was taken to the spot and a few wrappers retrieved from the lot. The women cut a few sticks and pinned them to the ground forming a circle. With the cloths they covered the space from the preying eyes of the men and children.

Mary herself did not really understand what was happening to her – the contractions, the mucus-like trickle and the fluid – she assumed that they resulted from the strain of the long trek. The women made the enclosure as comfortable as they could, but no one was interested in comfort. Babies had been born in more precarious settings. Eringa worked tirelessly and strained every nerve to ensure the safe delivery of the baby. About six O'clock that evening, the women yelled with joy in spite of the obvious danger facing them. At least nightfall was usually after broad daylight. Soon Eringa was carrying a baby girl wrapped in a clean piece of cloth. She showed it to Anselem. The other women could not control their ecstasy.

Singing their songs in mumbled tones, they danced in circles and offered praises to God:

"God who gives children, has given us another,
"God who gives children, has given us another,
"We thank Him, we thank Him."

The children joined the women, clapping their hands to the rhythm of the songs, and swaying their famished buttocks. For once smiles played on the faces of the young and the old as they defied the harmattan cold. Mary called its name "Oguaa" meaning "This War".

That night, nudged by the cold wind and weakened by the journey through the forest, the people slept like logs of wood. Before the third cock crow they were suddenly awakened by the deadly 'dum dum' of cannon fire.

They frantically gathered their things and headed for

Uzoagba. Mary clutched her baby tenderly to her breast. She felt the joy of motherhood as she wrapped the baby with a long piece of cloth and made a small opening to enable it breathe.

Eringa took pride in herself for delivering Mary of her baby. She kept a constant watch on the baby and her mother and even added Mary's load to hers. As long as the convoy was moving, she paid less attention to her own children and more to Mary.

The children chatted and pulled at one another. Martina rehearsed the birth song of the evening but she mixed the lines.

"Look at you, you can't sing a simple song", jeered Udoka.

"Does it concern you," Martina querried.

"It doesn't. If you can't sing a simple song why don't you shut your dirty mouth."

"Don't trouble that girl", roared Nneji. "Leave her alone or …"

"I…. I didn't do anything to her."

"Udoka, Udoka, be careful before I strike you with my walking stick," warned Anselem.

There was instant silence. The early morning wind blew gently at first. Soon the speed increased and raised a few dry leaves and sand particles into the air as if propelled by a devilish force. Beckoned by the wind, two kites flew in the air and sniffed round and round. All of a sudden two mysterious hawks appeared in the sky while the two kites disappeared. Like angels of death, the hawks stormed the air dropping their lethal loads. The convoy scattered. People dived and threw their loads everywhere and anywhere. They took refuge under shrubs. But it seemed as if they were noticed by the hawks which also dived and startled the forest to comb their enemy's positions. They flew back into the air, refilled their bowels with death warrants, then came back again and pounded the whole forest. They had wrested the life out of many men, women and children.

There were cries and moanings; sniffing and gnashing of teeth. It took a long time before they could assemble to count their dead. The losses were many. Bleeding limbs severed from their owners littered the forest. Brains gushed open and a river of blood flowed. After regrouping they counted their number and found many people missing. Mary was located with her baby thrown beside her. She was speechless. The baby was picked up by one of the old men.

He unwrapped it and felt its pulse. It was still breathing. Mary was almost dead with fright.

A few metres away was one half of the body of Eringa. But Mary had not noticed the bleeding half. Eringa's eyes were wide open and unblinking. Blood gushed out of her open mouth. The other half lay some metres away. Soon the two halves were brought together and the young boys, helped by the old men, cleared a spot in the forest. With their machetes and hoes, they dug a few metres deep and dumped her lifeless body.

The forest and farms had been turned into slaughter houses. The towns had been reduced to nibble upon their human inhabitants, and like the forest, their walls were coated with the blood and brains of the men, women and children who inhabited them. Fear cast its shadows everywhere. The depths of suffering and the pit of anguish inflicted by the bombardment were indeterminate. It was an excruciating experience and for many years after, it was like a spear into the heart of Mary.

2

To Pa Anselem the weight of being distanced from his native village to the cold bitter environs of a refugee camp was devastating. He had never been outside his home for more than four days at a time since he was demobilised after the great war. Of course on each of those occasions he travelled out with great enthusiasm for he was never forced. Now he was outside his hut, nothing could be more painful for a man of his age. It was unthinkable that he could be forced out of his homestead in a rather humiliating manner.

Added to the sadness of moving out of the warmth and relative security of his hut, was the death of his second wife. The manner in which Eringa died was excruciating to his huge frame. It was like a man, the lord of his family, supposed to be its guardian, standing by and watching helplessly as a mysterious assailant struck and dismembered a member. He could and did not raise a hand of protection. He could not ask the assailant, "who are you?" What explanation would he give the offsprings of Eringa in future when they demand the circumstances surrounding their mother's death?

Since they camped at Uzoagba, life, if it could be so called had become dreary. His existence had become one of walking, dozing, biting refugee meals once or twice daily and shouting at the children whenever the buzing of planes was overheard. He started as if he foresaw an empty tomorrow.

He talked little. He had no one to unburden his heart to. Anyamba was away in the war-front. His brother Jim was still young to understand the family secrets, who owned or owed what, the extent of their farmland. These secrets must be bequeathed to the younger generation just in case. The thought of dying and being buried in Uzoagba a strange village, incapacitated him. God, may it not be! He did not die in the thickets of Burma. He was not buried in the swamps of Bulgaria during the great war. Why then would the idea strike him now?

He stretched his arms and noticed that they had become more shrivelled than he had known. From time to time he tried to remind himself of how it all began. He wished his life could be replayed to him for final editing.

"Papa, here's your food", said Agnes as she set Anselem's food before him. Her presence startled him as he awoke from his meditation.

The food was made from powdered oat meal distributed to the refugees by the local Red Cross. He had come to prefer this meal to others. Agnes had specialised in preparing it for her father. She made it in various ways to make it palatable to the old man's receding appetite. She would add vegetables and ground dried fish and stir them in boiling water until they changed colour. She then emptied a cupful of the powdered oat-meal, a little quantity at a time into the bowl. Other times she would grind small pieces of stockfish and add it to the boiling water before adding the oat-meal. Onion and pepper were added as spices. As soon as the oat-meal boiled, she carefully removed the aluminium pot from the fire.

She served it hot to her father for at that stage it was eaten with a spoon and needed little or no munching. Even toothless babies could take it. But if left longer, it would solidify and create problems for Anselem.

He was without appetite and no one could urge him to eat. If Eringa was alive, she would have cajoled the old man into eating what she cooked no matter the circumstances. She knew how to make Anselem taste her own dishes even if he did not want to eat.

Agnes watched her father from a distance as he struggled to eat. He had started to exhibit signs of weakness and dejection. She attributed it to the general uneasy atmosphere in the land. She made to go back and urge him on but just about that time, Anselem picked up his spoon from the wooden bench that served as a dining table.

He held it with the fingers of his left hand and ran his right thumb through its face to assure himself that it contained no dirt. He closed his eyes and made the sign of the cross before he casually scooped a spoonful and emptied it into his mouth. He scooped a second time. He swallowed it weakly. He had no appetite for the food. The food, like life itself, was losing meaning and appeal to him.

After a few more spoonfuls, he called out to Agnes to come and pick up the plate and its contents. She came as soon as she heard the call, collected the plate and cup and ran back to the shade that had become their abode. She placed it on the ground which had been covered with palm fronds to keep off dust. As if a whistle had been blown all the children descended on the plate to get a bite of its content.

Pa Anselem was not the only one whose disposition exposed the attendant consequences which the dual incidents of death and residing in a strange land engendered. Martina knew her late mother as a hard working and self-dependent woman who not only loved children but also extended this quality to others. The birth of Oguaa was a glaring case in point.

On arrival at the refugee camp at Uzoagba, Martina had felt like a fish that had been forcibly driven out of its aquatic environment. The thought of her junior brothers, Nneji and Udoka added more to her misery. They were boys but all the same they were young and needed some maternal protection which death had suddenly denied him.

"Marti why are you always staying by yourself?" Agnes her half sister had asked one day.

"There is nothing wrong with me Agnes."

"I know you miss your mother."

"That's life my sister," replied Martina.

"Cheer up. My mother has promised to take good care of you and your brothers".

Martina was a wily one. She knew that Agnes mother Nwayieze could not do much to solve her present predicament. As Pa Anselem's first wife, she had nothing to worry except taking care of her husband and her last child Agnes who was almost the same age with her.

However, while at Uzoagba, Martina made a lot of friends among their hosts and also among other refugees. Many sympathized with her especially when they learnt about the tragic circumstances surrounding the death of Martina's mother.

As a young woman growing into maturity, there was no doubt that many young men who resided at Uzoagba held some admiration for her. She knew the unpleasant consequences that could develop if she bluntly turned down their advances. She would definitely appreciate their compliments. Most of these men were home guards and they held the key to the survival of most people especially the poverty-stricken refugees. There were however, some other men who would rightly be referred to as loafers since they did nothing other than while away their time in idleness and took to flight each time they were alerted that there was a conscription drive by the men in uniform.

With her amiable and social disposition, Martina succeeded in joining one of the International Charitable Organisations that provided relief materials. This afforded her the opportunity to provide relief materials in form of clothing and food to the large extended family which her father Pa Anselem brought to Uzoagba.

Although, her father's wives Nwayieze and Adaugo appreciated Martina's gestures, the women regarded her daring attitude as highly overbearing. Occasionally, they made cynical remarks which would definitely leave any listener with the impression that the young girl was gradually treading on slippery grounds.

Martina, who knew about her stepmother's gossipy remarks ignored them or rather dismissed them as mere trifles. She knew her cause was a just one and her mission was not in any way permissive. She was not selling her body to sustain the family. She was primarily working very hard so that her two brothers who were now motherless did not suffer neglect and die of hunger.

Her daring attitude was further reinforced by her astute determination that her cousin Jim should not join the army. To her, Jim's presence in the refugee camp was a moral booster to the almost female herd at Uzoagba. Should he abandon the flock for the force, the family's grief would be highly intensified since there will be no adult male to assist the ageing Pa Anselem.

Unfortunately, the situation in the refugee camp deteriorated as many people, especially the children, daily became highly malnourished. There was an urgent need to save this deplorable situation and some of the charitable organisations came to the rescue. Martina soon became one of the guards who ensured that these unfortunate children were safely transported to an emergency air strip from where they were flown out of the war zones to some neighbouring countries. Her tight schedule eventually alienated her from her family at Uzoagba. She was later to know what happened to her cousin Jim and the rest of the family.

Mary's attention was wholly absorbed in the care of her baby, Oguaa. Except while the baby was in her usual bouts of sleep, Mary was often seen cuddling it. Its food constituted of breast milk and warm water. Mary often felt tired as she was left famished after bouts of sucking by her baby. Food was scarce and so she obtained little replacement from eating.

At night she clutched the baby closely by her side and woke up several times to breast feed and give it water. She replaced her wrapper or turned it the other side each time the baby defecated on it. At such times, it cried to indicate its discomfort. After each feeding she changed her sleeping position on the coarse mat softened by palm leaves laid below.

Her mind often wandered to her husband. Is Anyamba

alive? Is he wounded or hospitalised? Did he receive any shell shock? Has he lost his limbs? She would drive away her fears of Anyamba's death by singing faith-sustaining religious songs. She would endlessly debate in which of the three conditions Anyamba might be-hospitalized, shell shocked or dead. She often pushed death behind the back of her mind. Hospitalisation was better although it could also mean amputation or surgical operation. Such events were common and the pressure on the hospitals often caused them to attend to very serious cases first.

Shell shock could, as in most cases, impair some of the senses. She consoled herself with the belief that impairment was only temporary. At least the victim would be existing. It carried with it the added advantage that the victim could either be redeployed to the rear or demobilised. All the same, she did not know whether to prefer this or that.

Her mind wandered to Ogele, a soldier from Umuayalu who returned home from the war front with an untreated shell shock. No one knew accurately the circumstances surrounding his ailment. Everything remained a matter of conjecture.

One theory had it that the vandals pounded Ogele's location for several hours with mortar and artillery. Several of these landed near his trench, but did not kill him. At the end of the battle, he was seen spreadagled in his trench and picked up unconscious by his fellow combatants. Others say he was overwhelmed by the number of deaths and desertions of his soldiers that he pretended to have received a shell-shock to save his life.

He was said to be unusually unnerved by the thought of death, being the only boy in his family. In a society where lands owned by individuals and communities from time immemorial were forced out of their weak hands by their more powerful and wealthier neighbours, the fate of a family without a male offspring was sealed.

Whatever his case, Sergeant Ogele roamed the length and breadth of Umuayalu daily.

"Ogele, how are you?" a villager would ask.

"Em-em-em-em on the head", he would force himself to stammer.

"Ogele, are you still receiving some treatment?"

"La-la-la-la armour", and he would point at his head.

"Do you apply hot water and balm on the affected parts?" another villager would encourage him.

"My my-my-my mother", Ogele would reply always bringing down his head to signal the end of each answer to a question.

The villagers often wondered whether he would eventually regain his senses. His mother, Naomi, a woman of two daughters and one son, consoled herself with the fact that her son was still alive and walking about. At least he was not mad for he attacked no one in this daily tramping.

Well-built, handsome and 1.7 metres tall, Sergent Ogele was often the victim of conscriptors who regularly swooped on the villages to recruit reluctant men for the secessionist army. But he had to return home to his mother the same day or the next. It was often said that he was a brave soldier who led his platoon to numerous successful surprise attacks on enemy positions before he got the shock.

"What affected Ogele this much?" Since he came back to the village, Ogele had always worn his army uniform.

He often used sign language to narrate his exploits in

battles but most people did not understand him. Whether they understood him or not, the important thing was that he was alive and would not be dragged to the scene of battle again.

Mary preferred Anyamba to be like Ogele, rather than be dead or amputated. In fact in her prayers, she would go out of her way to ask God to return her husband to her deaf and dumb instead of allowing him to die.

Though they were married a few years before Anyamba was forced into the war, the warmth between them was deep-seated. She could not think of life without him.

*   *   *   *   *   *   *

On January 2, Corporal Anyamba struggled out of his trench after a nap at dawn. The previous night had witnessed another exchange of fire between the vandals and the secessionist troops along Isiukwuator sector of the war.

At exactly 1.30am the vandals opened fire, with shells and cluster bombs, to pummel the secessionists and dislodge their positions. Rockets launched from the air swooped on their positions and caused them to pull back from their trenches. The vandals shouted and booed as they pursued their enemies. The attack was a mere diversion, not meant for any advance in their positions. Sensing that, the secessionists launched a counter-attack, repulsed the move and regained their positions. After the ding-dong affair, both sides seemed satisfied with the discomfort caused the other. The guns were silenced and the soldiers went home to roost.

Anyamba suddenly saw himself in the arms of his mother. A face not distinct but resembling his father's smiled briefly at him. His mother clutched him tightly to her breasts. She moved briskly but her feet seemed clogged up with heavy beads. He opened his mouth but could not utter any audible sound. His gasp for breath resulted into his screaming. Like a bolt from the blue, Corporal Anyamba's uncle, Anselem emerged and shielded him from the ravenous embrace of an advancing dog. The dog, barking, bared its fangs and rushed for Anyamba's leg. Anselem quickly picked up a club and made for the dog. It reversed, and took to its heels.

Startled by the action of the dog, Anyamba battled to free himself from his mother's firm but tender embrace. His struggle brought him to reality as his elbows hit the barrel of the rifle he had placed between his legs while he slept. He woke up to notice beads of perspiration around his neck and forehead. He was afraid. He took several seconds to recognise that he was still in his trench. It was a frightening dream. When he regained his consciousness, Corporal Anyamba's first resolve was to obtain a pass to go home. The dream had unsettled him; he must meet the adjutant for a four-day pass to enable him travel home to see his wife especially.

"Morning sir", Corporal Anyamba saluted Captain Nwokocha of the 31 Infantry Battalion stationed at Nkpo/Isiukwuato axis.

"Yes, Corporal, how was last night?"

"No problem sir. Vandals routed".

"Good, Corporal. Any wounded?"

"Slight bruises, taken care of".

"Good".

Captain Nwokocha knew from experience that Corporal Anyamba had something more to say so he left the corridor of the hut that served as his office and entered the inner enclosure.

"Sir, I need a four-day pass to see my pregnant wife and children", Anyamba said. He had added "my children" to elicit a touch of sympathy from the Captain. Such sympathies were of course rare but had to be if the war must be prosecuted.

Corporal Anyamba had pulled off several daring moves since his redeployment to this sector. Many of his colleagues had come to recognise him as a dare-devil soldier who could do the yeoman's service when the going became tough.

As he came out of the adjutant's office, Corporal Anyamba folded the piece of paper twice and tucked it into his breast pocket. The paper showed the hour of departure, the date, expected designation and the date of return. He deposited his rifle and the few bullets left in the office of Adjutant Nwokocha and saluted.

It took him a whole day's journey on foot, passing through Nkpo, Amoji to Ibeku. He passed military check-points on his way. Deserted villages, overgrown paths and abandoned farmlands greeted his eyes. At each check-point the sentries peered at his pass, sized him up to satisfy themselves of his identity before they allowed him to continue.

At Ibeku he found a swarm of refugees camped at the Central School. Most of them were old men and women, young children and disabled soldiers. On enquiry he found out that his own town, Umuayalu had fallen. It was besieged for two days, pounded from air and land and finally fell to the vandals superior military power. No villagers remained behind in spite of vociferous assurances by the commanders of the vandals to keep them out of harm's reach. Such promises were better taken with a pinch of salt because those who reposed confidence in them did not live to recount their gory experiences. They were either consumed by fire set on them in churches or massacred and thrown together into a mass grave dug by their victims.

Further enquiries from officers of the local Red Cross revealed to Anyamba that more refugees from Umuayalu were camping at Uzoagba. It was another day's journey from Ibeku. He slept at the camp and received food and water from officials of the Red Cross. His anxiety to meet his wife knew no bounds. He wished he could continue his journey even at night. But tiredness, despair and anxiety had taken their toll on his body.

His journey did not begin until six O'clock the next morning. He wanted to be sure of his route. Moreover, danger could be lurking anywhere. The vandals could break the secessionist defence lines, attack and capture unsuspecting soldiers and civilians at the rear. His training experience had made him to expect the worst always.

On 4th January, at 5pm he finally reached Uzoagba. He did not take long to locate his kinsmen. The children shouted with joy as soon as they recognised him. They clustered around him, causing him a momentary stop to embrace some of them – whose protruding tummies did not impede the gesture.

Mary peeped from the opening of her hut and on noticing Anyamba, she rushed out like a dog sighting a piece of bone. Luckily for her Oguaa was sleeping. With only a few paces to Anyamba, she stopped. Anyamba held her tightly, embraced her and carried her into the hut. She withdrew for a moment, looked at Anyamba again as if to make doubly sure and then held him closely. The only movement was that of her mouth as she kissed him all over the face. Her excitement knew no bounds. She was speechless. She shed tears of joy. Her prayers had been answered. Nothing else mattered.

Anyamba's visit to his uncle, Anselem was rather brief. He thanked him for taking care of the entire family, especially his wife, Mary. He regretted the death of Eringa and promised to help the children as soon as the war ended. He noticed the subdued nature of the old man's voice and knew that his uncle had changed much. He knew the reasons. Jim had left the camp.

When he went back to his wife, Oguaa had woken up. Anyamba picked it up, from the bed and caressed her. He saw that the baby resembled his wife so much. The light skin, the oval face and rich hair, all belong to his wife. She served him the familiar refugee meal which he ate with relish.

Mary recounted the death of Eringa and her own experiences at childbirth. She narrated events that led to their leaving Umuayalu and how she could not retrieve any of the belongings. Anyamba listened with rapt attention and expressed sympathy at her various ordeals.

Later that night Anyamba went back to his uncle's hut where they stayed together for a long time. It was like a father and a lost son recovered. Anselem unburdened his mind to Anyamba giving definite instructions. He insisted on not being buried at the camp if he died. "My bones", he emphasized, "must not rest in a foreign land".

Anyamba was afraid. Was the old man about to die? He talked to him the way he had never done before. The family's secrets and long relations, almost forgotten, were recounted to the minutest details by Anselem. He must have been satisfied that he had achieved his wish. The gods must have brought back Anyamba at the momentous period. It was a peaceful moment for him. His bones could rest in peace.

Anyamba slept for sometime before he woke up again to ponder over all that Anselem had told him. He also thought of all that his wife had told him. Sleep left his eyes for the rest of the night.

Early the next morning, the wailing of the women and children caused a stir in the camp. Anyamba's body ran cold as if a shell had dropped beside him. Anselem had joined his ancestors.

3

Anyamba sneaked back to his location at Isiukwuato sector and for a few days after, he slept in peace. His nuclear family was intact. He was grateful to God. Exactly ten days after he returned from the journey to Uzoagba to see his family, Anyamba's company was ditched in a hot battle to save its headquarters from capture by the vandals. It was a do or die affair. The same day in the afternoon at far away Ezeukwu, the vandal forces swooped on the entire town and captured it including the environs. The shout of "One Nigeria" rented the air. A Major in the vandal forces addressed the refugees:

"The war don over. Make una comot go una villages. Na one Nigeria we be. Na broda and sista we be."

His heavy tribal marks shrunk and expanded as he pronounced those words with a lot of difficulty. A great trek back home began for many and the remaining household of Anselem. The reversal of the journey to Umuayalu it was, but this time they knew exactly where they were heading to, their villages and homesteads.

Women and children, shrivelled old men with walking sticks, young men with tattered dresses all littered the road as they trekked towards different directions-some to Umuayalu; others to Ezeukwu and Umukabia. The spiral of dust raised by the multitude blinded others and forced them to slow down their paces.

Mary strapped her baby firmly to her back and carried her basin which was filled to the brim with sundry items of clothing and cooking utensils. A few milk cups of the oat-meal fondly called "gari Gabon" remained with her. It was usually distributed to the refugees by the Red Cross in the various camps littered all over "Biafra".

"We shouldn't have fought this war", complained one of the youngmen in his early thirties".

"But, but I reason that the vandals would have descended on us after the pogrom in the North if they were not halted by the war".

Everybody agreed.

"We should have negotiated even when we were pushed to the wall", reasoned another man.

"No one would have done that after what we suffered in the hands of our so-called brothers and sisters in the North", argued another man.

"Did you have relations with severed limbs and gorged eyes thrown at you in 1966" questioned another man called Sergeant. He seemed infuriated by some of the womanish arguments raised by the travellers.

Suddenly a jet fighter flew over the air and most of them dived for cover. Most of the women threw away their loads and scampered for safety. Some disengaged there grips on their younger ones. Mary threw down her basin and stopped. She quickly unfolded her wrapper and held Oguaa.

"Who is sure my husband has not been killed in the last series of battle before surrender? If he is alive, will he not first travel to the refugee camp to search for us? He might even think we have been killed. This is a really dangerous and confused situation. Only God knows and only Him can help us out of this horrible situation", Mary thought all these to herself and prayed.

The plane merely circled round in the air several times and zoomed away in the distance. This time it did not discharge bombs and shells on innocent women and children. Rather it threw down hundreds of posters with the inscription, "One Nigeria. War is over." It also took snapshots of the milling populace.

Mary halted as she approached a bend on the bush path. The attention of some others was turned to her side. A soldier in a tattered uniform was lying face upwards on the path. Hordes of flies milled round his mouth and eyes. It was a blood-chilling spectacle for Mary and she was quite frightened. She shed few droplets of tears then increased her steps. The soldiers was obviously killed in the last attempt of the Biafrans to save their positions. The tattered uniform had an emblem of the rising sun on it.

Mary's house, like all others, had been broken into and looted by the victorious vandals, but she was relieved to see it standing.

The bungalow which Anyamba built in his first few years as a staff of the Obubra Bakery has always remained modern. The pattern was brought to him by Jasper, his friend who worked with an architectural firm at Ugep.

Jasper decided to change a few things in the original design. For instance, the windows and doors were to be made of aluminium and glass louvres; those were changed to carved wood with gold enamel paints. There was to be a toilet for each of the rooms. But in Anyamba's designs, none of the rooms except the master bedroom, had a separate toilet. There was a common toilet attached to the side of the kitchen.

The floor was tiled and the walls painted with sandtex. There was beautiful flowers around the building. The pavement was wide enough to accommodate a few chairs for evening relaxation.

But to Mary's surprise and shock, Anyamba was inside the house putting a few odd things together in a heap. Like a cat on a hot tin roof, he had been pacing up and down the rooms thinking of what fate might have befallen his wife and relations. At that point also Anselem's parting words struck him like a blow: "my bone must not rest in a foreign village for ever".

He picked up Oguaa from Mary's arms and touched her all over. She smiled and broadened her small dark eyes. He admired her.

"What a bouncing baby, born in the face of the miseries of war. My bouncing darling baby and my ever courageous darling wife. I'm happy to have survived to experience these bountiful mercies of God. The war is all over", the elated Anyamba exclaimed.

Agnes, her mother Nwayieze, Anselem's second surviving wife, Adaugo and her children came into the compound almost at the same time. They were exhausted.

Anyamba rushed across the space separating the houses and helped them put down their loads. He exchanged a few banal words with the wives. The later showed little interest in anything else.

"I thank God for sparing your life, my great husband", said Mary when Anyamba came back. As Anyamba sat down on the wooden stool, Mary looked over him to see if there were any serious injuries sustained by her man. The picture of the village vagrant, Ogele, rushed through her mind.

A few days after, Anyamba initiated plans to retrieve the remains of Anselem back to his village according to the man's dying wishes. He remembered every bit of the old man's words concerning himself.

*   *   *   *   *   *   *

Anyamba did not go back to his job after the war. That would be starting afresh. The years he had put in before the war, would be counted off. That too did not bother him. But the idea of some junior workers whom he taught the job, now being his bosses as a result of the war gave him no joy. But there was little option left for him. His self-contained house in the village gave him a lot of confidence.

After some years of hardwork, Anyamba established a poultry farm, with the help of his father-in-law. Mary gave up her search for a teaching job and helped in running the poultry business. Meanwhile, she had given birth to two more issues – a boy and a girl.

As Oguaa grew, Mary found time to inculcate into her the good ways of life as handed down by her own parents. Since she was a virgin bride, she felt proud enough to tell it to Oguaa as she was coming of age. She taught her the facts of life. To Mary, it was necessary those seeds of goodness, as Mary's mother would put it, were sowed. Mary was doing her duty. It thus did behove Oguaa to sow her own seed so that posterity would benefit in the end.

With time the family found it difficult to cope with life in the face of the double-digit inflation that had afflicted the society. The labour market grew as more students graduated yearly from institutions of higher learning. The unemployment rate soared higher. With the dwindling economy and the purchasing power of the naira, many families were finding it difficult to even afford one square meal.

Anyamba and his family had woken up one morning to discover that their poultry farm was in utter ruin. The broilers and layers had been instantly wiped out by an unknown malignant disease. This was indeed a pathetic incident – a devastating loss – how could the family cope with this streak of irrepairable misfortune?

Jim, who at this time had passed his three major papers in the Higher School Certificate Examination, could not further his education owing to Anyamba's situation, had resolved to look for a job, if only to help alleviate his elder brother's situation.

Things began to go very bad for Anyamba and the family. The children had to feed and go to school. Mary's parents offered help as much as they could. Anyamba was growing too shy to keep expecting help from them as they also have their own problems. He started doing odd jobs if only to feed the family who were already living from hand to mouth. The teaching job was not forthcoming for Mary either.

It was at this period of hardship that Anyamba's sister who owned a hair dressing salon and fashion shop in Port-Harcourt visited them and decided that Oguaa should accompany her. She wanted Oguaa to live with her in Port Harcourt and attend school there. Mary dissuaded Anyamba from consenting to his sister's request for Oguaa to stay in Port Harcourt and attend school. She however reluctantly acceded to the request for Oguaa to spend her holiday with her aunt.

"It is not good for Oguaa to stay away from us at this stage of her development. We need to continue with the kind of training we are giving her. No one will do it for us. I don't know your sister well," Mary had told her husband.

"Well, it's only a holiday. It wouldn't affect her. I mean, we cannot fold our hands and reject help from people who are willing; from people who will not use it against us later", Anyamba had replied. It was not until Jim secured a job that Anyamba and the family were happy and somewhat relieved.

4

Jim approached the semi-detached hut cautiously. As he came closer to the door, the slow wind raised the faded white curtain tied to the transom. It caressed his face but he quickly tucked in his lips to avoid it kissing him. He knocked weakly and peeped.

"Come in", a female voice rang out. It was the clerk of the pool office. He stepped in and asked to see the Manager.

"He's out to the Head office", said the Clerk, and added instinctively, "please can I help you?"

Piled on top of each of two opposite wooden tables were heaps of old SPORTING RECORD, SPORTING TRIBUNE and WORLDWIDE FOOTBALL. Splashed on their pages were cartoons of different sizes and shapes. On one page, Jim saw a cartoon showing a man with oversized tommy and bulging cheeks with a smile on his cicatrical face.

He was dragging a bag containing hundreds of thousands of naira.

At the end of the table a middle aged man was busy studying each page of one of the copies. Opposite him but closer to the door, another man in his late fifties was equally absorbed in writing across the Kings fixed odd coupon in front of him. In between the two men sat two others of about the same age. They were equally busy studying the pages.

"See, I could have hit them below the belt last week but for one slight error", the middle-aged man nearer the door interposed.

"Just like me. If I had dropped number 13 and inserted 2 in front of the 3, I would have ended my poverty by last Monday".

"It was the cartoon on page 15 that deceived me. It indicated three strokes on the player's jersey and I failed to realise that I should have put 2 in front of 3 to make it 23".

"Just see", another of the men said, "if I had played perm 3 from 5 instead of betting the three numbers, I would have got something instead of losing my money".

"I'll lick them well-well come next Monday", the first man said, and continued, "it will be my game. I'll declare surplus. I've seen the trick and they'll go bankrupt." Jim watched the drama with a lot of interest. Some of the questions on his mind were being answered.

He began to see himself counting some of the naira notes the next week.

He turned to the girl to inquire if she could oblige him with some winning numbers.

Jim's question caused a stir among the pool pundits.

Here was a novice; a greenhorn openely declaring interest in the world of get-rich-quick mania. Another fish is being entrapped into the net of the ever-hopeful dreamers. Joblessness has led him into this. He had only two naira in his pocket. He thought of a way of investing just one naira to obtain some dividends by the beginning of next week. He could manage the other one naira on transportation, groundnuts and bananas.

This joblessness has become a source of retrieval for Jim. From time to time he thought he had committed a sin by coming down to Lagos. He had come to Lagos in search of a job at the end of his Higher School Certificate Examination. He lived with his maternal uncle and his wife. The man worked in the Federal Ministry of Transport.

Jim had written several applications for a job. Only a few had invited him for interview but none had considered him for employment. As days grew into weeks and the weeks lengthened into months, Jim's hope of getting even a menial job began to get dim.

The hospitality of his uncle's family gradually faded as he became a parasite in the family. At times he could be asked to fan one of the young cousins to sleep.

Quite occasionally he did jobs customarily reserved for maids and teenage girls.

He swept the open court-yard and dusted the louvres. He ironed the family's dresses on weekends and fetched water from the well. But amidst all inconveniences he remained cheerful and was grateful to his uncle for the opportunity afforded him to live in Lagos.

Now he no longer wrote to his friends or relations at home. "No money, no friend", he often reminded himself. He even hardly wrote home to his brother Anyamba. But occasionally he posted a letter to his sister, Nnenna who was living in Port Harcourt.

Nnenna was an attractive lady, usually soft-spoken but loquacious when she was making points in arguments. She was broad minded and her charismatic personality drew people, male and female, young and old to her. She was a self-made woman in a man's world and her astute disposition made her a successful business woman.

When the civil war broke out she had thought that the hostilities would last only a few days. No sooner had they remained in Lagos than they became an endangered species. Nnenna adroitly changed her name to Celina, and spoke the Lagos species of Yoruba all the time. She quickly, adjusted her mode of dressing. Clad in lro and Buba or in Aso oke, fluffy headgear and bold ear rings, she is Yoruba. Weaving the Okuku hairstyle with beads attached to the strands of woven hair, she would pass for an Edo woman.

Celina cultivated friends with her acquaintances. She ran a food canteen in one of the dark corners of Ojuelegba Road junction. She prepared stew in the grand style: reddened with tomapep, spiced with thymes and curry and sweetened with maggi cubes. Meat of various types and from different animal parts invaded the stew pot. The aroma taunted the nostrils and drew customers as flowers drew butterflies. Her eating house drew many customers. She soon accumulated money, but avoided ostentatious living and flamboyant dressing. Electricity power supply was quite irregular. A few hours of current graced every night on normal times. That notwithstanding, Celina had made a decision not to sell her wears as soon as the heavens withdrew their lights. Experience taught her that miscreants, emboldened by the tension in the country, wrecked havoc on lgbos at the slightest excuse for the law gave no protection to such victims.

Nnenna's husband, Uko left his home town, Akwete on

Saturday 24th June, 1961, barely six months after his Cambridge school certificate examination in 1960. He had roamed the streets of Owerri for those six months looking for a job that never appeared. His daily trips to the shell camp in Owerri yielded no dividend, as the shell oil company was more in need of artisans than unskilled clerical staff.

So when the ferry from the Onitsha end of the River Niger crossed him into Asaba, he heaved a sign of relief. Lagos would offer him the eldorado he failed to grasp at Owerri. His journey into the land of opportunities had begun.

When he wrote to his parents five years later to get him a pretty, sweet natured, family oriented girl as a wife, his family knew he had made it.

Though Nnenna was married to him by proxy, he nevertheless admired his parent's choice as soon as he set eyes on her at Yaba bus stop. In fact he has admired her right from the time he received her black and white picture posted to him months earlier. Their bus had run late, arriving Lagos in the early hours of the morning. Uko was on hand to receive her. He recognized her as soon as he saw her.

They had lived together for less than eighteen months before the hostilities broke out.

* * * * * * *

"Your travails as an applicant upset me a lot", wrote Nnenna in one of her infrequent letters to Jim. Sometime l feel like asking you to join me in Port-Harcourt but the time is inauspicious as there is yet a love lost relationship between indigenes and lgbo visitors here.

"You are a man which means more than it says. Keep

searching. You'll eventually strike the luck. Do not be daunted by the great disappointment."

"A certain Makanjuola was a good friend of my husband until events separated them. In fact he continued his affection until I left Lagos after the war. He had two little boys then, Dotun and Majek. He held a high position in the Department of Customs and Excise. I do not know where he lives now but before I left Lagos he lived at Herbert Macaulay Road, Yaba. You should make enquiries about him at Customs House in Kakawa Street. I wish you could locate him or his office."

Each time Celina remembered her stay in Lagos, it filled her with mixed feelings. It was while in Lagos that her husband disappeared after an air raid in some parts of the Mainland.

It was said that a few people lost their lives in the raid. Her visit to the mortuaries did not yield any result. She gave tips and descriptions of her man to mortuary attendants but none confirmed seeing any corpse resembling such a description. On one occasion she braved it to the mortuary. The awe and stench shocked her beyond control and she was later hospitalised for a few days. But she did not relent in her search.

It was also said that an enraged mob picked up quite a few Igbos after the raid and lynched them while few were saved by the eventual intervention of armed soldiers. These few were cast into protective detention. Celina trudged the length and breadth of Lagos. She visited every known detention camp. She got the reply: Uko was not an inmate. Her anxiety mounted.

With her husband's whereabouts uncertain, and her security unassured, she decided to take the bull by the horns by opening a food canteen. She ran it with all the sense of devotion she could muster.

* * * * * * *

Mr. Adefolahan Makanjuola was a humble man in his middle fifties. He was rich but he did not allow his riches to get into his head. Although he was not born with a silver spoon in his mouth, Pa Makanjuola made his money through his position as an Assistant Director of Customs. He was one of the few Nigerians to attain that position few years after independence. He attended few social occasions, and never paraded his wealth in the eyes of his neighbours.

Makanjuola was the main prop of Celina after her husband's disappearance. He had watched with satisfaction the struggles and tenacity of purpose of Uko as a bachelor. They lived in the same area of Yaba. They were not friends but Pa Makanjuola was impressed that Uko never went around with spinsters. His was a decent life for a young man of his means. Uko deserved accolades from men and women who were concerned with the moral decay of the society.

"Tinubu, Obalende straight-o."

"Federal Palace, Bar Beach, straight."

"Wharf, Apapa Wharf, no half-way-o."

"Eko, Ebute Ero, hold your money."

That was the music rendered in bass and alto at Lawanson Bus Stop. It was about 7 O'clock that Tuesday morning when Jim reached the chaotic arena. It was like bedlam let loose. People shoved and cursed. Market women dumped their baskets and basins on neatly dressed young men in an attempt to struggle into the buses. Several commuters stuffed the entrance with their massive bodies making it impossible for others to have an easy entrance.

"Oh! oh! they have taken my purse. Oh my God, what will I do. My family food money for the month has gone, just like that."

"Aunty, don't cry like that" replied a female voice.

"Shango strike him dead. May he not see the light of tomorrow. Shango do me this favour," she cried as she beat her chest.

As soon as the wailing started, the crowd at the entrance fizzled out. Passengers walked in twos and threes and settled on their seats. Jim felt exasperated at the bizarre drama, nonetheless he settled himself on one of the wooden seats in the bus in which the driver's mate was wailing.

"Federal Palace, Bar Beach, Maroko straight."

Since he was not sure where exactly to locate Kakawa Street, he made enquiries in the bus and was told that he should have boarded the enroute Tinubu Square. All he had to do was stop at the Bar Beach, cross over to the opposite of the road and board the bus going to Race Course, Tinubu. He wondered why the same bus could not make a detour and go to Tinubu Square.

At the Bar Beach Bus Stop, he stopped, looked around and saw the famous Bar Beach. It's lure was irresistible. The freshness of the early morning wind enticed him closer to the sand embarkments. He stretched his eyes to behold an interminable body of water. The waves rolled forward to embrace the shore and backward to join the entire ocean.

It looked as if it would consume any visitor. Littered here and there were groups of religious charlatans who worshipped at the Beach. They were adorned in their white robes and headgear. Smaller groups of young men also dotted the sandy area.

"With this you win and with this you lose," a young man about the same age as Jim was saying.

"I tell you, the early morning promises a lucky day. I saw it coming to you", said his accomplice.

Their appeals were directed at no person in particular. One held the cards, rolled his red shot eyes, adjusted his dark glasses and continued:

"Watch me carefully, play this joker with only ten kobo and you will win thirty kobo. You'll surely win as much times as you play. He exhibited three cards to the full view of the new spectators who had started gathering. One was red spades, another black crosses and the third a joker.

Jim felt his pockets and knew that he had thirty kobo. He was tempted to play the cards. It was clear. The joker was usually dropped at the man's right side. Just turn it up and he will gain another thirty kobo with only ten kobo. He needed money. It was easy to win and the temptation was high.

"Play your game, and take your win. Can you throw away such a chance," they urged him.

Jim finally succumbed. He diped his hands into his left pocket, felt the coins again and withdrew only ten kobo.

"Okay, I'm ready to play", he said. He dropped the coin in front of the young man and went straight to the card he saw as the joker.

It was usually dropped at the man's right side. He picked it, paused before he opened it. As soon as he opened it, the small gathering yelled and jeered.

"You missed it narrowly," one of them said. "You didn't watch me carefully, but don't worry. Try again."

They appealed to him again and again. He stood transfixed to the sandy soil and speechless. The man exposed the cards again, showed them to all and sundry and asked Jim to try his luck. If he won, he would have recovered his lost ten kobo.

That last statement was like oil in troubled water. Jim picked up the advice and fished out another ten kobo piece. He dropped it in front of the man and went straight to the card he thought was the joker. Again it showed only spades. He turned, rubbed his eyes then looked at the face of each spectator. They were full of pity for him. However, they urged him to have a third try.

"Three" they said, "is always a lucky number. The third try will eventually give you your whole money. Remember things happen in threes".

When he left the group, Jim had lost thirty kobo, enough to take him from Lawanson and back to the Bar beach. He could not believe it. He was quite convinced that he saw the joker card. But how it changed each time he touched it was unimaginable.

One or two of the supposed spectators followed him with entreaties. They wanted him to try again. If his home was near, he should go and collect more money. The more he played, the more he won.

He felt uneasy as he trekked all the way from Bar Beach to Tinubu. As his eyes darted on the sparsely populated bus, they suddenly rested on a boy of about the same height. He was neatly dressed in his white shirt neatly tucked into his trousers. He wore a pair of sandals. He peered closely and saw the boy clearly.

"Odeka", he shouted. "Is it you or your ghost? What

brought you here?" They exchanged greetings and soon stories of disappointment were exchanged. Addresses were also exchanged. "My-name-too-long," how is it with you in Lagos? Are you working?"

Odeka was Jim's classmate back home in Umuayalu. He was popular among his classmates for two reasons. His Father was a non-indigene who worked with Shell Company. Odeka was always neatly dressed and looked well fed than the others. In addition he had caused a prolonged laughter in their class "Two" at the beginning of that particular session.

One of the new teachers wanted to know the names of the students in his class. When it came to Odeka to tell the teacher his name, he paused and said;

"Sir my name is Odeka, my surname is too long". The class roared in laughter and even the teacher himself could not control his emotion. Before the class ended the students were already calling him "my name-is-too long". He had met the teacher at the end of the lesson and wrote out his name ODEKA OSEZEMAGHONOGBON in block letters.

Jim finally reached Tinubu Square and after asking two or three passers-by, located the Customs House at Kakawa Street. He made inquiries and was told that Mr. Adefolahan Makanjuola had retired as Assistant Director of Customs. His Yaba address was given to him by a lady whom Jim later came to know as his former confidential secretary.

With the address in his pocket, Jim felt happy in a day that started roughly. He put the piece of paper into his purse and put it safely into his pocket. But he was not satisfied. He did not want to take chances. Here might lie his luck. He retrieved the purse, opened it and recopied the address into three different pieces of paper which he distributed into his two side pockets and the back one. At least no pickpocket can make away with the three even if his purse is tampered with. No. He must be careful for also in his purse was a fifty kobo note which Odeka had given him.

5

"This man has come again today with his troubles. The sleep that is in my eyes has just disappeared as he opened his mouth that looks like fish own." Some of the passengers especially the women giggled over the last statement. It was a rather funny one which also drew the attention of a well dressed gentleman. A man looked up from the copy of a news magazine to behold the presence of an itinerant drug peddler.

"When will the country get rid of this practice? He is a nuisance", the gentleman muttered to himself and bent once again to pay more attention to his magazine. No sooner had he started reading than the voice of the peddler rang out.

"Good morning my people-o. I greet all of you fine fine. The journey to Lagos is not easy so you people should take it easy. To come to Lagos is not hard but to come back is problem".

Most of the passengers laughed out. One remembered that he only visited his village once every eight or more years, deliberately avoiding the festive occasions when the hikes on transport fares assumed very alarming dimensions.

"Yes, before I continue, let us pray for long life, prosperity, good health, many wives, many children, many husbands, many...."

Another bout of laughter cut him short as he screwed his face to indicate the reverence attendant to the ritual he was about to perform.

"In the name of the Father, the Son, and the Holy Ghost, Amen. Our Father, we your sinful sons and daughters in this bus thank you for the blessings you gave us plenty so that we can live happily in this wicked world. You made this world a happy place for us your children, but we turned it into a wicked place for others".

He paused, "help us to know what to do and do it quickly. Help us to have the money to pay for the things to buy. In the name of your Son, Jesus Christ we pray, Amen".

He made the sign of the cross again as he opened his eyes.

Some of the seemingly pious passengers also chorused 'Amen' and opened their eyes. The females had made a show of religiosity by placing a copy of a magazine or newspaper on their heads.

"Don't disturb us. We have spent all our money in the village. We only managed to save transport fare", Festus, one of the more outspoken passengers said.

Though the passengers did not address the peddler by name, every one knew that the jibes were aimed at him. Of course no one knew his name but he called himself "Young Doctor, Quality control Manager of Pharmizico Drug Manufacturing Company, alias lover of humanity".

"I know that you people don't have plenty money, so I have cut my prices to reach everyone. This special capsule is for all the stomach troubles that affect the homo sapiens. It was manufactured only one month ago in our laboratory at Ketu, manufactured to international standards, in fact to the standard of the British Phamacopia".

As he reeled off those bombastic words, some passengers clapped and called him "Young Lecturer".

"Do you think I didn't go to school? Truely, truely I went to school. I read standard, not elementary. Even I lectured in the University before my love for humanity propelled me into drug laboratory. In fact my students cried and demonstrated the day I handed in my stick of chalk to the Vice-Chancellor".

More laughter and cat-calls.

"The capsule can kill the poison inside all the bad well water you drink at Mushin, Okota and Ajegunle. Buy it now. Prevention is better than cure."

"Uncle Jim, do you think these drugs being peddled are genuine?" Oguaa asked.

"As much as possible, avoid them like a plague, unless where inevitable. They could cause and have caused death to many unsuspecting people who patronise them."

"Why? They are seen everywhere in towns and villages and no one stops them", argued Oguaa.

"Yes, that's the tragedy of our system. Since drugs are not available to the generality of the people through qualified hands, they are forced to patronise the quacks".

"But uncle Jim, in many cases the so-called quacks save many lives and are more readily available".

"I know Oguaa but their availability does not make them proper or safe. They have ruined many lives. Avoid them", concluded Jim.

"Yes, as I was saying, when you reach Lagos, even from Benin, you will eat soup and stew full of pepper, thirty minutes after, your stomach will run like tap water which children opened in the street. So you should buy this capsule now to avoid the running stomach. Had I known is brother to mister late".

"How much do you sell it, Young Doctor?" Another passenger asked.

"Don't worry about the cost, you just raise your hand, I will give you. It will help you, your wife, your husband, your children, even your girl friends. I can sell it anything because I'm the quality control manager of my company. Nobody can query me. It's only fifty Naira a satchet of six capsules. One capsule is 500 milligram.

"Give me two sachets", said Festus.

"Give me one sachet", said another passenger.

"Can you sell half sachet?" Asked a man nearest the peddler. He had just cleared his nostrils of brownish powdery tobacco. Tears rolled down his cheeks as he wiped them with the back of his hand. Some of the passengers burst into laughter.

"Oga", said Young Doctor, "I don't have fraternity with poverty. In fact I hate poverty like I hate accident. Even now, I'm not married. I don't have money, but my uncle promised to give me two of his twelve children. I don't need a wife now. I'm waiting for five years time. That is the year of free house, free health, free education and of free wives".

Most passengers could not hold their laughter. They

could not understand the year of free wives.

By the time he disembarked at Benin, all passengers who bought had paid for their drugs. God answered his prayer and he joined another bus en-route Onitsha with his pocket bulging with naira notes.

Oguaa wondered at the man's sweet tongue and how he wove the jokes he emitted to the delight of the passengers. Jim told her that the man was popular among regular commuters between Onitsha and Lagos.

When the luxurious bus, "Safe Journey", with registration Number LA 2964 MJ glided into the usually chaotic Yaba Bus Stop and came to a halt at 8.05 p.m., Jim heaved a sign of relief.

The driver's mate heaved the side booth open and Jim extricated his luggage from the numerous bags of garri, yams, and helped Oguaa to balance it on her head. A few metres away he flagged down a Surulere-bound taxi and chartered it for a smoother journey to his apartment.

Oguaa beheld Lagos and it enraptured her. She was spontaneously absorbed in the spectacle that was unfolding before her eyes. She was like the child in the adage who rested and slept after possessing what had kept her awake. It was a triumphant entry into a different world of red, white and blue lights. A world where the sun refuses to set.

Her wonder knew no bounds. The super highways that emerged as they entered into the Ojota end of Lagos, spanned through Ikorodu road and terminated at Yaba Bus Stop, beat her imagination. Hundreds of cars of various sizes and shapes blared out as they zoomed past in their regulated competition to outrace the others. She thought the pedestrians would fall to pieces through the bridges. Lagos must be the loveliest city in the world.

The house was a two-bedroom flat situated at New Surulere. The living room and bedrooms were neat, and spacious. It was rugged from wall to wall and decorated with modern furnishings. One chandelier hung at the entrance to one of the bedrooms while another hung nearer the kitchen door. On the shelf were a twelve-inch television set, a good musical set, books and colourful artificial flowers arranged in proper order. Two framed pictures of Jim also occupied some spaces on the large shelf.

This was the accommodation that Jim was given after the successful completion of his course and subsequent promotion in the Customs and Excise Department, where he worked. To him it was a world of difference, a refreshing change from the one bedroom apartment he lived in when he just started work.

Jim resumed work two days after his arrival with Oguaa. He had enjoyed a good rest during his period of leave. He was on afternoon duty.

"Oguaa, I'm going to work. I shall be back in the night as I told you. Make yourself comfortable. You can read your books. You can watch the television, play and listen to music. There are provisions and foodstuffs in the kitchen. Cook and eat whatever you like. Take care. Don't be afraid."

Just at that moment someone knocked at the door three times consecutively. Jim could guess who it was but all the same he decided to ask who it was. Before he could do that, a young handsome man, tall and dark – complexioned threw the wooden door ajar. He wore a broad smile, a pair of spectacles and was clean-shaven.

"Jim, when did you arrive?" he enthused.

"Good afternoon sir", Oguaa greeted the man meekly.

"Good afternoon lady. How are you?"

"I'm fine sir, thank you", Oguaa replied and immediately went into one of the rooms allocated her by Jim.

"Oh Jim, you came back since two days and no one has set eyes on you. Perhaps you've been busy with..", he said pointing at the door into which Oguaa had disappeared.

"Stop your jibes and be sensible", Jim said in a hilarious tone.

"Wait a minute, boy you came back with that beautiful one? Na your wife?" the man asked Jim in a low tone.

"You hardly keep your senses after sighting a beautiful lady. Well, she's my niece. She has come to spend her holiday with me".

"Wow. She's beautiful, just like a dream".

"Don't start getting excited, Dotun. She's only sixteen. It's just that she grew rapidly like a young sucker. Besides she is only in junior secondary three, so marriage for her now is out of the way. You can admire her, but hide your affection so that she doesn't start getting wrong ideas. She's too young to know she is beautiful".

"Jim you can trust me. I'm so harmless, that I can't hurt a fly even if it falls in between my laps."

"By the way Dotun, did you come in your car?" Jim asked.

"Yes, I did. I thought I could just drive in to check whether you were back, say hello and then run off."

"Haba, then you came at the right time. You would have missed me for I was about leaving. I resumed duty only today."

Oguaa walked out of her room and pretended to have heard no word of their humorous conversation. When she reached Jim's settee she held it with her left hand, then lowered her knee and greeted Dotun the second time.

"Dotun and his brother, Majek are very important to my life. We are intimate friends. You'll meet his brother, Majek, soon. Hardly a day passes without our seeing each other. I shall tell you more about them."

"Welcome sir", Oguaa beamed a little smile and greeted Dotun.

"I'm pleased to meet you, Oguaa. I welcome you to Eko City. I must confess you're charming. You need to be taken to places that make Lagos throb."

"Of course, she must be taken to all the beautiful places in the city", Jim emphasized as if to reassure Oguaa.

"Dotun, I am late for work. Let's start going. Oguaa take good care".

"Okay, Oguaa, I'll see you later," Dotun told her and gave a smile.

Oguaa held the front door of the house momentarily to wave bye to Uncle Jim before bolting it. She looked carefully as Jim held the door of the car and saw that there was another girl. Although she did not see her face, she noticed that the luxuriance of her shiny hair was superb.

She closed the door and peeped through the curtain to watch the car zoom off.

"Kemi, meet my friend, Jim. He works with the Customs and Excise", Dotun said as he smiled into Kemi's face.

"Good afternoon sir," Kemi greeted Jim.

"Afternoon, how are you?"

"But, Dotun, why did you keep Kemi waiting in the car? It was unkind of you."

"She insisted on staying inside the car to enjoy the cool music and the air-conditioner, so I couldn't force her."

"Ah, Kemi, so you refused to enter my house because I have neither an air-conditioner nor a stereo set?" Jim laughed as he asked.

"No-o-o. Don't say a thing like that, sir. I knew Dotun would be faster if he remembered that I was in the car."

"And I was fast", Dotun said proudly.

"Yes, you were as fast as a snail," Kemi replied jokingly.

Kemisola Ogundare was a third year student of the Mass communication Department of the University of Lagos. She occasionally spent her weekends with Dotun, especially when she ran short of funds. She had copies of several magazines of general interest scattered on the floor of the front seat.

Kemi's cordiality for Jim began as soon as she heard that he worked with the Customs. She asked generally about Jim's work and family.

Dotun chuckled as soon as he heard the word "family", the three of them laughed raucously as the car moved on towards Ikeja.

"Lest I forget," Dotun began, "I met Agnes yesterday evening. She complained bitterly about you."

"What sort of complaint?" Jim asked Dotun.

"She doesn't seem to have the confidence you would marry her in the end. She says you don't take her seriously any more. You don't take her out. You don't give her things the way you used to do. And that you don't ever talk of going to her parents as a sign that you're serious with her." Jim pinched Kemi as he made that last statement.

"And you Dotun, what do you think about such a woman?"

"You need to pet her more. Keep having fun. Marriage will come at last."

"Men? Keep having fun". Kemi repeated as she slapped Dotun on the right shoulder with the magazine she was reading. The slap was loud enough.

"Good for you, Dotun. Sometimes you act crazily. How do you want me to continue having fun with a woman I don't ever hope to marry."

Kemi continued to tap on her knee in rhythm with the music that was on. She enjoyed all the three activities, reading, the music and Dotun's conversation at the same time.

"She must be day-dreaming. Or you must be kidding. By the way, she is no spring chicken and besides, I don't approve of her ways. I met her at a night club in company of no one. I wouldn't marry such a woman. That issue should be understood. I'm not thinking of marriage now. When I'm ready to marry, I'll look for a well-brought up one".

"Like Oguaa, your niece," Dotun put in. And added as an after thought, "I like my Kemi."

"Yes, Oguaa my niece is well brought-up".

Jim got out of the car when they got to his office at the Customs Long room of the Murtala Muhammed Airport, Ikeja.

Dotun slammed the door and walked to Jim's office leaving Kemi in the car.

"I wouldn't like you to admire Oguaa openly like you did. You'll put ideas into her head and spoil her. She is very young and naive. Such open admiration you made isn't good for her."

"I hear you Jim", Dotun laughed heavily. "Nevertheless Oguaa is beautiful and ravishing. When I saw her, I thought she was your wife. I thought you had abandoned Agnes."

"And picked up Kemi?", Jim asked in between his laughter.

"Jim, I'm driving straight to the Model market. Kemi wants to do some shopping. She will be back to campus in the evening. Today is Sunday. She must be ready for lectures tomorrow.

Kemi and Dotun waved as the car drove off and Jim turned back to the office.

Dotun and Majek were important to Jim's life. Without them, Jim would not have had this job.

Jim travelled to Lagos in search of a job at the end of his Higher School Certificate examinations. He roamed the streets of Lagos and wrote dozens of applications without success. It was his aunt, Nnenna's letter that led him into a long search for Dotun's Father.

"Tanie?", a woman's voice rang out as Jim knocked on the door of one of the houses in Plot 347 Herbert Macaulay Road, Yaba.

Jim recoiled, but kept his composure. He summoned enough courage to ask the question on his lips. Although he did not understand Yoruba, he greeted the unseen voice that asked the question.

Jim tapped again and the door was opened by a young man of about Jim's age.

"Good afternoon ma", Jim greeted Dotun's mother. She

was an old woman with strands of grey hair on her head. She was fat and her heavy arms were flabby. She sat on a low stool padded on the top.

"Afternoon. Who are you looking for?"

"Please Ma, I'm looking for the house of Mr. Makanjuola of the Customs."

"Yes, this is the house. Can we help you?" the old woman asked.

Jim told his story mentioning his senior sister Nnenna and his trip to the Customs House in Kakawa Street, Lagos.

Dotun and Majek joined their mother to listen to Jim's story. They felt sorry. They sat him down and offered him a bottle of mineral. As he drank, Mr. Makanjuola emerged from the bedroom. Jim greeted and bowed as the man sat down.

The parlour was large and contained art works from various countries. A large framed photograph of the man in his Customs uniform was leaning on one foot of a large ebony black cupboard. The rug sank as Jim stepped on it. The curtains were heavy and imported. On the wall were photograph of Mr. and Mrs. Makanjuola. Although the photograph looked new, the man and his wife were ageing. Jim was afraid. He narrated his story again to Mr. Makanjuola who listened passionately before he gave Jim details and an accompanying note to his application.

Three weeks after the application was handed in, Jim received an invitation for an interview. He prayed, hoped and read for the exercise. But it was a mere formality. The ex-Assistant Director's letter had employed him.

He was grateful to God, to Mr. Makanjuola and to his sister, Nnenna.

6

"Boy, I tell you something. Jim has a chummy chick in town, says she's his niece. I'll pay any thing to have her".

"Good heavens! When? How? Dotun you can't have her. Your hands are full and overflowing".

"Your hands are full as well. I was the first to see her. Remember, first come first served", Dotun intoned.

"Yes, but remember also that he who laughs last laughs best. I've been the patient dog: I must eat the fattest bone".

"But you haven't even seen her".

"Well, I trust your assessment. You're never off the mark. Tell me more. How is she?"

"Fresh from the village, unspoilt, light complexioned, succulent, bashful and naturally beautiful. Give her to me and give me three months, I'll make her elegant and charming."

"But who will give her to you? Jim or me? Tell that to the marines. You're more married than a married man".

"Majek, don't slaughter me. I make them happy, that's

why they rush me. It's not my fault."

"What will you do if Jim disapproves of your approaches?"

"Well, what would I do? Can he really stop me?" Oguaa spent some time to survey the whole flat of two rooms and a spacious parlour. She first entered Jim's room and arranged the dresses scattered on the bed and she then picked up the black plastic comb also from the bed and ran her fingers through the teeth to remove strands of hair.

She dusted the louvres and drew the curtains. She dusted the cabinet bed and with a sheet of tissue paper, she cleaned the dressing mirror. She brushed the three pairs of shoes and arranged them beside the dressing mirror. She cleaned the parlour very carefully before she came to the room Jim allocated to her.

The ringing of the door bell caused Oguaa to stop. She could not guess who it was. But she peeped through the curtain and saw Dotun making frantic effort to peep through the key hole.

Oguaa opened the door slightly to let in Dotun. This time he came alone. He had left Kemi in his suite in the Hotel and hurried out on the pretext that he was going to purchase spare parts for his car. He so painted the picture of the dubiousness of his mechanic that he wanted to join him in the search of genuine spare parts.

He assured Kemi that he would be back though it might be little late since they would comb the whole of Idumota to search for the parts. But Kemi was not easily taken in. She smelt a rat and decided to try her luck.

"How are you dear?" Dotun was saying as he slumped into the sofa in Jim's parlour. Before Oguaa could answer, Dotun asked for a cup of cold water.

"Fine," said Oguaa and ran into the kitchen for the water.

"Thank you, Oguaa, you've saved a life. I was almost dying of thirst".

"Thanks, I'm happy to be helpful to you."

Dotun held out the empty glass cup for Oguaa. As she was receiving it, he used the opportunity to caress her hand.

Oguaa came out of the kitchen and sat slightly opposite Dotun. He zipped open his brief-case and emptied it of its non-paper contents. Two packets of chocolate biscuits and two boxes of fruit drinks.

"One for you and one for me. You don't have anything to fear. Jim has already told you of the strong relationship between us."

She took one packet of biscuit and one of the fruit drinks in both hands and kept them on top of the short stool beside her.

"Jim is a good friend of my family. We do everything together and he has been helpful to me in particular. He helps me clear my consignments at the airport without extra kobo.

"Yes, uncle Jim is nice. He inundates us with gifts when he visits home."

"Jim is a busy bee. In fact he is so important in his office that occasionally he travels outside Lagos on duty".

"Oh no! I don't pray for him to travel out now. I'll be left alone in this whole house".

"You don't say so. We're here to take care of you. After all, my best friend's niece is also my niece. In fact, he has already asked me to take you out to see some interesting areas of Lagos."

Oguaa jumped at the idea. She was ready to absorb Lagos. That's good of uncle Jim, she thought.

She went into her room and dabbed her face with white talcum powder. She then picked out the dress which she thought was fanciful: a red blouse atop a black skirt. She had high-heeled black shoes to match. She also picked up her handbag and slung it over the shoulder.

As soon as she came out of the room, Dotun chuckled his approval and drew nearer to hold her hand. She looked around the parlour to re-assure herself that everything was in order. Satisfied with her survey, she banged the door and turned the key.

Because Dotun's car had been in the blazing sun for several minutes, the inside was hot. As he opened the doors to allow the hot air escape, he also utilized the opportunity to wipe the windscreen a second time. Satisfied, he asked Oguaa in and strapped the safety belt across himself.

"How nice! My goodness! I knew it. I guessed right. So that's the mechanic? That's the spare parts shop? Your car indeed."

"Kemi, stop it! Don't create a scene with me here. Respect yourself".

"Did you respect yourself in the first place? You dumped me in the chalet and here you are with this ……..this village girl," Kemi shouted pointing at Oguaa.

"No, Kemi, it's enough. Calm down and let's go together. I left every goodie in the chalet to keep you cheerful."

"Go together ke? Together with this rat. She must have been imported for you by Jim. Or you tapped the opportunity of his absence to indulge his niece".

"And you village girl", pointing at Oguaa, "do you just join any man with a car that comes your way? Was that what your poor mother in the village taught you? Ah! Ah! A village girl who should be busy sweeping her uncle's house is here running after a man. You'll soak in them, I'll teach you the way about town".

A few passers-by stopped to see the end of it. They seemed used to such free entertainments.

"Kemi, it's enough! I'll get you locked up for this nonsense."

"Don't think you'll insult me publicly and get away with it. You will certainly pay dearly for this, I promise you."

"But what have I done to you?" Oguaa asked. "I didn't even talk to you".

"I'll teach you some sense. You can't steal my man and claim innocence."

More passers-by also stopped to swell the crowd. Some put in few words to the charged air. Young children merely giggled and clapped their hands as Kemi displayed and swore from the bonnet of Dotun's car to its bumper.

"Don't agree! If anybody touches your man, don't leave her. Grab her by the breasts and teach her sense!" a man shouted. Others laughed wildly.

"Man is hard to get now. Kill any girl who thinks she can joke with your man. Afterall magun is at Ijebu-Ode," another man chipped in. More people laughed and clapped.

"It's true", said another man whose feet were covered with dust. Dotun smiled but it was a smile that had frustration written on it. Oguaa merely looked in bewilderment.

"Who told you that men are hard to get? I have more than five men who are worrying me", a woman in her late forties said.

Dotun could not stand the commotion any longer. He seized the last chance and drove off leaving a trail of dust in the air. Kemi was left yelling at the moving car.

She swore to inform Jim of his niece's waywardness.

When they entered the hotel room Dotun was still infuriated. Nevertheless he distributed his smiles to a few customers in the drinking parlour. Some of them recognised him and bowed.

While in the car, he had appealed to Oguaa to forget the incident. Oguaa herself was shocked. She could neither believe nor comprehend what had already happened.

She remembered that she had witnessed such scenes twice or thrice at Port-Harcourt, but they were not so aggressive. It was usually two girls exchanging blows or tearing their dresses over a sugar daddy or a rich young man. But here was a young girl and another girl – all in the open street.

Dotun got her seated and ordered cold drinks – a bottle of malt drink for Oguaa and a bottle of lemon for himself.

"It's rather early for alcohol", he announced to no one in particular.

"What will you eat"? he asked as the waiter set down the drinks.

"Em, em, anything, just anything."

The choice is yours to make. I'm at your beck and call. Okay, eba, or pounded yam or fried rice?"

Finally Oguaa nodded at the mention of fried rice. She ate to her satisfaction and consumed the four pieces of meat with relish. She found the meal delicious to her taste but as good manners dictated, she left some grains of rice in the plate.

"I prayed hard today for the jackpot", a man was saying.

"I play only when I'm happy, then I'll be sure to win", said another addict at the casino.

"Man I was living on this before you were born, so steer clear until I finish playing," joked a third man.

Oguaa was shocked to see men falling over one another to throw coins into the gaming machine. Few of them won but failure did not deter others. They kept on playing. It seemed they remembered only when they won but forgot the dozens of losses they encountered.

Oguaa drained the bottle of malt of its liquid content and felt satisfied. She had tasted beer once or twice in Port Harcourt at aunty Nnenna's house but she did not find it pleasant. She had wondered why men, including some women, consumed the bitter liquid with much relish.

Dotun could not get the shock of the altercation with Kemi off him. Despite all attempts, he found it difficult to push it to the back of his mind. Occasionally he would bang at the black mahogany table to emphasize the resolve which was forming in his mind. He swore to make Kemi regret her action. He was afraid the gossip of the affray might reach Jim and further embarrass Oguaa. He pleaded with Oguaa not to allow Jim get wind of what had happened.

At a few minutes past six that evening, Dotun dropped Oguaa in front of Jim's flat. He had touched her tenderly at some sensitive part of her body while they were alone in the car. She had offered a pretended resistance. There was a lot of time. Dotun assured himself. But the effect of Kemi's action earlier in the day was not to be glossed over. Its effect on the future relationship with Oguaa should not be under-estimated.

*   *   *   *   *   *   *

Jim opened the door of Majek's car and alighted as the car pulled up in front of his apartment. They were in an animated mood. At 9.30 that evening, some thirty minutes before Jim closed for the afternoon shift at the Customs Long Room in Ikeja Airport, Majek was waiting to take him home. The news of Oguaa's arrival hinted him by Dotun, had aroused his curiosity.

He found a decent way of climbing to Oguaa through the steps paved by his relationship with Jim. To take Jim home would be a welcome opportunity and pretext for going to Jim's flat.

When Oguaa opened the door to welcome uncle Jim, she was greeted by the beaming face of Majek. He wore a finely embroidered long-sleeved shirt which was recently delivered to him. He looked more like a prince than an aspiring under-graduate.

"Uncle Jim, welcome". Oguaa greeted, bowed and left for the kitchen.

Jim stopped her, asked how she enjoyed the whole afternoon and introduced his friend Majek as the brother of Dotun.

"Good evening sir," Oguaa greeted Majek.

"Evening". Said Majek as he surveyed Oguaa quickly before their eyes could meet.

"Bring me a dish, Oguaa", Jim said as he sat down, yawned and dropped his briefcase on the centre table. He brought out two bundles wrapped with sheets of old newspaper.

It was suya – a popular delicacy of roasted beef. Jim asked Oguaa to retrieve two bottles of beer from the refrigerator for Majek and himself. They drank the beer and munched pieces of the roasted beef spiced with fresh onion, sliced red tomato and ground pepper.

"This sudden trip does not go down well with me?" Jim complained between mouthfuls of meat.

"Why? You'll enjoy it! I wish I were in your shoes, Jim".

"I've just come back from home. Moreover, here's my niece, Oguaa. She'll be left alone for these days. I can't fancy it. It looks an interminable period".

"You needn't worry about that. We're on hand to help her until you come back. My sister Doyin will keep her company so."

"That your boss nominated you again for the job indicated how important you are in the Department. The sky is your limit".

"This is the third time I'm getting involved in this type of assignment – investigating one's colleagues in another zone is not a Christmas jamboree for me".

"You shouldn't worry. Just report what you find out. Honesty is the best policy".

"It could be detrimental to one's promotion prospect if one were to be transferred to that zone later in one's career."

"Do your work and damn whose ox is gored. As my father used to say, the truth will always prevail".

"In Nigeria fraud is everywhere. Small fishes like me

should not be made scape-goats. The suspects, who are to be let off the hook could be one's bosses."

"Remember the popular saying that cowards die many times before they're finally buried. You aren't a coward. Cheers Jim".

As soon as Jim closed the door after waving bye to Majek, he called Oguaa to his side in the parlour. He told her the news of his emergency departure to Kaduna. He could not reject the task; it was part of his job. It was sudden that there was little time to make any arrangements. He was kind to Oguaa and wished her the best in his absence.

"Don't go out unnecessarily. Remember, you don't know any place yet. When I come back, I'll take you to nice and interesting places in Lagos. Read your books to improve your position next term".

"Thank you uncle Jim. I'll not disobey you. I know that you love me and want the best for me."

"Yes, I'll buy you things at Kaduna and when I come back, we shall go shopping".

"Uncle Jim you're good. I will always remember you. You have been so good to me. Take me with you to Kaduna. I'll feel lonely without you".

"Don't worry, I've told Majek to send his sister Doyin to keep you company. She's a good girl. You'll learn a lot from her."

"Uncle Jim, I can't thank you enough for such an arrangement. I'll wait for Doyin and we shall study together".

"There's enough food in the house to last even one month. I'll leave you with some money to buy other food items which might interest you."

"Thanks uncle, God bless you."

"And you too," said Jim. He pulled out his wallet and counted forty naira in five naira notes and gave to Oguaa. She was happy.

Jim slept little that night. He woke up before five O'clock and got ready. He ate bread and few slices of fried plantain. He also prepared scrambled egg and made two cups of coffee. He usually preferred coffee to tea when going on a distant journey. In fact, he took with him a small flask in which's contained three cups of coffee.

When he got ready, he woke up Oguaa and gave her few other instructions, emphasizing that she should not go out without Doyin.

Jim left early for the airport in order to catch the first morning flight. Being early at the airport would help him obtain a boarding pass without the menace of the touts. However, with the Nigerian Airways, getting a boarding pass was not a guarantee that one would get a place in the flight. On still had to struggle for a seat.

7

It would be about a quarter to nine in the morning. I had been out of bed alright but I was lazying about all morning with the hope that I could take my time to do the morning chores.

The doorbell rang. I knew it was Doyin and the thought was quite reassuring. But I had thought she would come alone. She came with her brother Majek in one of their family cars. Majek's face was the more visible one when I peeped through the window blind. Beside him was Doyin. She was radiant and exuded happiness.

I opened the door and greeted them. Doyin and I held hands momentarily and she slapped my shoulder as a show of affection. They asked if I slept well in the night and if I had taken my breakfast. We exchanged news of the day. They knew I was lonely in the flat. I felt the absence of my uncle and the effect was already visible on me.

*   *   *   *   *   *   *

"Men are monsters!" They would go for anything in skirt. How nauseating! Me? Share my hubby with a maid? I can't imagine it."

"Yes, men, you don't know them. They are callous.

They are animals of the basest order. They don't mind that the maid cleans and scrubs the floor and toilet for them", said a second lady as she readjusted her head cocked in the dryer of "Elegant Salon".

"I pity women who claim their readiness to die for them. Die for men? What for? For someone who might later dump me for a house girl? Not me", said a third lady.

That was the type of conversation that went on in the salon. I was in the salon. I was shocked. Women peering into the private lives of their men or their friend's men and disclosing their findings for all and sundry to hear. My mother wouldn't have said that of my father.

I recoiled at the vogue of men taking their teenage house-maids, not even their nannies, to bed. I shrugged at the idea of a father and a house girl on one mat.

One of the women swore she would beat the hell out of such a maid. Another promised with a bang on the centre table of the salon that she would rub red hot pepper into the girl's private part and pour iced water on her. Yet another lady, sitting immediately beside Doyin in a dryer claimed she had seen with her two eyes where, in Amuwo a house-maid actually had hot pepper rubbed in her private and its surroundings and almost beaten to death after she was discovered to have tasted the same fruit which the mistress thought was exclusive for her.

I began to wonder whether the maids should be blamed. The blame should be laid on the doorstep of the man and his wife. They created the circumstances. Should one imagine a maid tapping at the master's door to rouse him up and remind him it was time? Isn't it always the other way round? And since he is the provider for the family, dare she disobey him? But we live and learn.

I could not leave Doyin in the salon and go home because we came together. I detested the conversation. On the other hand, Doyin herself seemed to be enjoying the abuse on the men. I noticed that men were the targets of all the conversations – their tricks, their foibles, their foolish excesses.

"I had to tell my man that the hairdresser charged one hundred naira for this particular style and not the twenty-five naira it usually costs. He must provide the money! No bargains! No haggling! After all I answer his name. I must make up to fit the status," boasted the lady nearest me to the left.

"Yes, good soup na money makeam," said another woman.

"To make us charming and delicious, they must pay for it. Let them pay. Men are meant to cater for us."

These utterances amused and annoyed me at the same time. Could women-folk be so blunt and abusive? I don't think men would marry if they knew what women discussed behind them. Or at least if they would commit their heart and soul to their women.

I sat long in the salon and waited for Doyin. There were many feminine magazines and I busied myself with some of them. Some of the fashion dresses in the pictures in them did not interest me. How women expose themselves for money or enjoyment.

Doyin also was busy with some of the magazines. She adjusted her head several times until her hair was dry.

Doyin was simply beautiful. Her rich, curly and long hair rested beyond her shoulder. I think it is the style they call 'V-Voot'. I admire Doyin. She is a girl that showed vivacity and amicability.

We left the salon a little before twelve noon. Majek was at hand to take us home. I went to their house for the first time. It was quite beautiful. Their mother showered me with a lot of affection and asked after my own mother.

Doyin prepared jollof rice and dodo, which she said, was her favourite dish. The meat was of various types and sizes. In fact there was too much meat in the rice. I remembered a cattle I had seen while the car raced towards Doyin's house. It trotted as the shepherd herded and flooged it along. It was like a sheep being led to the slaughter. "Poor creature." I had said to myself.

Soon Dotun came into the house with Kemi. I felt they had made up after that commotion. Oh how Kemi cursed and swore. The world of young people is a curious one. Enemies today, friends tomorrow.

Dotun smiled at me as he sat beside me in the parlour. He asked how I felt at the sudden departure of uncle Jim and also he joked if Doyin prepared Igbo dishes for me. We laughed. I looked at Kemi. She also laughed, but I think she was still suspicious and perhaps envious of me.

I soon found out that Doyin was a final year student at the Polytechnic, Ibadan. She spoke well and her intonation was superb. She advocated sex education for teenagers. I supposed she had been well groomed on the subject for she did not see anything wrong in sex education for students of our age. She had her points. Many girls who dropped out of school because of pregnancy would not have done so if they had received sex education.

In addition they would be able to guard themselves even

when they are married. Both husband and wife should know how to space out their offsprings. Females would need the exposure since they are the more easily guillible and the ones who carry the pregnancy and its guilt for nine months.

But Doyin forgot that it was like giving an adolescent a loaded pistol – he would shoot at the slightest opportunity – teenagers are emotionally immature and prone to the temptation of trying what they are taught as a show of rebellion against the dictates and advice of their teachers. It is like the question of allowing every citizen to bear a gun. Can its shooting be controlled?

The proponents of sex education for adolescent tell youngsters that sex is good and worthy but that they should await their turn. How and how do you expect impatient youth to await their turn to pluck something said to be good and juicy?

Astonishingly, Doyin will not be convinced. She concedes the fact that many of her students did pluck the forbidden fruit after several titillating lectures on the subject. Many people outside the school protested and parents also vented their displeasure. "What is good for the western world may not be good for Africans," they seemed to say.

Majek took us out again in a different car. I supposed he wanted me to know the various brands of cars owned by the family. I slumped into the rear with Doyin. It was another air-conditioned car and I enjoyed it.

Occasionally Majek and Doyin spoke in Yoruba-a language, which I did not understand. I supposed they were making comments about me. I heard such words like 'Omoge', Iyawo' Oko dada' but I could hardly understand their meaning.

Doyin smiled and giggled and seemed to be enjoying

every moment of the journey for a reason I could not perceive. I often looked out through the windscreen to catch glimpses of some areas of Yaba and Surulere.

Doyin reminded me of the mother-daughter arrangement in girl's school. A senior girl would cajole a first year into being her 'daughter'. Occasionally the Senior Prefect actually did the distribution of the first years to the final year students.

Thereafter the senior girls does whatever she likes with her daughter. These include snatching her best dress if they are about the same size and hatching every conceivable plan to trap the daughter for her brother or his boy friend. Many junior girls actually get messed up in the syndrome.

"Oguaa, I'll be coming down here. Majek will take you home. I just wish to see one of my friends at Lawani Street. Go over the front seat and don't make Majek a chauffeur by sitting at the owner's corner". She smiled again and held my shoulders.

I merely gave a wry smile for I had thought she would go back to Uncle Jim's house with me so that I could show her some of my latest pictures.

Majek also smiled and pretended to be embarrassed at Doyin's seemingly sudden decision to alight.

I remembered what uncle Jim told me about Dotun and Majek. Dotun was the manager of two big hotels in Lagos. The hotels were owned by his father. I supposed it was in one of those hotels that he occupied a chalet. This chalet he used conveniently as a nest for preying on his female victims outside the range of his parent's eyes. Not that they would quarrel.

Majek on the hand controlled three large supermarkets, along with the restaurant that houses a casino.

The super markets and restaurant were also owned by their father.

Dotun, uncle Jim told me, spent most of his leisure time running after women. He could pay and did pay any amount to satisfy his romantic urge. He made friends easily with any stranger who could be leading him to women. He never wished to read further. To him there was no need for further education when the money was there. The life of women and gambling had eaten deep inside him.

Majek was kind and willing to help anyone in difficulty. He liked making friends with intelligent and humorous people. He was interested in people and their well-being. He hoped to further his education and become a lawyer. Not that he cared less about beautiful girls. It seems no man cared less.

"You enjoyed Doyin's cooking?" Majek asked without looking at me.

"Yes, she is a good cook. In fact all girls are good cooks."

"No, not at all Oguaa. You're being presumptous. I disagree. Nine in ten don't know how to slice an onion bulb. But they claim to be better cooks than their mothers," he laughed and pretending to have missed his hold on the gear handle at the floor of the car. He utilized the opportunity to caress my exposed laps.

I laughed and it just occurred to me that boy's generally don't enjoy hearing praises heaped on girls.

Running through the streets of Yaba and Surulere could be an interesting but frustrating experience to newcomers like me as well as to busy commuters. The traffic jam afforded the new comer an opportunity to look round to assimilate the interesting sights, and to assess his bearing. But the commuters are dragged on as it were, in the standstill.

Majek stopped at the parking lot of Mafedoy Restaurant. The large sign of the restaurant was beautiful by the neon lights which revolved in broad daylight. I supposed the workers forgot to switch them off.

A lot of customers were waiting to be served. Others were already eating and chatting while the take-away section busied itself with selling fried and roasted foods. It was a beehive and it looked as if the whole of Surulere patronised the place.

"Afternoon Sir", greeted one of the waiters who first noticed Majek. Others followed suit in a chorus and Majek merely nodded his head like the lord of a small world. Some of the customers waved.

I trailed behind him, unsure whether to acknowledge the greeting also.

"Take this", ordered Majek. He tossed a small piece of paper to one of the waiters.

He beckoned on me and I walked demurely beside him. Some of the customers stared at me. I didn't understand them.

"Come in and make yourself comfortable," announced Majek. He emphasized the word comfortable.

We were already in a large room adjoining the restaurant. My shoes sank in the rugged floor. I missed my steps and nearly fell down. I stopped momentarily to regain my balance.

Majek switched on the light which twinkled red, blue and amber alternatively. The curtains were double –a soft light blue lace material at the interior and heavy coloured cotton material to the exterior – the cushions were soft and hairy. They looked imported and superior to those in uncle Jim,'s house.

The deck played a cool Afro Juju number as soon as Majek pressed the button. Three minutes later, he picked up the remote control of the video cassette player and half nude dancers appeared twisting their breasts and kicking the empty air to expose their anatomy on a television screen.

"This is where I rest my bones after a hard day's labour", Majek said in a slow soprano voice.

I was still absorbing the room when a soft tap was heard on the door. The waiter to whom Majek had handed the note entered gingerly, bearing a brass tray containing two dishes. He set them down, genuflected, and left us alone.

Majek drew the refrigerator open and exposed rows of drinks of assorted types. He retrieved a bottle of cold water.

"I purposely ordered for snacks and chicken parts since you have already eaten with Doyin" he said.

"I don't mind. You guessed rightly. I'm not yet hungry", I said.

He uncovered each of the dishes and asked me to help myself. I ate a little and we discussed general on banal issues. We also sipped cold mineral drinks.

Soon the telephone rang and Majek picked up the receiver. He spoke all through in Yoruba not minding my presence.

After he said bye and dropped the receiver, he came and sat on the empty seat beside me. He picked up my left hand and caressed it tenderly. I didn't with hold my hand. His palms were so soft and comfortable . He pressed my arms tightly. I was helpless.

Then a thought struck me. How safe was uncle Jim's

flat? At the same time fear registered in my mind. I passed the question to Majek. As I expected, he assured me that the house was safe. He went on to say that part of Surulere is the safest from the records of burglary and robbery.

My fear of what Majek was up to dissipated each time I remember that uncle Jim trusted the family enough to hand me over to them. But Majek was insistent. He unbuttoned my skirt and pressed hard on my orange-sized breasts. I protested mildly by withdrawing his hand carefully. He merely smiled and kissed my lips. It was cool, soft and juicy.

Before I knew it Majek dug his fingers into my underwear and pulled it down. He held me tightly for some time and rubbed me for a fairly long time. Then he sunk himself into me and fumbled my womanhood. It hurt yet I did not want him to leave me. Majek struggled and struggled and I was soon tired out like a battered wrestler. When it was all over, I felt some cold liquid on my laps. I touched it and it was blood. I became weak. I didn't know how the blood came about.

Majek helped me to dress up. He patted my shoulders several times and assured me that I should not worry.

He drew out a tin of talcum powder, some of which I dabbed on my face.

I shed tears. I remember the warning of my mother. Would she find out? I kept wondering. I continued to feel hot between my thighs as I walked to the car outside. Majek had packed some of the chicken parts and tucked into my bag. I could not hold my tears. I did not have the courage to look him in the eyes. He took me straight to uncle Jim's house and deposited me on the double seater. He lifted my arm, kissed it lightly and smiled into my face.

I managed to stand up and lock the door as Majek left. I wept more. I wished I had not left uncle Jim's flat.

I lay on the cushion, barely taking off my dress. I was spread-eagled on the cushion to minimize the intense heat. I switched off the light. Soon I slept off. When will uncle Jim be back?

8

"Look, Mary, I'm not a party to this business".
"What business?"
"Our daughter, Oguaa."
"The angels protect us! We should just wait and see the type of boy Oguaa has inflicted on herself".

As Majek entered Anyamba's house, Oguaa ran and hugged him.

"Hello, Oguaa! How are you doing with village life?"
"Majek, it's nice to see you again".
"You meet my parents. That's my mother", said Oguaa as she pointed at Mary.
"Hi, mum. You're kicking fine," said Majek as she and Majek drew closer to the couple.
"And, this is my father".
"Hi, dad. You're feeling, fine men", asked Majek. He tilted himself one side and lamely shot out his hand for a handshake.
"I'm feeling good, men", replied Anyamba and added, "May the bright sun melt you! Is that the way they greet adults in your area?"
"Don't mind dad, Majek. He seems to be in a sour

mood. Pardon his inconsiderate nature."

"Okay, thank you, Oguaa."

And quickly, Oguaa added, "Will you have something to cool off?"

"I won't mind, but what do you have in the house?" enquired Majek.

"That's when I'm dead, buried and forgotten. You, Oguaa, feed this thing in my house with my own food, the result of my sweat".

"Calm down Anyamba", pleaded Mary.

"Look young man, move out of my house before I call Amadioha to strike you dead with its lightning. I can't stand your stench. You're a fool. You can't marry my daughter."

"Oguaa, I can't stand this. I'm going back. I don't want this family again. Never in my life," Majek screamed.

"Darling, come back," pleaded Oguaa. "Please come back to me", she added.

"Daddy, see what you've done to me. I'm not staying in this house again. I'm going to stay with my Majek", Oguaa concluded as she stormed out of the house.

Mary called and rushed to stop Oguaa but the latter was running fast towards Majek.

The door-bell terminated my dream. I was perspiring hard and breathing fast. It was a fearful dream. I woke up, rubbed my face and went to the door. It was Doyin. She had come to see me after yesterday's episode.

She asked after my general well-being. She observed that my face was slightly swollen but I didn't know. I suppose it was because I had just woken up from sleep. She said her mother was pleased with my visit the previous day. I suppose

Majek had asked her to find out about my condition. Doyin smiled and her face radiated friendliness. She kept on observing my movements, possibly to notice any show of pain. She felt relaxed and was not in the mood of leaving our house early.

We conversed on sundry topics ranging from private schools to public schools; from friendship to holidays and from strict parents to loose ones. Doyin was good in conversation and through her mannerisms I saw the mustard seed of a woman giant. When she finally left the house I was relaxed and fresh. But my dream frightened me each time the details appeared in my mind. I did not tell Doyin, for I did not know what she might think of it.

"Hi, Oguaa how are you? How was the night? Did you sleep well?" That was Majek's voice. I hardly knew when he entered the house.

"I slept fine, thank you".

"I sent Doyin to you but when she didn't come back in time, I got worried hence I decided to come."

"Don't mind Doyin, she is trying to be caring and supportive. I'm feeling fine. I only felt lonely because of uncle Jim's absence and your own absence."

Majek smiled at the last statement. "I'm happy to take care of you in the absence of Jim".

"Thank you."

"Now, Oguaa, you should be taken around to places in the city. I mean places of interest. So, go inside, put on your Sunday best for we're going to see some beautiful places in town".

I was elated. I had longed for such a proposal. I wanted to see Lagos.

As I walked inside my room to change, Majek murmured to himself and smiled. I didn't hear him clearly, but I suppose that he seemed stunned by my shape and beauty.

I didn't spend time. I was dressed in a blue skirt, white T-shirt and blue shoes. I hung my white bag over my left shoulder.

"You should have been more cute and smashing in jeans, Oguaa. Anyway, you're still a young student. I admire your demure appearance. Let's go. We are painting the town red," Majek joked.

The first place Majek was driving to was the Bar Beach. While at the top of Eko Bridge Oguaa looked down to behold rows of hundreds of cars parked at the Marina, she wondered whether the cars were for sale or for exhibition.

Instead of driving straight to the Bar Beach, Majek swerved left into Onikan to look around the Museum. A few poles away from the Museum opposite a high commission building, Oguaa noticed children clapping in an excited mood.

They were obviously pursuing a habitual sight. But the elderly people around the scene were oblivious of the children's excitement.

Majek had realised what it was and he drew a red herring across the trail by opening a conversation on the busy nature of Lagos roads. "They are usually congested causing traffic to traverse at snail speed". He narrated the incident in which it took him more than six hours to drive from Lagos Island to Yaba. He did not have any mechanical fault in his car. The traffic was just at a standstill.

Majek's ploy achieved only a momentary success. The children's ecstasy increased as they drummed on empty cans and tins. Oguaa was forced to look more closely and she beheld a mortifying sight as the children shouted "Mascaras" "Mascaras". Mascaras was the name of an indomitable popular television wrestler. Was he on the streets of Lagos or just in passing car? Human excreta was being conveyed on giant buckets by men in the heart of Lagos. Oguaa was shocked. Obviously the work dress of the conservancy workers resembled that of the great wrestler Mascaras.

Oguaa wondered at the beauty of the ocean and the beach when they alighted from the car and walked through the sandy surrounding. The water stretched as far as the eye could reach. She wondered at the rolling and rumbling currents of water from the Atlantic Ocean. The noise was reverberating like that of thunder. The large heap of sand at the coast amazed her. She wondered and asked Majek how it came to be there as the two pulled off their shoes and walked hand in hand, wading through the sand at the coast. At intervals, Majek would stop by one of the numerous spots to buy snacks and soft drinks for their refreshment. Sometimes they would just sit close together and watch other picnickers swim in their suits while others sunbathed in their bikinis. At other times they would stop and watch people shout and gamble at card games. Some children of school age played football with improvised goal-posts at the sandy beach.

They dusted themselves of the wet sand and drove to the National Theatre where Oguaa had the opportunity to watch a film full of violent incidents. There were ruthless killings which made her shudder. The climax was the cold-blooded assassination of Celina Regin whose father had suffered a similar shocking fate. She had recoiled at such scenes and held tightly to

Majek's left hand as if she was trying to avert the tragedy.

Oguaa saw familiar sights as they drove next to the National Stadium in Surulere. Although no match was on, Majek wanted her to see the Stadium and compare it with the television version. The rows of empty stands gave little excitement to Oguaa. She was not usually gamesome but her enthusiasm was rekindled when she saw the empty spots in the VIP stand from where the television and radio broadcasts were respectively beamed to the world.

Eventually, Oguaa was driven to the same casino where people gathered around both day and night and gambled at machines. The casino was as usual half filled with young people of both sexes. Some drank while others smoked different kinds of stuff. Few others chatted loudly and watched as if waiting their turn to try their hands at the machines. Disco music played loudly and many people danced.

Majek took her to the gambling machines where she gambled several times but never won. Later they went to sit and Majek beckoned on the bar man to take his order. "Gin and lime for me. And what for you?"

"Soft drink", Oguaa requested.

"Get her malt drink and roasted chicken, too?" Majek added as the bar man left.

"Oguaa, you have to taste a little gin and lime today. It's sweet. You can even add the mixture to the malt drink."

Oguaa mused. As she ate the chicken parts and sipped her soft drink, she felt rather uncomfortable in the midst of the faces in the casino. Some would drink a bottle of beer at a gulp, smoke and blow their cigar fumes on other's faces and shout at the top of their voices in the sweet name of conversation. Some became drunk and exhibited all kinds of rude mannerisms.

The men who sat immediately behind Oguaa and Majek were no exception. They drank, smiled and blew their cigarette smoke across Oguaa's ears. She looked at Majek who seemed unperturbed by the goings-on. He seriously sipped his gin and lime and nodded at any music, local or foreign that blared from the amplifier. He seemed to know the rhythm of every record being played.

Latter, Majek beckoned on the bar man to bring more drinks. Oguaa declined the offer but rather requested that they should hurry up and leave the venue.

"O. K. Just help me with this quantity of gin in the glass, then we can go. It's sweet. Taste it and you'll find out."

Oguaa, discovering that it tasted good, drank the whole content of the glass in one gulp.

"Let's go."

Meanwhile the gin and lime taken by Oguaa had made her become slightly dizzy. The music from the car stereo boomed as they drove to Majek's rendezvous. Majek held on to the steering with his left hand. All the while, he whistled, snapped his fingers and nodded rhymically to the music from the car stereo. Occasionally he allowed his hand to wander into the public area of Oguaa.

Oguaa was beginning to muse over the life she was going through. Was this what holiday in Lagos was about?

Was it the sweet life? Though dizzy, she was still in control of her senses when they got to Majek's rendezvous.

Majek helped Oguaa to sit on one of the three-seaters. It was the room she had come into only yesterday. But the whole place seemed re-arranged. The window blinds had been changed.

The television and video sets were still the same but their position had changed along with their coverings.

Oguaa was feeling comfortable though she looked a little tired. She smiled from time to time as she picked up each of the several video cassette tapes to see the cover pictures.

Majek stood up, made straight to the television and switched it on. He slot in a video cassette and went back to his seat.

On the screen were revolving pictures of naked men and woman having sex in different positions. While the act was on, some screamed like wild animals while others hissed like snakes all in ecstasy.

At first, it was all strange to Oguaa. She had never seen such a sight before-men, and women naked and doing their thing – unable to control his sexual urge, Majek drew Oguaa closer and rumbled through her breast and sensitive parts – Oguaa's eagerness knew no bounds. But Majek took his time.

Soon she slept off on the soft rug and Majek lay also beside her. When he knew that she was fast asleep, he unbuttoned her skirt and pulled it down. He also gradually drew her elastic underwear. Her public hair concealed her sanctuary. Majek merely ruffled the lock of her hair and inserted the forefinger of his left hand inside her. He parted her legs wider. He ran inside the back of his shelf and removed his Yashica camera. He took several shots of her then returned the camera. He then came back and pulled back both the underwear and skirt.

Majek left Oguaa to sleep while he went out to inspect the engine of his car and top the water and oil respectively. He also tightened few bolts and nuts. With a wet towel he wiped the car clean although it was still shining its true monaco blue colour.

He came in and had a cool bath. At a few minutes past seven he woke Oguaa. She rubbed her eyes several times and could not locate her whereabouts. When she knew her setting, Majek told her to take a bath. She came out fresh and radiant after combing her hair and patting it at the middle.

When they arrived at the place located at Ikeja, Oguaa noticed several young men and women in the large hall. Many of the women were in their early twenties, while others were teenagers. They conversed in hilarious tones and their sense of freedom and amicability was high.

When they went to their corner, Oguaa held Majek tightly at the right hand for she did not know what it was all about.

The bulbs of the different hues twinkled their 20-watt power and revealed the faces of the inmates. Laughter rolled and cat-calls reverberated the whole place.

At first, it looked like a cocktail. Glasses clinked and spirits were poured into them. But the men were lightly dressed, no three piece suits, no agbada; only casual wears. Most of the women were similarly dressed.

Majek urged Oguaa to quickly swallow the content of her glass. Other women were also doing the same. It looked as if a signal had been given but only the initiated would understand. The women were handing the glasses over to their men while the men were drifting to one side as if to deposit the glasses at a central pool.

Suddenly music blared from invisible loud speakers and the men and women picked up the rhythm. They slowly giggled in happiness. Oguaa danced with uncertain steps but no one noticed she was a greenhorn in the venue. Everyone thought the other experienced in every event in the hall.

Oguaa's song of innocence did not last long for she quickly picked the popular dance steps and made her mark. Majek was elated. He held her tightly to his breasts for several minutes.

The music changed several times but it was hardly noticeable. Each new rhythm started right inside the dying one and one could hardly know at what point to cool off. Music continued and the men and women danced and danced as if waiting for a signal that never seemed to arrive.

More music and the lights dimmed more and finally died. There was shuffle of feet on the rugged floor.

There were screams and hissing on the floor. The wriggling and gyrations that filled the air was immeasurable.

The music continued to play but no one seamed to care whose partner he held so long as he felt a pair of breasts on the upper abdomen.

After several minutes had ticked away there was renewed activity as if they changed partners. The female partners enjoyed it more and more.

When it was all over, the lights came on gradually. The women fidgeted for their skirt. Others with long gowns merely pulled them up. Several underwear's littered the floor. No one seemed to want them. Their owners must have been people who knew little of where they were going. The women merely giggled at such. The men simply zipped their trousers and smiled into faces closest to them. No one knew whom his or her partner had been.

Majek searched for Oguaa. He did not search long as the lights were now brighter. He held her warmly to him and smiled into her face. He never bothered of such rare opportunities in picking a pretty girl since he had his fill of her earlier. It was past midnight and as he could not drive Oguaa home, he simply took her back to his own chalet until early morning.

Oguaa slept until five-thirty in the morning. When she woke up and got dressed, they headed for Jim's house.

At the door of Jim's house, Oguaa inserted the key, turned it but it got stuck. She could not turn it. Her heart beat missed. Perhaps thieves had burgled the house. Majek was impatiently waiting for her to step into the sitting room before he drove off. But that was not to be for the noise had awakened Jim who opened the door from the inside. He had come home by the night flight and was shocked to find Oguaa out of the house. He opened the door to behold Oguaa standing in front with the key in her hand.

He raised his eyes to see Majek who was ready to drive off. Majek merely waved and promised to come back later in the day. Jim opened the door wider to let his niece in.

"Good morning uncle Jim", Oguaa greeted.

"Morning".

He sought no explanations.

He received none.

9

"The full effect of the war on the moral fabric of our society will be immeasurable," said Mary.

"You're quite correct. Our society is in a big mess. It has not dawned on us", agreed Nwayieze, Anselem's wife.

"Imagine young girls taunting their bodies to the embrace of any man who cared", Mary added.

"You see them in the barracks hawking their wares just for a mere cup of salt and some heads of stockfish. Most annoying is the case of the so-called liberated women who join the young girls in this disgusting trade."

"Yes, the irony is that many of such women have sons and daughters fighting for Biafra. I don't know whether they didn't know that whatever they sold to the enemy strengthened him to slaughter their own children in the various sectors of the war", said Mary.

"Our girls sold their bodies for a mere pitance and my God, the ugliness of the men didn't repulse them," Nwayieze said as she screwed her face to indicate disgust.

"In most cases, no one forced them. They first used

what they have to obtain whatever they wanted."

"And do they expect decent men to marry them at normal times?" Mary asked.

"It isn't easy to say, but they will all get married some day. And who knows the type of disease that changed hands in such a free-for-all affair", said Nwayieze.

"They'll be married. Anything goes in our society. Men will always run after a shapely thing in skirt no matter the past history. You may not be surprised that such shameless girls pick up partners first. They know what the man wants they offer it in large doses and cart away their prizes," Nwanyieze reasoned.

"A particular one in our refugee camp literally begged the men to have her. Sometimes she was beaten up mercilessly. The next day you would see her there again. We all wondered whether she still had any sense left," added Mary.

"My sister, it was horrible. I know her. In fact every mother knew her for we all cautioned our daughters against any association with her. But she always succeeded in entrapping younger girls into her fold. Yes, Comfort was her name".

"I notice that such girls never bear their real names, or rather, they hide their names while perpetrating their nefarious activities. God forgive them", Nwanyieze said.

Their conversation was interrupted by the arrival of Loretta, Oguaa's bossom friend. Among her friends, Loretta was the closest and dearest. Oguaa and Loretta came from the same village. In fact her parents were Loretta's god-parents.

The two families are close.

Loretta was a year younger than Oguaa. At the end of their primary education, both girls gained admission into the same Girls' Grammar School in Owerri. They lived in the boarding house.

Oguaa and Loretta got on very well. They did everything in common-eating, playing and working. They came out in flying colours after each examination.

The Girl's Grammar School was fenced round with barbed wire. Some distance away from the entrance gate was a mango tree. It was under this tree that a group of girls found pleasure, and relaxed whenever they had nothing doing. Oguaa and Loretta also enjoyed this past time.

Just outside the school compound along the sides of the main road were hawkers who sold a variety of things to students. Young boys, some of them in bawdy appearances also loitered outside the school compound. For a chat they beckoned on any of the girls they saw coming out of the school compound.

Funny enough, some of the approaches always met with rebuff when they called on any of the girls.

The girls would cock their snook at them and sometimes call them names like truants, ragamuffins and hooligans. They kept on trying, hoping to win one of them for friendship. And they did win on few occasions.

One evening, Oguaa and Loretta were under the mango tree. "Oguaa, I didn't tell you. One of those ragamuffins, putting on dirty jeans and a worn-out polo shirt, whistled and called me yesterday when I went to buy a biro. I insulted him.

He drew nearer to touch me while I was going. I was mad with anger and of course, I gave him the treatment he deserved".

"How did you treat him?" Oguaa asked Loretta.

"I gave him the length of my tongue. The idiot was indeed a nuisance and more still a college drop-out. I wondered if he had even had his bath for two weeks. Oguaa, the pigsty stank like a cesspit".

"It's good you told him off. I suppose he would go back home and think", Oguaa put in.

As Oguaa and Loretta were still chatting, a 504 saloon car pulled up just outside the entrance gate. Emerging from it were two well-dressed men and a girl.

"Oguaa, see that girl coming out of the car. It's Lizzy. Do you know she is repeating class two? She will fail again if she continues to go about with men. She is the girl they made a caricature of yesterday in class Two C.

"Why", Oguaa inquired.

"The letter she wrote to one of her male friends was picked up on the floor of her classroom and was pasted on the notice board and read by several girls before she found out."

"And you know what, Oguaa? Lizzy has no shame. She doesn't seem to be moved even by the taunting given her by some of her classmates, since the letter scandal. She had even proudly told them they were too young for her to talk to them. That they knew next to nothing and would never mind their business. I learnt that she begged and even offered money before the letter was given back to her".

"Look at her walking as if she is a queen. Her beauty has gone into her head. She sees only herself", Oguaa said.

Just at that moment, the school bell rang.

"Oguaa, let's go. It's supper time."

"Beans again. I hate to eat their beans. Just beans, nothing added to make it palatable", Oguaa complained as they left.

Indeed, Oguaa and Loretta's friendship was growing

by leaps and bounds. Most of the time they travelled home together on weekends, both visiting each other's home and spending hours with the parents. Their parents would ask them questions about their studies and life in school.

This was the good, peaceful and friendly atmosphere existing between them before Oguaa travelled to Port Harcourt and Lagos respectively on holidays. After her trips, things began to go sour.

Oguaa came back a changed girl. She no longer saw things the way she used to. She had abandoned the good ways taught her by her parents and sustained by her friendship with Loretta.

In Port-Harcourt, Oguaa had been exposed to beauty, make-up and fashion. Anyamba's sister, Nnenna hadn't enough time to keep an eye on her. She rather spent most of her time travelling overseas or working in her hair-dressing salon where customers streamed in endlessly. Her two maids took care of her house and most of the time they cooked for her.

This tight schedule which Nnenna had, made Oguaa spend all her time with the maids throughout her holidays at Port Harcourt.

It was most unfortunate for Oguaa for these maids who were by far older than her had a lot of influence over her. They were of low morals. Their gossips revolved around the secret faults of others and their discussions often centred on men, money, fashion and sex. They often taunted Oguaa for being timid, naïve and shy. "By the time you leave this place" Adaku, the short abrasive one would say, "you'll abandon your timidity." Their discussion made a lot of impressions for Oguaa soon began to detest life in the village.

In Lagos she had been brain-washed by Majek, Dotun and Jim in their various ways. All she could think about now was beauty, fashion and romance. These made up the new world as taught her by Majek.

While Loretta thought of morals and studies, Oguaa thought of comfort and easy life. To worsen it all, she started developing hatred for Loretta and even despised her.

"Be there. Don't open your eyes to modernity. Keep preaching what you don't know. You will live and die in the old world of your grand parents, if you don't fight to free yourself".

"Are you crazy? Have you gone out of your mind, Oguaa? What's come over you? Your behaviour changed when you came back from Port-Harcourt. You speak strangely to me and I no longer worth anything to you. What have I done to you? Are you under a spell? You came back from Lagos only to look down on people and see things strangely."

"Loretta, you talk a lot. It's love. I found a new world. A world of love and class. Not the old world in which you're still living. The bus of modernity will abandon you."

Oguaa had formed the habit of courting many of their students as friends, particularly, those whose "eyes are open" as she puts it.

To Loretta's bitter and utter disappointment, Oguaa had become friendly with the despised Lizzy. She also became friendly with Tolu an intimate friend of Lizzy.

At the beginning of her friendship with Tolu, Loretta had warned her saying:

"Oguaa, this friendship with Tolu is not healthy for you. Tolu and Lizzy are friends and they are tarred with the same brush. Remember the saying, show me your friends and I will tell you who you are. They will succeed in bringing you into their fold of disrepute."

"Loretta, I had in the past joined you in despising Lizzy and her friends. That was when I was a novice. Lizzy and her friends are not as bad as they have been painted. You tend to judge people you don't know much about. My short contact with Tolu and others shows me there is a method in the madness of those people we despise. They have their own lives and you have yours to live. They mind their own business. Let's mind ours. Leave them alone. As for me, I know myself, and I am old enough to know what is right and what is wrong for me."

"I can see you have gone far, Oguaa. Preservation and good manners do not mean anything to you again. You have to bear in mind that what you think is right may not necessarily be right for you. You still have to be guided."

"Loretta! Nobody talks about virgins these days. You just have to fight and free yourself."

Oguaa was undaunted, She had lost interest in reading and had begun to join Lizzy and her friends at sneaking in and out of the school to attend parties and dally with men.

Loretta was in fact overwhelmed by these strange happenings. Her efforts to win Oguaa away from that life proved futile. She would cry her heart out at Oguaa's behaviour. She would go to her parents to let them know what has been happening to their daughter.

Oguaa's parents could not believe Loretta for certain reasons. Their daughter was still visiting home as usual. She still performed well at the end-of-term examination. Loretta could neither convince Mary nor Anyamba.

Oguaa saw Loretta's recent moves as one borne out of

envy. She complained to her parents who though believed her, still advised that she should not break up her long lasting frendship with Loretta.

Loretta and Oguaa never came home together again. Oguaa had stopped going to Loretta's place but Loretta was still visiting Oguaa's parents.

Loretta would cry her heart out. Teardrops would gently roll down her cheeks as she thought of her long lasting relationship with Oguaa. A relationship which had been well nurtured and gradually built up into a sisterly affair.

"What went wrong?"

"What forces of evil are work?"

"Who is responsible for this unfortunate and untimely estragement?"

"How can this monstrous situation be remedied?"

As Loretta pondered over these unanswered questions, the teardrops rolled down to wet her pillow. She must find a solution. She must seek for a reconciliation fast.

With such determination, Loretta slowly drifted into a nightmarish sleep.

10

The fever had subsided. He lay quietly on the bed. It was not an ordinary fever. Its effect had taken some toll on his lean figure. The whole picture seems to unfold.

Yes. It all began about three or rather four days ago at about 4 O'clock on that fateful evening. He had left his parent's house and after visiting the two supermarkets to assess the progress of sales for the day, he had left for the restaurant. As he stepped into his private apartment within the restaurant, he realized that the air-conditioners were still on and the whole room was very chilly. At his parent's house he had complained of having a mild headache which he thought, was an excuse to leave. He wanted to be alone, so leaving them was good riddance.

He also remembered that at about 9.00 p.m., he had switched off the air-conditioners as well as the fluorescent lights before going to bed.

"Oh what a relief", he thought. "I can have rest before midnight." Meanwhile, he could hear the faint noises of music blarring downstairs in the lobby of the restaurant. Obviously one of those crazy juju minstrels was taking care of a ceremony whose reception had been scheduled to take place at his restaurant. He let out a faint smile, mused to himself as he imagined the scenes that would be created downstairs before the ceremony winds up at the dawn of the next day. The parade of beautiful ladies in elegant attires; the preying eyes of bachelors and sugar daddies; the show of affluence in terms of the variety of cars that will be parked outside the restaurant; the spraying sessions and a lot more. Having over-stretched his imagination, he fell asleep.

Majek woke up in the morning feeling rather uneasy. Trickles of sweat bathed his frame. He was feeling very hot and his body shook feverishly.

He was not going to take chances. He had actually felt sick at his parent's house although he never expected that the feeling would degenerate to the situation he has suddenly woken up to find himself. He managed to get up. On reaching the bathroom cabinet, he retrieved two tablets of analgesic drug. With a little water from the flask, he swallowed the pills and retired to bed.

That was three days ago. The medicine did not seem to have helped as he surveyed the skeletal frame, which was all that was left of his once enviable physique.

"Why should Jim do this to me? At least he should have informed me before sending his niece back to the East. I may have behaved badly but my apologies should have appeased him. Oguaa is a very nice girl. Quiet, intelligent though naïve. She would make a good wife for any eligible bachelor for she is a rare and priceless gem. Oh Oguaa! I have treated you badly. No parting words. No farewell gifts. Your uncle never gave me the opportunity to appreciate. How do I make up for this lack? How do I stop your memories from haunting me like a vengeful ghost? I have been miserable for sometime now. I am undergoing a crisis period of mental torture. Oguaa, please forgive me."

A sharp knock on the door interrupted Majek's thought as he quickly reacted and asked the caller to come inside. It was Doyin his sister.

As Doyin came into Majek's apartment, she stood speechless. Her brother's highly emaciated body was a big surprise. Majek slowly lifted himself from his lying position and sat on the bed. Doyin moved over and sat beside him.

"What is the matter?" Doyin asked in a tearful voice.

"Nothing?"

"Yes Nothing."

"And you expect me to believe you. You have been away from home for almost four days."

"I have not been feeling fine."

"And you did not deem it necessary to inform anyone? Majek! What is eating you up?"

Doyin walked up to a side table and handed a mirror over to Majek.

"Take a look at yourself. You look like a scare crow. I am sure you have not tasted any food for some days not to talk of having a bath and a clean shave."

Doyin's word struck Majek like a thunder bolt. He had not realised the extent of damage which has been inflicted on him as a result of his illness and his condition. How can he explain that his illness had been compounded by his endless thoughts about Oguaa? Oguaa, his heart-throb whose absence has created a vacuum in his innermost being.

As Doyin ranted, raved and fumed, Majek simply stared

at her.

"I shall not stay here and watch you kill yourself. First of all, you must eat something before I call mum and dad on the phone. After that we shall leave for the hospital."

"No! Don't tell them Doyin. You will only succeed in getting them worried. Remember that they are getting old and mama is hypertensive case. Don't raise any false alarm so as not to put the entire family in a panicky situation. The crisis period is over and I shall soon be well and strong enough to explain things if the need arises.

Doyin sat still as if weighing Majek's utterances. She then got up and walked towards the cupboard from where she fetched some beverages, milk and sugar. Soon Majek was enjoying the hot beverage drink to Doyin's delight.

Having gulped down two cupfuls of the Bournvita drink, Doyin surveyed the apartment. Everything looked out of place. Everywhere was in a mess for the apartment had not been swept for some days.

"Now Majek. All you need is a little rest before we go to see the doctor. While you rest, I shall try to tidy up your apartment."

"Why don't you leave that for the cleaners?" Majek interrupted.

"I am not doing the sweeping. I just want to make sure nobody comes in to see this place in such an awful condition", Doyin replied.

Majek was not prepared to argue. Rather he quietly rested his head on the pillow and was soon fast asleep.

Meanwhile Doyin got busy dusting the entire apartment. She removed the bedsheets on the other bed and replaced them with new ones. She washed up the cup from which Majek drank and returned the beverages and other food items into the drawer. As she opened the drawer, she noticed that there was a fat envelope. Looking closely Doyin saw that the envelope contained printed photographs as well as the negative of the printed pictures. While her brother slept, Doyin glanced through the photographs. She was amused as she saw pictures of herself which Majek took. She was even more excited when she noticed that the pictures of Majek and Oguaa which were taken by her turned out good. There were beautiful shots of her brother and Oguaa entering the car, relaxing at the Beach and posing before the grand statue that graced the National Theatre. She admired the pictures and praised her dexterity in the art of photography.

"That is not a bad start for an amateur", Doyin mused, as she continued to look at the other photographs in the envelope.

*   *   *   *   *   *   *

"I can't understand the girls of nowdays. Does she have to buy a whole house before she returns to school?"

"Ade, I don't understand why you should be worried. Doyin is not asking for any financial assistance from you."

"Yes, Iya Doyin. I know you will say that. But you forget that her brothers will always help her out no matter what it costs them."

"That's what brothers are meant for. You don't expect a girl of her age to go about begging for money. That will not tell good on the family Ade".

"I only hope those children do not put me out of business."

Iya Doyin let out a quiet smile before she again addressed

her husband.

"Ade, your little boys are doing well in the business. You should be proud of them. Each time I think of these two little gifts from God, I feel younger and happier".

Iya Doyin as she was fondly called always, referred to her husband as Ade the short form of Adefolahan. Their conversation which centered on Doyin was taking place as Pa Makanjuola was treating himself to a delicious meal of amala with ewedu soup. As he ate the slimy sauce with the processed yam flour, his face radiated happiness and pleasure.

He ate with relish while his wife patiently waited and watched as each ball of moulded yam flour immersed in the slimy sauce disappeared into the mouth of her husband. After more balls had disappeared, Ade belched and washed down the food with some cold water which was served in a large bowl.

"Iya Doyin", her husband called.

"I am listening", replied his wife.

"Don't you think that Majek looks more promising and enterprising?"

"How, Ade?"

"In every way."

"I don't understand you."

Every event points towards what I am saying. From their returns you can see that the supermarkets and restaurant are really making fantastic gain", Pa Makanjuola said.

"So also are the Hotels", his wife replied.

"You don't understand. Dotun is not as organised as Majek. If only he can be a little more shrewd and serious, he will improve in his turnout."

"Ade, don't forget that Majek's restaurant also houses

a casino. I remember your telling me one day that casino is a public room used for gambling and other forms of entertainment. Times may be difficult but despite that Majek tells me that many people especially the moneybags, both black and white besiege the casino every night. They are of course trying their luck to see if fortune will smile on them and give them the rare opportunity to triple their millions. It is not fair to compare my two boys. Running a hotel is quite different from running a restaurant and casino."

Pa Makanjuola was not ready to go into further arguments with his wife. He knew it would be a futile attempt since Dotun has always been his mother's favourite and pet. Pa Makanjuola also knew that Dotun's love for the opposite sex knew no bounds for he at one time or the other brought home a new female visitor. This was not the case with Majek who his father saw as one woman man. It was thus wise for him to reluctantly agree to his wife's views. At least the postponement of the issue would enable him enjoy the good meal. However he still felt Doyin was becoming too demanding. But as a young lady still in school, her needs have to be met in order to ensure that she does not stray away from her academic pursuits.

*   *   *   *   *   *   *

"Majek! Majek! Wake up". It was Doyin shouting at her brother who had fallen asleep after taking his drink. Majek rolled over and answered in a sleepy voice.

"I say wake up!" Doyin repeated.

"What is the matter?", replied her brother.

"Everything is the matter. Wake up and explain what you have here".

Doyin was holding a photograph which was among the pile of printed ones contained in the fat envelope which Doyin had earlier seen in Majek's drawer. The picture was a nude photograph of Oguaa. This unusual discovery had greatly infuriated Doyin hence her aggressive mood.

"Majek why did you have to do this?"

Majek who was now wide awake saw the photograph and immediately pounced on his sister in a bid to retrieve the picture. But he had been sick, so no matter how hard he tried, he could not get the photograph from Doyin.

"Why are men so unreliable? What have we done to deserve this human degradation? What have you done to this innocent girl? Tell me Majek! Tell me", Doyin lamented.

"I did it with her consent. Oguaa agreed to pose for me. I paid her well", Majek managed to say.

"You are a liar. Oguaa is a decent girl and would never have subjected herself to such an indecent exposure. Look Majek, I am very much ashamed of you. I hate you! You are a disgrace to the men folk".

Majek could not cope with Doyin's aggressive mood. He saw her as a wounded lioness who would never spare any prey that fell on her way. He could not look into Doyin's ferocious eyes. He simply sat with his head bent low staring at the floor. But Doyin would not relent.

"When have you stooped so low as to indulge in pornographic displays? How would you feel if it was your sister that is being treated this way?" Doyin continued despite Majek's pleading that she should take it easy.

"I will not stop. In fact I am going to show Jim this picture so that he will know exactly what you did with his niece.

I will also inform mum and dad so that they will rejoice for having a son with loose morals. Majek! By the time I finish with you, you will not be able to walk along the streets without feeling the pangs of guilt. Women will dread any encounter with you. I don't need to talk more for you will soon be a laughing stock all over town."

Doyin's rantings were interrupted by a hard knock on the door. Silence reigned as Doyin quickly wiped her tear-stained face and simultaneously put the nude photograph inside her hand bag. The caller was Dotun. But he was not alone for behind him trailed Kemi his girl friend.

As soon as Kemi stepped into the room she sensed that all was not well. One look at Doyin told her that the former had been crying. But she decided to keep quiet since she was in the midst of two brothers and a sister.

"Hello Doyin, how are you?" Kemi greeted.

"I am fine and what about you", Doyin asked.

"I am alright, as you can see", replied Kemi.

However Kemi noticed that Doyin did not greet Dotun. No doubt she was still nursing the grievances she had just acquired over the men folk.

"Little sister, why did you fail to tell me that Majek has been ill?" Dotun asked.

"That's true Doyin", Kemi interjected. "At least we would have come earlier to see him."

"Don't worry Dotun, Majek said. I was not really sick. Just a little tired. You know we have been very busy all through the weekend at the restaurant. How are you Kemi?"

"Fit as a fiddle as you can see", replied Kemi.

Majek managed to give her a faint smile.

"You have lost much weight", Dotun said to Majek.

"Better explain to the doctor that you need some blood tonic before you end up as thin as a rake".

"Doyin is taking good care of me. I'm almost feeling fine. I just need some rest and within a few days I shall be strong again."

"Kemi and I were on our way to see mum and dad but decided to check on you first. More still I wanted to have a private discussion with you and Doyin but we can talk some other time".

"No, Dotun. That is not fair, Kemi said. I can wait inside the car while you discuss your family affairs."

Dotun was quite surprised at Kemi's reaction.

When did she acquire the pleasant habit of showing such a sense of maturity by asking to be excused? Nevertheless, he gave the car key to Kemi who left immediately, leaving the two brothers and their sister to discuss.

"Now Majek," Dotun started. "What is wrong with you? As I was coming in I heard Doyin screaming, shouting and cursing. Was she trying to cast out the demons that may be responsible for your sickness?"

"There was nothing like that", Doyin replied. "I was simply expressing my annoyance over Majek's inability to get any member of the family informed that he was sick".

"Are you sure there isn't more to what you have just said Doyin?"

"She is right Dotun. You know that Doyin easily gets temperamental so I wouldn't like you to get worried over her momentary tantrums".

Dotun knew both of them were trying to cover up.

"That's alright by me. I suppose I can now leave".

"Majek please get well quick and promise never to fall sick again as a result of the loss of a woman."

"Which woman?" Majek inquired.

"You are love sick my dear brother. Oguaa may have forgotten you by now. You should never trust any woman."

Dotun's gaze immediately fell on Doyin and he could see anger radiating from his sister's eyes. Nevertheless he bade them good bye and promised to call back the next day.

"Where are we going to?" inquired Kemi as Dotun drove off.

"To see Jim… Any objections?"

Kemi did not reply.

As soon as Dotun left, Doyin once more resumed her threats and warning over the nude photograph of Oguaa. But this time she was talking to a sober Majek. On noticing that her brother was indeed ashamed of his act, Doyin's utterances became more of an advice than a reprimand.

"Jim's niece is still in the secondary school Majek. It was very wrong of you to have taken an undue advantage of her innocence. Think of what the fate of this little girl would be should this photograph get outside this apartment".

"I did not mean to keep it", Majek said.

"Good then. I will destroy it immediately but that will be on the condition that you also let me have the negative", said Doyin.

"What do you need the negative for?"

"Just in case you fail to meet up with my financial demands. You know I shall soon be going back to school."

"That is blackmail Doyin. You are not being fair."

"No way dear brother. It is a deal. You are supposed to be a businessman. I shall destroy the photograph before I leave. But I can only destroy the negative when you have signed the cheque for my up-keep while on campus. What do you say Majek?"

Majek was silent for a while. He thought of women and their wily ways. He definitely knew he had no options so he asked his sister to get him his brief case.

When Doyin handed over the brief case to his brother, Majek brought out his cheque book and wrote out a cheque which he gave Doyin. Doyin looked at the cheque and smiled. At least with five thousand naira she can purchase some beautiful dresses as well as get herself initiated in the most popular Ivy League Club on the campus. Of course she still has to collect more money from Dotun. She bent and kissed her brother very passionately on the cheeks. Having expressed her delight and appreciation for the wonderful gift from Majek, she picked up a pair of scissors from the drawer and cut both the negative and the nude picture into shreds. She then went into the toilet and soon every shred had been flushed down the drains.

"Now brother Majek, your secret has at last been buried down the drains. Get dressed and let's go and see the doctor."

As the two approached the door on heir way out Doyin held on to her brother and asked.

"Now tell me, Dotun may be right. Are you love sick?"

Majek suddenly burst into an uncontrollable fit of laughter. Doyin soon joined him. After some time Doyin repeated her question.

Majek smiled this time and said:
"I don't know."

11

Pa Adefolahan Makanjuola seemed to have taken a liking to Oguaa right from the first day the pretty girl visited him in company of his daughter Doyin. After brief introduction, Pa Adefolahan asked:

"My daughter, where do you come from?"

"I am Ibo sir," replied Oguaa. My father hails from Umuayalu one of the villages in the Eastern part of the country."

"You are welcome. I supposed you have come to Lagos to spend some part of your holidays with your uncle Jim?"

"Yes sir".

"I hope you find your stay in Lagos a pleasant one. Doyin, please make sure that Oguaa is well taken care of."

"You bet I will father", replied Doyin.

As soon as Doyin and Oguaa left for Doyin's room, Doyin's mother emerged from the bedroom and inquired who the caller was. Before her husband could reply, Doyin and Oguaa once more emerged from the house.

"Mama, this is Oguaa, brother Jim's niece".

"How are you my daughter?"

"I am fine," replied Oguaa.

"Mama. We want to pick up some food items from our supermarket. We will soon be back."

Without waiting for a reply, Doyin took Oguaa's hand and the two girls left the compound. Husband and wife exchanged glances. The message was clear. Doyin is an excellent schemer and matchmaker. And her brother Majek is the target.

All these are far-fetched now. Oguaa has learnt a lot in Lagos. She has returned to school to form an unholy alliance with Lizzy. Loretta her best friend can go to hell for all she cared.

Lizzy was happy over her newly acquired convert. To Lizzy, Oguaa was a new weapon that had been added to her deadly arsenal.

* * * * * * *

For two weeks Jim had worked tirelessly in his office without asking for his normal off days. This was however deliberate for he wanted to get over the rude shock he had experienced on the night he arrived home, only to discover that Oguaa was not in the house. He had contemplated going to report to the Police Station but had later decided to wait until morning before taking any action.

It was thus a great relief when he opened the door in the morning only to find Oguaa standing in front of him. He also noticed that Majek brought her but since he did not wait to offer any explanation, he decided to let the sleeping dog lie in the meantime.

For Oguaa, her uncle's cold reception immediately sent shivers running down her spine. Her entire frame was ridden with guilt but she summoned up courage and disappeared into her room. She soon re-emerged and walked straight to the bathroom to have a shower. It was not until two days later that Jim confronted his niece and demanded an explanation for her spending the night out with Majek. Oguaa could not offer any explanation. In fact she did not utter a word but rather replied with streams of tears running down her face. Jim remained calm but deep down in his mind, the die was cast. Majek had betrayed him and Oguaa had been foolish to fall into his trap. He had to play safe and the only option left was to arrange for Oguaa to leave for home the following morning.

It was the day that Oguaa left that Majek paid a visit to Jim in his office. He sounded apologetic but Jim merely accepted his apologies as a purely routine exercise. The harm had been done but thank God Oguaa was already on her way back to her parents, Mary and Anyamba. For old time sake, Jim decided to maintain the cordial relationship and let bye gone be bye gone. But for the Makanjuolas, he may still have been trotting the streets of Lagos as a miserable applicant.

*　　*　　*　　*　　*　　*　　*

Mister Ndu taught Mathematics at the Girls' Grammar School, Owerri. He was a very quiet man but took no insults from anybody especially the students. He was aware that most female students generally regarded Mathematics as a very difficult subject, so he tried his best to make the subject interesting and entertaining.

However there were students who despite the Mathematics teacher's effort, had already written off the subject as a no-go area. They did not attend the maths classes neither did they attempt to do the assignments. Two students championed the rebellion against this monstrous subject. They were Lizzy who was repeating form two, and her friend Tolu. When all attempts to get these two rebels attend the Maths classes failed, Mister Ndu gave up and saw them as a lost cause.

Lizzy's dislike for the subject had been borne out of the embarrassing situation she once found herself. During one of the Maths classes (Geometry), Mister Ndu had asked Lizzy to explain to the class what complimentary angles were. Lizzy, who had never read or heard about angles being complimentary simply stood and stared at the teacher.

"Yes Lizzy. What are complimentary angles?" Mister Ndu repeated. Lizzy still remained silent. After asking the question for the third time, Mister Ndu was annoyed.

"I didn't expect a reply from you after all. You feel too big to answer my question. I only pray that you don't repeat this class a third time", Mister Ndu said.

Lizzy was embarrassed over the teacher's blunt remarks. She was equally annoyed that she should be addressed thus. So she quickly said to the teacher, "I hope you do not intend to embarrass me".

Mister Ndu screwed up his face and looking at Lizzy yelled out.

"You think you are pretty. But nobody in his right senses takes pleasure in only admiring pretty faces. You've got to combine beauty with brains my young lady. You know my wife who works in the Ministry. Is she not prettier than you?"

Lizzy did not wait for the teacher to conclude before she snapped back at him.

"Your wife? Who is her? Who is she?"

The whole class burst into laughter and at the same time

chorused an answer to Lizzy's double-edged question. "All of the above". This answer generated more laughter especially from the other students who did not take part in the first segment of the laughing scene.

Lizzy quickly gathered her text books and exercise books and walked out of the class. That was the end of Mathematics for Lizzy. It was also the beginning of enmity between her and Mister Ndu, her Mathematics teacher.

Loretta was determined to end the unholy alliance which now existed between Oguaa and Lizzy. She could not afford an open confrontation with Lizzy, since the latter's notoriety was already a household topic among the students.

She could also not summon up courage to advise Lizzy whose immoral acts were already beyond redemption. Day by day she thought and thought. The opportunity then came and she did not hesitate in utilising it. Her target was of course Tolu, Lizzy's best friend. However she did not anticipate that her actions may lead to some miserable consequences.

Loretta set her plans in motion by pretending to be friendly with Tolu. Oguaa was very much excited with this new development. She rejoiced with Loretta and praised her for seeing reason at last. With this assurance granted, Oguaa took Loretta into confidence and disclosed that Tolu and Lizzy were often in the habit of visiting a chemist store near the post office. There they procured some drugs.

"What for?" inquired the curious Loretta.

Oguaa laughed until tears flowed freely from her eyes down to cover her face. As she wiped the tears with her handkerchief, Oguaa explained in detail.

"Loretta. That is why I keep telling you to grow up.

My association with those girls really opened my eyes. It is true that I have been to Port Harcourt and Lagos. But nothing is as satisfying as freedom. Freedom to do whatever you feel like doing. How, when and where to do it. I was heavily guarded when I visited my aunty, Nnenna at Port Harcourt and my uncle Jim in Lagos. I could not learn much because I was always afraid of the consequences of my action. My association with Lizzy and Tolu gave me that freedom, the confidence and of course, the wisdom to accept challenges and deal with issues single-handedly."

"Oguaa", Loretta called out. You have not told me exactly what takes Lizzy and Tolu to the Chemist."

"Well if you insist, I will. But don't ever mention it to anyone."

Oguaa moved closer to Loretta and whispered into the latter's left ear. Loretta was surprised at what she had just heard from Oguaa.

"But that was dangerous. I wouldn't have taken such a risk."

"It is not risk", Oguaa corrected. "Afterall, I had already told you that it is not their first visit. That man is a wizard. His experience is incredible. I have even accompanied them twice."

"Well, I wish them well," Loretta concluded.

"You can now understand why Lizzy has not been attending classes for some days now. The crisis period will soon be over and she will be fit again to enjoy the fruits of her labour," Oguaa said.

Just as the discussion was coming to an end, the school bell rang signifying the end of the break period. Both girls hurried back with the other students in order to meet up with the Geography lesson.

Unlike Miss Theodora Uwakwe who was the former principal of the Girls' Secondary School, Owerri, Madam Uzor Ezechi was a mother of three, and strict disciplinarian. Within months of resumption of duty in her new station, Madam Ezechi knew that the high moral standards, which earlier characterized her Alma Mater, had fallen greatly.

She had observed that most of the senior girls no longer wore their day dresses which was the official uniform meant to be worn as soon as classes were over. She had also received reports that most of the students left the school premises after class periods and were often seen in town making purchases at the supermarkets. Initially she thought those students did not live in the dormitories but on further investigations, she discovered that most of the defaulting students were residing in the boarding houses. They had no reason to leave for town without obtaining official permission from their various house mistresses or from herself as their Principal. She was determined to curb these excesses.

Contrary to Oguaa's story, Lizzy's recovery did not come as early as anticipated. Rather her condition was growing worse. Lizzy on her own part was becoming sad and afraid for very soon, her predicament would be exposed. She thus resolved to travel home as soon as the Friday classes were over. The pain inside her was becoming unbearable. Some minutes later the pain seemed to subside. She heaved a sign of relief and crawled out of her bed. She was feeling uneasy and needed to visit the ladies'.

*   *   *   *   *   *   *

The Principal, Madam Uzor Ezechi had just completed a tour of House B, which was made up of four large dormitories. As one of her attempts toward the upliftment of the moral standard of her school, she had started paying surprise visits to the dormitories during school hours. After inspecting House B, she was tired but on impulse, she decided to make a quick trip to House C before returning to her office.

House C was made up of three dormitories and a common room. The junior dormitory and the common room were downstairs while the two senior dormitories were located upstairs.

On reaching House C, Madam Ezechi noticed that the door leading to the junior dormitory was wide open.

"Who is the careless prefect who forgot to lock up this dormitory before leaving the classes?" she thought.

Nevertheless she walked into the dormitory and was very much impressed with the tidy manner in which the junior girls arranged their beds and lockers. Everywhere looked neat and perfect and everything seemed to be in their right places. She did not have to go further for House C had won her admiration as well as brought back some degree of re-assurance that sanity was gradually filtering back into the school. She smiled to herself, closed the door and made for the corridor on her way out. Her exit was however temporarily halted. She heard the fast flow of running water. The noise came from the place which housed the toilets and bathrooms.

"Certainly somebody is there. That must be the prefect who had left the door open. Madam Ezechi stopped and waited patiently for the prefect to finish up and come out of the toilet.

Some minutes later the figure appeared. You can imagine the surprise that registered on the Principal's face when she realised that the prefect was no other person than Lizzy. More startling was the fact that Lizzy held tightly to a white towel. This towel can rightly be called red for blood stains had completely changed the colour of the towel.

"What is happening here?" Madam Ezechi asked. Lizzy had been stuck dumb since she could hardly utter a word.

"Why are you not in school?"

"I am not feeling well madam," Lizzy managed to say.

"What is that stuff in your hand?" Madam Ezechi further asked as she looked at the towel.

Lizzy could no longer offer any explanation. The Principal asked her to step aside while she inspected the toilet. One look at the place told her the entire story.

"Now young girl, you have some explanations to do. Wrap up that towel in your palm and follow me immediately to my office".

12

"I don't think this place will be able to accommodate us. You may have to pack and go to the village and stay with your grandmother."

"You are not being fair, mama."

"What else do you want me to say? I can't afford to feed an extra mouth. I have been trying to survive. I can hardly make ends meet. With your presence, I can hardly earn half of what I used to make when you were away."

"I am sorry, mama."

"That's not the solution. Look my daughter, your presence scares some of them. More still my daughter, the profession is neither a noble nor an enviable one. The village is the best place for you."

"I can't stay in the village: You know how granny behaves. I prefer to stay here at Aba, and suffer hunger or starvation than go to the village."

"Well, you have to look for your own accommodation. After all you are a big girl now and must have made huge sums of money."

"I don't have much on me presently. The hospital bill took nearly all the money I had. Mama I almost bled to death. It was my principal who saved my life."

"And expelled you after saving your life", Mama added.

"Yes. But I was not the only one that was punished."

"Of course not. You and your disciples deserved that punishment. Afterall what do they say? Birds with same feathers flock together."

"You are beginning to get on my nerves mama. You talk as if you are a saint. This is just the case of the kettle calling the pot black."

Mama could not stand such an insult. She immediately raised her right hand and the five fingers of her palm descended in one single swoop on her daughter's left cheek. She fell on the bed and started screaming and wailing.

"Serves you right you ungrateful girl. As soon as you are through with those crocodile tears of yours, go and pack your things and leave at once."

The scene was one of the many scenes that took place when Lizzy joined her mother, Monica, at Aba.

As Lizzy cried, she recapitulated her sudden change of fortune as well as the way fate had twisted her life. She blamed only one individual for her ill-luck, and swore to take vengeance on Loretta should the latter ever have the misfortune of coming across her way. But was Loretta really responsible for Lizzy's dramatic exit from the Girls' Grammar School?

*　　　*　　　*　　　*　　　*　　　*　　　*

Uncle Dike, as he was popularly known, had been on hunger strike for two days. Despite all pleadings, he had refused to taste the food which his wife brought him in his cell at the Central Police Station. He was very bitter as well as angry with the girls whose statements before the Disciplinary Committee had brought him into this cell.

Throughout his nine-year practice as a druggist, he had been the darling of many young girls whom he had saved from unwanted pregnancies. The proceeds from his sales and medication had enriched him so much that he had eventually opened a Chemist Shop very close to the General post Office.

As his business boomed, his clientele equally increased to accommodate mainly some wayward housewives, motor-park touts, prostitutes as well as the likes of Lizzy and Tolu. Their indiscriminate love affairs always led them to his store. Uncle Dike was not only good in terminating unwanted pregnancies, he was also an expert in diagnosing and providing cures to various types of venereal diseases. His store was always a behive of activities. As a friend to the law enforcement agents, he was adequately protected against the incessant raids often carried out by the Ministry of Health on the illegal operators of Chemists shops and the attendant sale of fake drugs. Uncle Dike has enjoyed this immunity until Lizzy's case exposed his nefarious activities.

When Lizzy followed Madam Ezechi to the office, the Principal immediately summoned an emergency staff meeting and a panel was set up to investigate and submit a report on their findings in connection with Lizzy's sickness. With the help of the doctor who eventually saved Lizzy from an untimely death, and from the statements made by Tolu, Oguaa, Loretta and some senior girls in the school, Madam Ezechi was forced to subject the entire students population to a thorough medical cheek-up. Lizzy was the only victim of attempted abortion while Tolu and

Oguaa were healthy carriers of venereal diseases. Loretta was discharged and uncle Dike was arrested and detained pending when he would appear in Court.

The penalties for the individual student's crimes ranged from indefinite suspension to outright dismissal from school. Lizzy was sent away from school as soon as she was discharged from the hopital while Oguaa and Tolu were given indefinite suspension. Fate had eventually caught up with the "excited trio" as Lizzy, Oguaa and Tolu were popularly known.

Lizzy was not bothered over her dismissal. She was a dunce hence her exit was a welcome relief from the rigours and boredom, which the phenomenon called "Education" engendered. She knew what to do and felt no remorse for her action. She thanked God for saving her life but left the Girl's Grammar School with a personal grudge. This grudge was no doubt directed at Loretta whose statement Lizzy believed helped the panel in bringing her to book.

She had under-estimated her mother's reaction. Mama would not mind for after all she Monica was equally a popular prostitute. Since the death of Lizzy's father in a fatal car accident, five years ago, Monica had lived at Aba and financed her daughter's education with the proceeds she made from her shaddy profession.

"I will leave", Lizzy muttered to herself. "I cannot cope with Mama's persistent nagging and unnecessary bickering."

*   *   *   *   *   *   *

The wide open space which was a courtyard in Anyamba's compound could contain two mini-football fields. At the center of the open space was the ageless "Udala" tree whose fruits have been tasted by generation of villagers in

Umuayalu. As the need to erect more houses in the compound arose, Mary had advised her husband to cut down the tree. But despite Mary's incessant appeals, Anyamba had remained adamant. The tree was indeed an obstruction but its presence always brought back historical memories to Anyamba.

The foot of the Udala tree housed a make-shift grave where Anselem, Anyamba's uncle, who died during the war was buried. Anyamba had obeyed his uncle's last wish that if he died in the refugee camp, his bones should be brought back to Umuayalu and buried in his ancestral home. To cut down this hitorical tree which was planted by Anselem when he was a little boy, would be sacrilegious and its consequences might spell doom for the entire kindred and even the whole of Umuayalu.

Anyamba was not the superstitious type but the thought of obliterating the memories of his kind uncle deterred him from carrying out his wife's wish. More still Anyamba did not know how Anselem's two widows would take the decision of his meddling with the remains of their late husband. Anyamba knew all these but did not want to disclose his reasons to anybody. Why should he? Afterall his uncle was a good man while he lived. His ghost had never haunted any member of his family. He had weighed all these conditions and finally resolved never to disturb the dead. Activities in the compound were at its peak when a taxi cab blarred its horn and screeched to a halt inside the big compound. At the back of the cab sat a woman who was past her middle age. As she alighted, the children stopped playing their different games. They did not recognise the stranger- a gaily-dressed woman who emerged from the cab.

The noise of the taxi cab also attracted some older members of the family for they hurried out of their individual houses to know what was amiss.

"Nnenna", shouted Nwayieze, who was the first to recognise the strange visitor. It is "Sisi Potacot", Nwayieze who again shouted.

The children gazed at the visitor. Most of them hardly knew Nnenna. Some of the older ones could not even recognise her for the dark complexioned woman who visited the village as soon as the war was over was now a different woman. Her hitherto dark complexion had been highly bleached that she should aptly pass for a half-caste. Affluence radiated all over her perfumed body as the ageless woman smiled, greeted, hugged, and embraced all who had come to welcome her. Mary was one of them.

"Where is my brother?" Nnenna asked Mary as soon as the excitement had subsided.

"He is inside the house. For some days now, he has been weighed down by fever."

"Please take me to him."

As Mary and Nnenna walked towards Anyamba's house, Adaugo who had been busy emerged with her entire palms soiled with red palm oil. As she greeted Nnenna, the later secretly surveyed her and quickly hastened her step so that Adaugo would not see the tear drops fall from her eyes. After wiping the tear, Nnenna now turned and spoke.

"How are you Adaugo?"

"We are surviving my husband", replied Adaugo.

"And your children?"

"We are grateful to God. How is Potacot?"

"Port-Harcourt is fine but I have left that city for good".

Nnenna went into Anyamba's house accompanied by

Mary. Seated on a long form was Anyamba. As he saw his sister, his eyes lit up with pleasure. He also put down the cup of hot tea which he had been drinking.

"Welcome Nne", Anyamba managed to say.

"Anya. Your wife said you have been sick. How are you feeling now? Any improvement?"

"I am getting better," replied Anyamba.

As Nnenna joined her brother on the long form, she further asked: "What medicines have you taken? Have you visited the doctor in town?"

"Adaugo prepared some native herbs for me. It is made from the leaves of a popular tree called Dogonyaro mixed with some other spices like Agbo. Quite a bitter concoction but I am happy it is working", Anyamba concluded.

"Let me prepare some food for you my husband. You must be hungry after making such a long trip to the village", Mary said.

"No need, Mary. Just ask some of the boys to help you bring out my belongings from the boot of the taxi cab. After that, you can dismiss the driver for I have already paid him off."

When Mary left to see the cab driver, Oguaa emerged from an inner room and greeted her aunty.

"Ah Oguaa, my daughter! How are you?"

"I am well aunty", replied Oguaa.

"You don't need to say it. It's quite obvious."

"Jim took her to Lagos on a holiday trip", Anyamba said.

"No wonder! You are a naughty girl. Why have you failed to write me since you came back from Lagos?"

Aunty Nnenna was not surprised to see Oguaa at home.

It was a weekend so she presumed the girl had come to the village to spend her weekend. Nature's handiwork had done quite a lot on Oguaa. She had blossomed into a full fledged woman and her radiant beauty was enchanting.

"How are you enjoying your school?" Nnenna demanded. Oguaa hesitated before giving an answer.

"We are trying, aunty."

"I am happy to hear that. Now that I have moved to Aba, I will one day invite you to come and spend some time with me".

Oguaa was beginning to feel uncomfortable as she stood before her father Anyamba and her aunt Nnenna. She feigned an excuse and left.

"I saw Adaugo when I was coming in Anya. That woman had greatly emaciated. I have been very much worried since I saw her. I hope she and her children are not suffering much since the death of her husband, Pa Anselem."

"Times are hard for all, Nne. We may be poor but thank God nobody is starving. Adaugo has been working hard and I am happy that she and her mate Nwayieze are getting on well. All the same they need help. I can only do my best, but to be candid with you my sister, my best is not good enough."

Nnenna nodded as Anyamba narrated the situation at home. She had anticipated such conditions hence did not come home unprepared.

"I'll see what I can do. I must however thank you for all the assistance you have so far given them since Pa Anselem died. Now what about your children? Oguaa is a big girl now. I hope she is doing well at school?"

Anyamba did not reply to Nnenna's question. He looked around to see if Mary his wife was around but she was nowhere in sight.

"I asked about Oguaa, Anya. You have not answered my question".

"Yes, Nne. Oguaa's story is a long one. You have just arrived and I would not want to bore you with long tales. We shall talk later in the evening."

Before Nnenna could press further, Mary came in dragging along with her two medium sized suitcases. As she wheeled the boxes along, behind her trailed two youths carrying two jute bags, which were very much pregnant. The bags obviously contained some goodies. Anyamba asked Mary to take his sister's belongings into one of the rooms. Mary obeyed and left.

"As I told you", Anyamba continued, "Oguaa's story is a sad one. It will be better if she were present to narrate her ordeal by herself. I can already see that you are growing impatient and would not be able to wait till evening."

"You are right Anya. I cannot wait to satisfy my curiosity."

Anyamba called Oguaa thrice but there was no reply.

"What is the matter Anya? Please tell me".

Oguaa had deliberately sneaked out of the house.

"My sister, Oguaa had been suspended indefinitely from school."

"Why?"

"She and some of her friends were found guilty of having committed some immoral acts. The Principal had to send them home pending the outcome of investigations".

"I can't understand you, Anya".

As Anyamba tried to explain more, Mary came out to the sitting room. Anyamba tried immediately to change the topic and told his wife to prepare some water for Nnenna to take her bath.

"I'll take my bath then if that is your wish Anya. But first I have to unpack and after taking a wash, I will visit Adaugo and Nwayieze. I have something to discuss with them".

With that Nnenna followed Mary. Anyamba watched the two women disappear into the room Mary had prepared for her sister-in-law. Anyamba once more lifted his cup to his lips. He tasted the tea but dropped the cup almost immediately. His tea had gone cold.

*   *   *   *   *   *   *

Lizzy could no longer bear her mother's aggressive attitude and heart-breaking utterances. Her four days with her mother in the one room apartment had been one of misery, sorrow and regrets. She wanted to leave but where would she go?

As she packed her belongings the clouds began to gather. Dusk was approaching and the chilly weather was indicative that a downpour was imminent. Her mother had noticed the inclement weather and hence had asked Lizzy where she was going. Lizzy's mean look at her mother was enough reply. She quietly packed her few belongings into a suit case and a travelling bag.

"Where are you going? It is already dark," Monica asked. Lizzy did not need her advice. She took one last look at her mother and quickly left the house.

Monica stood by the door and watched her daughter disappear into the twilight. As Monica walked back into her room, she looked at the old clock that hung on the wall. The time was twenty minutes to the hour of seven in the evening. The day was Tuesday.

13

Nnenna spent six days in Umuayalu before she finally decided to leave for Aba. But they were days of strain and stress which in the end left her completely exhausted.

Her conversation with Adaugo and Nwayieze revealed that women are generally more open and frank when they are in the midst of their own sex. Adaugo had told Nnenna how uncompromising Nwayieze had been since they came back to Umuayalu after the civil war. Nwayieze had attributed her action to Adaugo's disrespectful attitude. Nnenna did not mince words in telling them that as widows, they have a lot at stake. If they should continue with their uncompromising attitude, they may resort to anti-social acts like adultery and petty pilfering which would bring disgrace and shame to the family.

As Nnenna explained the consequences of the women's actions, her mind went back to the bitter strife which claimed Eringa's life. Eringa was Pa Anselem's second wife. She had learnt about the woeful tale as soon as the civil war ended and she got in touch with her family at Umuayalu. She also remembered the mysterious disappearance of her own husband. All these are history now. It is better to let the dead rest but no matter how hard one tried, their memories would still linger.

"Look at yourselves," Nnenna admonished the two women. "You are mothers and even grandmothers. But your behaviour can be likened to those of a three-year old baby."

"We have heard all you said. We promise never to disappoint you. At least I can vouch for myself,", said Nwayieze.

"You have spoken at length my husband. I have nothing to add. But please I would like you to appeal to my senior. Her children are older. I work myself to death yet she never asked them to help me out."

Adaugo paused as if she was running out of breath. She shook her head then continued. But this time her voice was highly charged with emotions.

"Look at me my husband. Look at my body. What do I look like? Worse than a dish rag I suppose? My husband, do you know what the villagers call me?"

Nwayieze looked away while Nnenna looked sternly at Adaugo.

"My husband. The villagers now refer to me as the "living ghost." Of course I bear no grudge against anyone. I know I am now a shadow of my past self but I blame no one for my present plight." Adaugo has finally ended her pathetic oration.

Before Nnenna left the two women, she distributed all that she brought for them. To Adaugo she gave two pieces of "Abada" materials, a headgear to match, a blouse made of lace material, some trinkets and lots of food items. Nwayieze received almost the same items but Nnenna, had added a piece of "George" materials to the rest of her presents.

The two women thanked Nnenna, prayed for her, and

wished her well in her business. They were very found of Sisi Potacot. That is why they often referred to her as their husband.

*   *   *   *   *   *   *   *

Lizzy stood forlorn near the motor park. She sat on her box and held her handbag tightly to her bosom. It was getting dark and she was afraid. Many thoughts ran across her mind as she watched the teeming mass of humanity hurrying past her. Nobody seemed to pay any attention to her for they were obviously trying to get home before darkness fully engulfed the entire atmosphere. There were no vehicles in the park but she silently prayed that one would come so that she could leave the unholy surrounding and get to her village at Nkwerre. Each time she looked back, she became more frightened. She prayed that those hoodlums who hovered behind her would not pounce on her and cart away her belongings. The thought of rape crossed her mind as she pondered over a lot of strange imagination. She tried not to listen to some cynical and vulgar remarks which transpired between the touts standing behind her.

"This lady thinks that she will fine motor."

"Which one is your concern? It looks as if we have gotten bush meat tonight."

"I'm the first to sight her."

"Okay, all of us will share her."

This vulgar conversation was becoming too deafening for Lizzy's ears, so she quietly moved a little further away from the maddening mob. The showers of rain began to drop. A red Daewoo Racer car stopped right in front of the spot where the confused Lizzy stood.

"Care for a lift young lady", a male voice asked from the driver's seat of the car.

Lizzy did not give any reply. The rains would soon come pouring in torrents. It was safer to be with the unknown stranger than to be stranded and left at the mercy of those motor park touts. She simply opened the passenger door of the car and entered. The driver smiled, and drove away.

"Where are you going to?", the male voice asked. Lizzy started to cry.

"Don't cry. I wouldn't want you to ruin that beautiful face with tears. Don't you think it may help if we talk things over?"

"Good. We are making progress".

*   *   *   *   *   *   *   *

Before aunty Nnnenna left Umuayalu, Anyamba had fully recovered. Seeing that he was strong enough, his sister now engaged him in a long discussion. Mary too was present.

"Oguaa's story is pathetic. But I would want you and your wife to handle it with a great sense of maturity and care. Her age is one of the trying periods every young girl is bound to undergo. You may not understand but these things do happen. I have spoken to Oguaa. She is sad over the unfortunate development but even more unhappy for she cannot face your wrath or that of Mary. Give her some time and she will be alright."

Anyamba was surprised over the rather relaxed manner in which Nnenna viewed Oguaa's case.

"You know what her waywardness has caused her?" Anyamba asked Nnenna.

"Yes," the latter replied. "But she has paid the price."

"But what about the dent she has inflicted on herself and the family at large?"

Nnenna laughed and patted her brother slightly on the shoulder.

"Anya, I have not been idle since I came. Oguaa has already received a clean bill of health. I took her to the doctor a day after my arrival. Her case of venereal infection was a mild one and needed just a little medication to purge her of the disease."

Mary who had patiently listened to the conversation now asked Nnenna.

"My husband, I am at a loss for I don't know what to say. I am grateful for your help. Oguaa has really disappointed me. The news is all over the village and I can hardly walk without bending my head in shame."

"The village is the custodian of gossips and rumours," Nnenna cut in. "In the city nobody would even care or blink an eyelid over Oguaa's actions. I am not trying to hold brief for Oguaa, Mary. I strongly feel bad and condemn her action. But as I was saying, unlike in the village, people in the city mind their own business."

Mary looked at Anyamba. She wanted to say something but she was not sure how he would react. But she had to break the silence.

"My husband", Mary said this time referring to Anyamba. "If I had my way, I would advice that Oguaa goes away for sometime."

"Where will she go to?" Anyamba retorted.

"We can send her to stay with Loretta and her parents.

Oguaa should utilize that opportunity to make up her differences with Loretta".

When Mary realized that Anyamba was silent on her suggestion, she pressed further.

"You may not understand. I have heard a lot, my husband. Oguaa's continuous presence in this house will keep tongues wagging and eventually send me crazy."

Anyamba was surprised at his wife's suggestion. At least the issue has changed from one of confrontation to that of mutual understanding. Was Nnenna's visit responsible for this turn of events? All along Anyamba has borne the brunt of Oguaa's ultimate moral decline. Her visits to Port Harcourt and Lagos according to Mary had triggered off series of chain reactions, which finally culminated in this final disgrace. How could Mary allow Oguaa to get out of her sight once more?

"Mary is right," Nnenna said. "A change of environment often helps to ameliorate situations such as the prevailing one. Give it a trial please Anya, and inform me about any development. I have given Oguaa my address at Aba."

Mary and her husband thanked Nnenna for all she had done during her brief visit home. They prayed the Almighty to reward her for her kind gesture and inestimable generosity.

Unknown to anyone, Oguaa was eaves-dropping and heard all that transpired between her parents and aunty Nnenna. She was happy with the manner her aunt had handled her situation. But what bothered her most was the suggestion by her mother that she should spend sometime with Loretta and her people. Despite the fact that Oguaa's parents had investigated and were convinced that Loretta had no hand in Oguaa's suspension, Oguaa still felt bitter towards her friend and assumed that Loretta might have betrayed her by telling people about their secret visit to the Chemist Shop. Oguaa quietly tiptoed outside.

She patiently waited as the whole family trooped out to see aunty Nnenna off. Nwayieze and Adaugo also joined. Soon a large crowd was heading for the village square where Nnenna will board a vehicle that would take her to the motor park in town.

By the time they got to the square, Chinwe, Mary, Oguaa and Adaugo were the only ones left. The others had retired after bidding farewell to the kind lady whose brief visit had brought happiness to all in the family.

Mary noticed that Nnenna was quite apprehensive when she noticed a-not-too-well-dressed figure quickly walk past them. Soon the figure turned again and joined the group going towards the square. She tried to allay her sister-in-law's fears by speaking to the figure.

"Ah Ogele! how are you today?" asked Mary.

The figure did not reply but continued to follow closely.

Mary turned to Nnenna

"Don't mind him?"

"Is he a lunatic?", Nnenna asked.

"He is not, my husband. Just a victim of the civil war. He has been like that since he returned from the war zone. It is only God who can restore his health."

"What is wrong with him" Nnenna asked.

"They say he is suffering from shell shock. The noise from the canon fire used during the war affected his sense of hearing while he was in the trench. Ever since he has not been able to speak or hear properly," Oguaa tried to explain.

"He should have been sent to the hospital for thorough medical attention," said Nnenna.

"Who would do it for him?" said little Chinwe who spoke for the first time. "People say that it is his present condition that led to his mother's death."

Nnenna was deeply moved as she surveyed the pathetic figure that stood very close to where they were waiting for a taxi to take her to town. She could physically count the ribs on the highly emaciated body of Ogele. She was so deeply engrossed in her thought about Ogele that she did not notice the taxi cab that pulled up and halted where they stood.

"It was a senseless war", she said as she entered the cab and the driver drove away.

Oguaa, Chinwe, Adaugo and Mary waved until a huge cloud of dust prevented them from seeing the cab fade into the retreating horizon.

*   *   *   *   *   *   *   *

"C'mon let's go and dance."

Lizzy got up and followed her partner. Soon they were swinging away to a melodious tune that was blarring from a giant loud speaker.

"Dreams Night Club" was a popular rendezvous situated in the heart of the highly commercial town of Aba. The club was not only popular but also notorious for it harboured all types of individuals ranging from the affluent businessmen to men of the underworld.

The club was always dimly lit so no one knew or cared who patronised it. It was to this club that Samson Otani look

Lizzy to.

Samson was the good samaritan who gave Lizzy a lift on that fateful night when she had walked out on her mother with the intention of going back to her village at Nkwerre.

Initially, Lizzy counted her blessings when she met this stranger. A conversation had transpired between them during which Samson informed Lizzy that he was not really travelling out of Aba. In fact he Samson lives at Aba and was actually going back to his house at Ulasi Road when he spotted Lizzy at the park.

He had sensed that the girl was in danger on seeing her in the midst of motor park touts, most of who made their living by engaging in vices like looting, rape, arson and abduction. He had seen the pretty but pathetic face stare as he drove past. His immediate intention was to get the girl out of the presence of those men.

Lizzy felt more relaxed as they drove away. On their way, Samson advised Lizzy not to make her intending trip home since it was already dark and the rains were pouring down in torrents. She as Samson hinted, could be faced with disastrous consequences. Lizzy saw with Samson's reasoning but confessed that she was a stranger in the city and had nowhere else to go.

As soon as Samson got this information, he smiled and assured her not to worry. He asked if she would mind sharing his little apartment with him, at least until the next day. Lizzy had no choice than to agree.

The days grew into weeks and Lizzy no longer indicated her desire to travel to her village. Samson had been kind and until then had not taken undue advantage of her beauty and desperate condition. He made sure the girl was comfortable and lizzy grew to admire this stranger whom she had come to see as God-sent.

That was how Lizzy came to stay with Samson Otani. Unknown to Lizzy, the little apartment at Ulasi Road was not actually Samson's apartment house. It was just one of his many guest houses.

14

Mary could not understand why her daughter had taken such a decision. She had spent three days thinking seriously on what to do. No doubt, her daughter's move was not a bad one. Her husband had consoled her.

Although Mary had agreed with Anyamba, she still felt that the problem would not be solved by Oguaa's decision. In order to pacify her and allay her fears, Anyamba had reluctantly agreed that his wife should make the proposed trip.

*   *   *   *   *

Despite Lizzy's ravishing qualities, her host Samson Otani saw her as a sister and nothing more.

The guest house consisted of four bedrooms and a large and well-furnished sitting room. Lizzy had one of the bed-rooms all to herself.

On the morning after Lizzy had come to stay with Samson, the latter had advised that it was now safe for her to travel back to her village. Lizzy, who had never intended going back to the village, confessed to her host that she would like to stay with him at Aba if he wouldn't mind.

"Why don't you want to go to the village?" Samson had asked.

"I come from a polygamous home. My parents are dead and my step mother is very wicked", Lizzy lied.

"I am sorry. I understand your plight for I am also an orphan. But that is not the end of the world. You are a student and as you told me the mid-term break will soon be over. Who pays your school fees?"

"Actually Sir, I was sent out of school since I could no longer pay my fees".

"If I provide you with funds, can you go back to school?" Samson asked.

"I am the eldest child of my mother. I have three younger ones who are all boys. They need at least basic education and I would like to help them achieve it. I feel bad bothering you with my domestic problems sir," Lizzy finally said.

Samson was silent for sometime. He could guess at what Lizzy wanted but he still wanted to be sure. She had not answered his question but rather evaded it. Many thoughts wondered in his mind. Had he done the right thing by coming to Lizzy's rescue? What if the police investigates and he is eventually charged for abduction? Who is this mystery girl whose sad plight was creating very anxious moments for him?

Lizzy's voice cut short Samson's thoughts.

"I know I can be useful to my brothers if I have some job to do. I will be very grateful if you can help me secure one. I promise never to disappoint you."

"I'll see what we can do. Meanwhile I shall be travelling to Port-Harcourt. I hope to be back before dusk. When I come back we shall discuss further on the issues you have raised.

Meanwhile take good care of yourself and please don't admit any visitor into the house while I am away."

With those parting words, Samson went into his bedroom and soon emerged well dressed. He bade Lizzy good bye and drove away in his car.

As Samson left, Lizzy sat in the living room. Her thoughts centred on her host, and she marvelled at the type of man he is. What type of life he lives and why he has not made any advances towards her. Why is he still a bachelor? One reason seemed to satisfy Lizzy's curiosity. Samson is not interested in women. He must be impotent.

*   *   *   *   *   *   *   *   *   *

As soon as Oguaa was officially informed that she would be staying with Loretta and her family for sometime, she made up her mind never to honor such a visit. On the morning of the day, she was to leave for Loretta's place, she packed a few of her belongings. Mary was not at home and Anyamba had gone to visit one of his friends who was also an ex-soldier.

When the couple came back, they were not surprised to learn that Oguaa had left for Loretta's place.

Mary prayed that the visit would eventually open up a new vista in the life of her daughter. Anyamba secretly wished her daughter well too.

It was three days later that Oguaa's visit took a dramatic turn. Mary and her husband were engaged in a serious discussion when Chinwe, Oguaa's junior sister came in.

"Yes, Chinwe," Mary said. "I would like you to go over to Loretta's place and see how Oguaa is faring."

"But mama, sister Oguaa did not go to sister Loretta's

place," Chinwe replied.

"Why are you always stubborn?" Anyamba fumed at her second daughter. "You will not go because you are lazy. I pity any young man who will have the misfortune of coming one day to ask for your hand in marriage."

Chinwe started crying and Mary drew her closer.

"Don't mind your father. He was only joking. When you get to Loretta's place, tell Loretta's mother that I shall see her tomorrow as we agreed. Tell Oguaa that I said she should respect herself and be of good behaviour.

Chinwe suddenly stopped crying and looked at her parents.

"But I had earlier told you that sister did not go to sister Loretta's place. She travelled to Aba."

"What!" shouted Anyamba.

"Sister Oguaa told me that she was going to see aunty Nnenna at Aba."

"And you never told us all this while?", Anyamba querried.

"Papa, I thought you knew. Aunty Nnenna gave her some money and she promised visiting her soon. Aunty also promised to secure admission for her at Aba. At least so sister Oguaa told me."

Chinwe's story sounded like a fairy tale to Anyamba and Mary. They eventually confirmed the news when Mary came back to tell her husband that Oguaa was not staying with Loretta's family. Chinwe was right.

Anyamba took the whole story calmly but Mary was as restless as a she-goat on heat. She shouted, fumed and raged at any slightest provocation.

When all attempts by Anyamba to appease her proved abortive, he finally consented to Mary's decision to travel to Aba.

*   *   *   *   *   *   *

Lizzy felt lonely and bored as Samson left for Port-Harcourt. She wanted to get busy but had nothing to work on. Nevertheless, she decided to make a tour of the entire guest house. This was not her first visit but she had to get herself occupied. The other two rooms were in order so there was no need to engage in any clean-up exercise. As she went back to her room, she stopped by Samson's room which was actually the master bedroom. Unlike the other rooms which had flush doors, the door leading to Samson's room was made of mahogany and had intricate patterns carved on it.

Lizzy stood and admired the door with its wonderful designs. The door handle caught her fancy and out of curiosity, she turned it. The door opened to reveal Samson's room.

She did not know what to do. Samson's bedroom was always locked. However she felt it was an opportunity to have a glimpse of the room.

The room was sparsely furnished. Apart from the Turkish rug that graced the floor, the entire furniture in the room looked inferior when compared with the ones in the other rooms. Out of curiosity, Lizzy continued her survey until she stood in front of the in-built wardrobe. Samson was always well dressed so his wardrobe must be rich in fashionable wears.

This move turned out to be Lizzy's undoing. No sooner had she opened the wardrobe than wads of Naira notes started cascading down from the topmost shelf of the wardrobe only to crumble like packs of cards on the floor of the room. This torrential movement of millions of notes did not seem to end. Rather the action seemed to intensify. After a while the wardrobe had been swept clean but lying scattered all over the floor of the room were millions of notes.

As soon as Lizzy recovered from the shock of her strange discovery, her first intention was to run out of the room and if possible escape from the house. On second thought, she changed her plans and summoned up courage. She bent down, began packing the notes and arranging them carefully inside the empty shelves.

Sampson would not come back until evening, so she would definitely conclude this self imposed assignment before her host returned. She was so deeply engrossed in her task that she did not notice the door open. She was no longer alone in the room.

*   *   *   *   *   *   *

Nnenna received her niece at her Aba residence with mixed feelings. After listening to Oguaa's narration and the circumstance that motivated the journey, she decided to welcome her niece.

Oguaa's visit to Aba was quite untimely since Nnenna's busy schedule could not allow her meet up with her niece's demands.

When Mary eventually arrived at Aba, Nnenna was not in.

She did not ask her daughter any question and Oguaa did not answer. Mary waited patiently at the Ehi Road residence until Nnenna came back. Both women had a brief discussion after which dinner was served and everybody went to bed.

Before cock crow in the morning of the next day, Mary was already on her way to Umuayalu. Her husband was just getting out of bed when she arrived.

"Did you find her?" Anyamba asked.

"Yes my husband," Mary responded.

"How is she?"

"Fine. She is staying with your sister."

Nothing was added to the brief dialogue but for Mary, a decision had been taken. Oguaa's matter was a closed chapter.

For Anyamba, the situation was only a temporary phase.

Oguaa has decided to throw a challenge at her father. He was determined to accept and if possible defeat his challenger.

He waited for two weeks before embarking on an unscheduled visit to Aba. On getting to Nnenna's residence, he learnt that his sister had travelled abroad on a business trip.

"What about Oguaa?" he inquired.

"Oguaa has left for Lagos."

Anyamba shook his head like a lizard that has fallen from a great height. He left and was soon on his way to Umuayalu.

*   *   *   *   *   *   *

"Wao! This girl you have become senior chick."

"Your head is not correct."

"What of you. Is your own head correct?"

"Well, one must survive whether hardship or no hardship."

"Haba, you have grown to be fine like this."

"Yes, taking care of myself is my most concern."

"Nne. God don't make mistake. I knew and said to myself that I must meet you one day."

"So what did you come to do in the market?"

"I just came to buy some cloths. I'm travelling."

"Where are you travelling to?"

"I'm going to Lagos. I'm tired of staying in this town."

"You and this your Lagos. The one you went before have you returned?"

"What will I do? I don't have a choice".

"I was with my Antie until this morning when I left her house".

"So your antie sent you to Lagos?"

"No way! My antie travelled to London. She doesn't know that I have left her house."

"Come. We have a long story."

"Where do we stay and talk? You didn't see everybody running out of the market?"

"Truely, you don't know anything. So you don't know Ure?".

"Who is Ure?"

"I will gist you later. Just follow me to my house. You may travel by air in the evening if you still want to go your Lagos".

"Where do you live?"

"Ulasi Road. Come quickly before this people begins their trouble again".

As the two ladies left their scene of discussion, a passer-by could not help wondering at what was amiss. Amidst the pandemonium that had suddenly broken out at the Ariaria market, people could still afford to indulge in idle gosspips such as the one he had just overheard.

The two ladies were none other than Lizzy and Oguaa. They had not seen each other since both were sent out of the Girls' Grammar School. Their meeting at Aba was as dramatic as their exit from school.

As the girls moved on, Lizzy counted her blessing and silently thanked Ure for being instrumental to their meeting. She had at last accomplished a task that had alluded her for days. Sampson and his friends will now be happy with her for in Oguaa, she, Lizzy has found a suitable replacement.

15

The figure which stood in front of Lizzy as she turned was not Samson Otani. It was not even one of the few friends who paid some casual visits since she started staying with her benefactor. Lizzy froze as she gazed at the stranger whose huge physique dwarfed her petite features.

The stranger looked at her and the bundles of notes that lay on the floor of Samson's bedroom. He slowly moved towards the girl.

Lizzy wanted to shout but her voice failed her. As the first blow descended on her head, she dropped the wad of notes in her hands and staggered blindly towards the bed. A second blow caught her on the bed.

*   *   *   *   *   *   *

"Lizzy!" Oguaa called

Lizzy did not reply for she was still engrossed in the mysterious circumstance under which she narrowly escaped death in the hands of the stranger who caught her in Samson's bedroom.

When Oguaa called Lizzy a second time and there was

no reply, the former presumed that Lizzy was simply taking a short nap. The cab driver glanced backwards and saw his sleeping passenger. There was no need to wake her up. She would pay the fare as soon as he stopped them at their destination.

*   *   *   *   *   *   *

Two men were engaged in a much heated debate.
"What do we do now that the girl has discovered our secret?"
"Kill her of course", replied one of the men.
"But we can't. You heard what, the medicine man said. The ritual forbids the use of twins."
"If she stays alive, how are you sure she would keep her mouth shut?"
"I agree with you but we cannot kill her."
Samson Otani remained silent as the two men argued. He could not understand what was happening.
On returning from Port-Harcourt, he had entered his house only to see Umeadi, one of his business partners sitting complacently in his sitting room. Umeadi did not speak to him when he inquired about Lizzy. Rather, he had led Samson into the bedroom where the unconscious girl lay among the scattered wads of notes on the floor.
On further inquiry, Umeadi told him about his unscheduled visit to the guest house and his strange discovery. However as Umeadi said, he had administered some sleeping drugs on the girl while he Umeadi patiently waited for Samson's return.
Samson was sad over the development but the situation

called for prompt action. The other business partner Kanu was immediately sent to the medicine man's house at Ogbor Hill. He later came back with the sad news that Lizzy was a wrong victim and any attempt to destroy her would spell doom for the whole group.

According to Kanu, the medicine man explained that Lizzy having lost her twin brother at birth was not a suitable candidate for the sacrifice. She is a strong willed child and her spirit is the vengeful type.

On further inquiry as to what was to be done, the medicine man advised that the girl should be revived and made to swear the oath of secrecy. She should be allowed to move about, but kept under strict surveillance, until she is able to find a suitable candidate.

Lizzy was happy to be alive. She readily took the oath of secrecy and immediately set out in a bid to accomplish her task of finding a substitute.

It was not an easy task. For many days Lizzy combed all the nooks and corners of Aba in a bid to achieve her objective. But luck was not on her side. Weary, tired and hungry after the fourth day of a fruitless search, she went into one of the eating houses at Ariaria Market to take a bite.

No sooner had she finished her meal than pandemonium broke out. A lunatic was on the rampage and people were closing their stalls in the hot afternoon and fleeing the market for their dear lives.

Among the fleeing masses was a young lady. This lady could not run very fast for the pair of high-heeled shoes which she wore impeded her movement. As the lady got to the eating house where Lizzy was, she stopped in a bid to take off her shoes. But that was a mistake for as soon as she bent down, the surging mass of humanity which ran behind her pushed her down.

As she yelled and begged for help, people came to her rescue and quickly brought her into the eating house. Some two pairs of eyes met each other but only one recognised the other. Lizzy ran and embraced the unfortunate and frightened lady and together they made their way to safety.

When the frightened lady regained consciousness, Lizzy introduced herself and called the lady by her name. It seemed some scales had fallen off the eyes of the unfortunate lady as she gazed at her caller.

"Oguaa?" Lizzy called again

"Lizzy," the lady replied.

The two ladies were soon locked in a warm embrace. The surging crowd was still fleeing from the pandemonium that had engulfed the market at Ariaria.

*   *   *   *   *   *   *

The taxi slowly took a sharp bend as it made its last lap towards Omasi Road.

"Where you de go?" Lizzy asked.

"No be Omasi Road you talk?" replied the driver.

"I no tell you Omasi Road. I said Ulasi."

"I no fit take five naira. That place too far," the driver complained.

"Na only five naira I get and na him I go give you", Lizzy answered back.

"If na so, I go carry una go back to Ariaria."

The argument continued but after a little intervention from Oguaa, the driver agreed to go to Ulasi Road for eight naira.

* * * * * * *

"Jim should receive this letter before the week runs out. I am going to town to post it. If I don't get his reply within two weeks, I will then know what to do."

Mary was busy shelling some egusi seeds, which she would use in preparing the afternoon meal. She heard her husband but merely looked up as Anyamba left the house for the post office.

"I will not die because of Oguaa. I must live in order to train my other children".

Mary continued shelling the egusi seeds.

* * * * * * *

Nobody could give a realistic account of Ure. Several stories had been woven around her. Nobody knew where she was born and how she came to occupy her former abode at the famous Eke Oha Market in Aba.

One story had it that Ure was once a very beautiful maiden whose vanity was responsible for her present plight. She was said to have been married to two men at the same time. This action which was a sacrilege made her first husband angry and he inflicted her with madness.

Another story spoke of Ure as a village beauty who as a priestess was capable of curing any ailment. Her clientele was innumerable until she disobeyed the river god whom she served by getting married. She had to pay for her disobedience. She was struck mad by the jealous river god.

Ironically, Ure's spot at the famous Eke Oha Market was a great scene of entertainment for Ure was a very good dancer. She entertained anybody who visited the market. Everybody liked her and showered her with gifts which ranged from money to food and clothing.

Events however took a different turn when Ure suddenly became pregnant. No one knew who the father of Ure's unborn child was. As she bore her pregnancy, the love people had for her turned to pity. She eventually gave birth to a handsome baby boy.

The market authorities tried to make Ure give up her baby to the Welfare Board but this attempt met with stiff resistance and aggression from the lunatic.

Ure's baby was about three years old when the famous Eke oha market was gutted by fire. Now homeless, Ure moved her abode to the newly constructed Ariaria market and had since remained there with her baby boy.

Ure was not the only lunatic that pitched her tent in the market at Ariaria. Several others like her existed. Among these was a very prominent one called Amosu. Amosu was already staying in the market before Ure's arrival.

Like Ure, Amosu was also a great entertainer. He was well versed in the art of dancing although his most favourite music was the one popularly referred to as "Ikwokirikwo". Each time Amosu took the floor to display these dance step, the crowd cheered and went wild. Little children loved him for he was very kind and often invited the children to partake of his food and other gifts.

The children usually refused and this made the lunatic sad. He loved children and wished he would have one as his own.

Ure's presence at the Ariaria market completely changed Amosu's life. The handsome lunatic who usually danced to the delight of the market audience at Ariaria was no longer the centre of attraction. Ure's beauty and highly seductive qualities soon made her the darling of the traders especially the male ones. The gifts often showered on Amosu changed hands leaving the male lunatic almost at the mercy of hunger and starvation.

Amosu new that Ure was responsible for the love-lost relationship which now characterized his existence in the market. He resolved to regain his popularity and schemed to outwit his rival Ure. Amosu's target for vengeance was none other than Ure's baby boy.

In the middle of the night preceehing the riot, Amosu sneaked into Ure's ramshackled den. He stole Ure's baby as the mother was fast asleep, and left the market.

Ure could not find her baby when the day broke. The boy who was now about four years old had been her source of happiness and her reason for existence. As soon as the market went into session, Ure began the search for her baby. At every stall she inquired, nobody listened to her. Some of the traders who had never liked her drove her away with curses. After about two hours of fruitless search, it dawned on the female lunatic that she may never see her baby again.

Ure knelt in front of her make-shift abode and evoked the spirit of her ancestors to deal with those who were responsible for her missing child.

After a long wailing which was accompanied by heart-rendering and thought-provoking utterances, Ure stood up and set her abode on fire. No one dared confront the lunatic for she soon carried her one man riot into some nearby stalls. Soon a part of the market was in flames. Ure laughed as she moved on to the next group of stalls.

The market was slowly getting engulfed in an inferno. Hell was let loose and everybody took to their heels. The few traders who tried to retrieve some of their wares from the fire were trapped while the wiser ones fled.

Ure was on the rampage. She screamed, yelled and pleaded that her son should be returned to her.

A fire brigade squad soon arrived and the fire was eventually brought under control. By the time of this event, Amosu who stole Ure's baby was far away from the commercial town of Aba. He had already passed Ovom and was on his way to the riverine town of Opobo. It was during this riotous moment that Lizzy and Oguaa met at the Ariaria market.

*　　　*　　　*　　　*　　　*　　　*　　　*

Samson was standing in front of the guest house when the two ladies stepped out of the taxi. One look at Lizzy and he knew that Oguaa was the substitute. He greeted them and when they were inside the house, brief introductions were made.

Plans had already been concluded by Samson and his business partners on what line of action to take should Lizzy accomplish her task. Everything had to go as arranged, so none of Samson's partners was to visit the guest house for the next three days. This move was to avoid any suspicion.

Lizzy and her host Samson treated Oguaa like a queen. Oguaa relished in the red carpet reception. Soon the unfortunate lady who was seen at the Ariaria Market forgot to make her purported trip to Lagos. She has seen Lizzy and so she too has finally arrived.

Lizzy and Oguaa shared Lizzy's room. While in bed, they shared their old school jokes and discussed some idle issues. Lizzy intimated Oguaa with the notion that Samson was a gentleman, an assertion which she supported by disclosing how they met and how he had not made any advances towards her not to talk of taking her to bed. When she told Oguaa about her suspicion that Samson might be impotent, Oguaa could not but agree.

"But he is not the only one", Oguaa said.

"How?"

"In my village there are two men who though married, are not the real fathers of their children."

"You mean they have children", Lizzy asked.

"These things can be arranged Lizzy. It is just a matter of secrecy. Some young virile men are paid to do the job for these impotent husbands."

"Tell me more, Oguaa".

"The poor wives have no choice because of the values tradition places on child bearing."

"That's strange. Society condemns prostitution yet encourage adultery", Lizzy reasoned.

"That's life Lizzy. Let us sleep for I am tired".

In the afternoon when Lizzy came back from the hair dressing salon, she could not find Oguaa. After sometime, she heard some whimperings coming from Samson's bedroom. Then there was laughter. She could not be mistaken for the female voice was certainly Oguaa's. She was having fun with Samson in the bedroom. She realised that she was wrong. Samson was a normal human being, virile and strong. He was far from being impotent.

* * * * * * *

Adaugo and Nwayieze had just had their launch which they brought with them to the farm. As the two women rested after the meal, they chatted.

"Adaugo. I feel sorry for Mary", said Nwanyieze.

"Why?"

"Oguaa's behaviour is really affecting her."

"It is not only her. The whole family is affected. You needed to hear what Nnadi the palm wine tapper told me the day I went to buy some wine at his house".

"What did he say?"

Nnadi said that he was not surprised at Oguaa's behaviour. He expected it afterall any dog that is nurtured by a woman will definitely eat eggs", Adaugo said.

"So Nnadi is blaming Mary for Oguaa's behaviour", Nwayieze interrupted.

"That's what it means. You know that Nnadi is a very good story teller. He even recounted how Oguaa was born as we were fleeing from the cannon fires during the civil war. It was then he knew that a child who was publicly given birth to in the midst of a crowd, will one day join that crowd", Adaugo concluded.

"But Oguaa had been a good girl. I think it was the idea of sending her to secondary school that is responsible for her bad behaviour".

"Nnadi may be right," Adaugo said. "But there is nothing wrong in allowing a girl to acquire the basic education. What about other girls whom I learnt attended universities?"

"Those ones are worse than Oguaa," Nwayieze said. "Don't you remember Pa Ozizioma's last daughter Elema who is a University graduate? Did you not hear how she later went to Lagos and eventually left for overseas with a white man whom she met in a hotel?"

"I heard the story." Adaugo sighed. "You are lucky that all your daughters are happily married. I pray my own children don't behave like Oguaa".

"God forbid!" Nwayieze spat out.

The conversation would have continued but for the sudden change of weather. The clouds had gathered and a mild darkness had engulfed the bright afternoon sun. Both women quickly collected their farming implements and left for home. They did not wait to be caught in the approaching thunderstorm.

16

The entire Umuayalu community were not the only ones who had learnt about what was happening to Anyamba and his family. As the news continued to spread, relatives, well-wishers, friends and foes from far and wide came to the little village of Umuayalu to visit Anyamba and express their concern.

As would be expected, the purpose of their trip was as diverse as the visitors themselves. Some came to console Mary and her husband. Others came to assess the situation which they would exaggerate and later narrate to others when they retire to their various homes.

The story continued to spread like wild fire until it got to the ears of Agnes, Nwayieze's third daughter who was now living with her husband in the far away town of Item.

As soon as Agnes arrived with her husband, they first went and greeted Anyamba and Mary before retiring to see Nwayieze.

"So this is what has been happening?" Agnes asked as soon as she sat down. Her husband Munachi also sat beside his wife. He was not much a talker. He simply listened as mother and daughter discussed.

"My daughter", Nwayieze said, "The issue is beyond

everybody's comprehension. The situation is highly unprecedented. However Anyamba is trying all his best to solve this unforeseen event".

"I can't still believe that story mama. Look at Oguaa. She was just a little baby still sucking her mother's breast when we were at the refugee camp."

Nwayieze did not want to think about the war for the memories only brought miseries and reminded her of her husband's death at the refugee camp. However, Pa Anselem has long been dead and his bones brought back and buried in the family compound. It is safer to let the dead rest.

Try as much as she would, Nwayieze could not hold back the tear drops that trickled down her sad face as she spoke to her daughter and son-in-law.

Munachi was moved but there was nothing he could do to salvage the present situation. However, he managed to console his mother-in-law by telling her that the crisis was not beyond redemption.

"How?" Nwayieze asked amidst tears.

"Anyamba is wearing himself out because of Oguaa. Mary has resigned herself to fate. I am afraid my in-law. Misery is clearly written all over everybody's face. Anyamba has been trying to bear it like a man. If he dies my children, what will become of me?"

Munachi was deeply moved as he watched his mother-in-law. He was even more disturbed when he noticed that his wife Agnes had joined her mother in crying. The atmosphere was becoming too tense so he excused himself and walked out of Nwayieze's house.

"How are you Muna? When did you arrive?"

Munachi turned and saw Adaugo. The latter was returning from the stream for on her head stood firmly a large earthenware pot no doubt filled with water.

"Not long ago, Adaugo. How are you?" Munachi answered back.

"We are alright," Adaugo wanted to continue but what else could she say.

Agnes got married to Munachi a year after the civil war ended. Unfortunately the marriage had not produced any offsprings. This seemingly barren condition that characterized Agnes' marriage was of great concern to Nwayieze and Agnes. Munachi however remained unperturbed. His moral upbringing has taught him that the child factor was God's gift and hence should not be an issue to ponder over.

When Adaugo put down her pot of water and came out of her house, she was surprised to see Munachi still standing quietly in front of Nwayieze's house.

She wanted to talk with him but she did not know how to start.

"How is your wife, Agnes?" she managed to say at last.

"I came with her. She is inside the house with her mother."

"I hope all is well," said Adaugo.

"Everything is fine. We came as a result of the news we heard about Anyamba's daughter."

Adaugo heaved a sigh. Oguaa's story was no longer news but she had to talk to Munachi.

"Children of these days are very unpredictable my in-law. I have personally left everything to God for it is only Him who knows best", Adaugo said.

"But what is Anyamba doing about it?" Munachi asked. "He has posted a letter to his junior brother Jim. I suppose you know Jim. The one who works in Lagos. Oguaa is supposed to be with him. The poor girl may have taken such steps to avoid the gossips that have engulfed the whole vicinity".

"That is not a bad idea anyway. It is just sad that Anyamba's daughter had to leave school in such a disgraceful manner. This is the aspect that gives me great concern. I know we live in a very permissive society. But we are not entirely morally bankrupt. Anyamba and Mary did not deserve this treatment from their daughter. The couple have shown exemplary qualities which are worthy of emulation by everybody."

Adaugo listened attentively until Munachi ended his speech.

"My in-law, I have heard all you said. You are right but often times the arrow misses and hits at the wrong target. Even from bad families are born good children. Oguaa has made her choice and I agree that she should be allowed to have it her own way."

Munachi took in every word said by Adaugo with a pinch of salt. He knew what to do but he did not want to interfere. At least not now that Oguaa was in Lagos with her uncle Jim.

As Adaugo returned to her house, Munachi decided to go back and see his wife and mother-in-law. While he walked into the house, another figure approached the compound and hurriedly walked towards Anyamba's house. Munachi turned but too late, the figure had entered Anyamba's house.

*　　*　　*　　*　　*　　*　　*

It was the third week at the Memorial Hospital situated in Lagos Island. He was no longer feeling the pains but the bruises which he had sustained were yet to be completely healed. He had been bored and had pleaded with the doctors to discharge him.

His pleas fell on deaf ears for his parents had hinted the doctors that he should remain in the hospital until his wounds were completely healed.

Beside his bed sat a lady. She had been his major companion since four days after that fateful evening during which the accident occurred. This was after he had recovered consciousness and inquired how he came to be admitted in the hospital. A week later the whole story unfolded. It was his father that broke the news to him. Dotun was driving on the fast lane when one of the front tyres of his car gave way. The car skidded, somersaulted and both driver and vehicle ended up in a ditch.

"My son we are grateful to God that you are alive. God in His infinite mercy rescued you from the cruel arms of death and brought you back to us", Pa Makanjuola said.

To all the prayers he offered on behalf of Dotun, his wife who sat beside him merely responded with the word "Ese". The lady companion also chorused "Ese" along with Dotun's mother Ma Makanjuola.

*   *   *   *   *   *   *

Eno worked as a receptionist in one of the Finance Houses at Ikeja. In spite of her long stay with the company, Eno's sense of decorum and her approach to work were impeccable. Punctuality was her watch-word and her polite quality especially in attending to callers who spoke with her boss on the telephone was exemplary.

Her boss was very pleased with her attitude to work and did not hesitate in showing his appreciation whenever the opportunity arose.

Eno also attended some extra-mural lectures after work. As an ambitious and brilliant student, she soon passed all her secretarial examinations and eventually became a qualified confidential secretary. In order to retain her services with the company, she was promoted and with time, she became one of the executives of the company.

Her meteoric rise in the company did not get into her head. She was still the humble, diligent and dedicated lady who joined the Albatros Finance House some eight years ago.

One day her boss noticed that Eno was not looking as cheerful as she had always been. She did not go for her lunch break but sat quietly behind her typewriter. She could not even type some important documents which her boss told her needed urgent attention.

When Biola, the office tea girl asked Eno what the matter was, the latter replied that she had been a victim of incessant stomach upset for sometime.

Biola was a notorious gossip and soon the news of Eno's ill-health spread to the ears of Eno's boss.

"I learnt you have been ill Eno", the boss asked. Eno could not but admit what her boss said.

"You can take the day off. Make sure you visit the clinic tomorrow. But before you go ask one of the typists in the pool to come to my office."

Eno thanked her boss and left. The doctor's diagnosis at the clinic confirmed that Eno was suffering from acute appendicitis. She was immediately referred to the Memorial Hospital in Lagos Island where she was operated upon. Two days after Eno's operation, an accident case was reported at the out patient department of the hospital and the accident victim was Dotun, Pa Makanjuola's son.

The Doctors worked all through the night and after three days Dotun was wheeled out of the intensive care unit to the male surgical ward. It was there that Eno met him.

She did not know whether the meeting could be described as love at first sight. As soon as she saw Dotun, an unusual sensation ran through her spine. With more visits, she grew to admire this handsome young man who had won an amazing victory over death. She was determined to help this young man regain his health hence continued to pay him occasional visits after work. It was on one of such visits that Eno met Dotun's parents the Makanjuolas.

*   *   *   *   *   *   *

As soon as Martina saw Anyamba and Mary, she broke down and cried.

"What's happening to us?" she lamented. Mary joined Martina and soon the whole house was thrown into a mournful mood.

Anyamba felt concerned but as a man he tried not to let the others see through him. He was no doubt worried but he firmly believed he would soon hear from Jim.

"Why should my late parents allow this happen to us? What sins have we committed that the family should be a laughing stock in the neighbourhood and even beyond?"

Martina would have continued with her lamentation but

for a harsh intervention.

"Why are you trying to create a scene? Oguaa is not dead, so why this display?"

It was Adaugo's voice. She had heard the wailing from Anyamba's house only to hurry down and see Martina in tears.

Martina was the figure Munachi could not recognise as she entered the compound. Unlike Agnes, Martina having lost her mother, Eringa during the air raid, had come to see life as a cipher. As her mother was being buried in a make-shift grave along their fleeing path, Martina had stared unbelievably at the rather mysterious way death had snatched her mother leaving her and her two brothers Udoka and Nneji at the mercy of fate.

Her stay at the refugee camp with the rest of the family was shortlived. She soon joined one of the international charitable organisations that provided relief materials to the war-torn Biafran children.

As if that was not sufficient, Martina carried her crusade to the war zone where she provided first aid treatment to the wounded Biafran soldiers. The soldiers marvelled at the guts of this brave lady as she darted with drugs from one trench to another.

During one of her adventurous quests to save humanity, she stumbled on a wounded soldier. Her casualty could not move for an enemy bullet had pierced his thighs. Blood flowed profusely covering almost the entire body of the soldier. Martina had summoned courage and single-handedly carried the wounded soldier through the lines of the enemy artillery fire until she reached the sick bay. It was when the soldier fully recovered from his wounds that Martina realised that the man she saved from the marshy trenches was a captain in the army.

Captain Obioha, for that was his name, could not conceal his excitement when he was informed of the circumstances in which his life had been saved. He prayed that he would one day meet this brave lady. Luck soon shone on him for one day Martina arrived at the sick bay and recognized the soldier. Both rejoiced over the captain's recovery. Their subsequent discussions revealed that the soldier hailed from the village of Umualumaku in Uzoagba. Strangely enough Uzoagba was also where Martina's family resided as refugees.

Captain Obioha was granted permission to visit home as soon as he was discharged from the sick bay. He insisted that Martina must accompany him. Martina did not refuse for the trip would afford her an opportunity to see her long-abandoned family.

Rumours already had it that Captain Obioha had been killed by the enemies. His return was thus seen as a miraculous act of God. The excitement within his family circle was further increased when he presented Martina as his deliverer.

Two days later the Captain and Martina left Umualumaku in search of Martina's family. Ironically, the excitement that greeted Martina and her male companion at the refugee camp was nothing to be compared with the red-carpet reception they received at Umualumaku. Martina was sad when she learnt that her aged father, Pa Anselem was dead.

"The war had claimed both Mama and Papa," she cried.

But for Obioha, the war had eventually provided him with a life partner.

Their marriage has been blessed with four children which included a set of twin boys. Obioha who was a graduate before the war took up a teaching appointment at the Community

Secondary School, Atta. His wife, Martina ran a sewing institute at the Eke Atta Market.

It was Obioha who heard Oguaa's story being discussed by his students. As soon as he communicated this information to his wife, Martina set out for Umuayalu.

*   *   *   *   *   *   *

Lizzy was jealous and angry when she realised that Samson had some designs for Oguaa. But she had to suppress this anger since she knew that Oguaa's days were numbered.

"She can have all the fun", Lizzy said to herself.

She, Lizzy has to be careful for if Oguaa should sense any foul play, she would definitely become suspicious. Any mistake on her own part would ruin their entire plan.

But for Samson, it was the beginning of a crisis period. On the day he slept with Oguaa, they had discussed at length. Samson had eventually learnt all about Lizzy's escapades and their strange meeting at the Ariaria Market. He could not bear to see Oguaa being sacrificed for wealth. He could also not compromise his life by letting the unfortunate lady into a joint secret. The oath of secrecy was irreversible so Oguaa must inevitably dance to her fate. He nevertheless wished that the procedures which were being adopted would fail. But he was wrong.

17

Soon Oguaa's health began to fail her. She started having nightmares which were soon replaced by early morning vomitting and occasional fever. Lizzy knew that the liquid which she secretly added to Oguaa's meals was responsible for her deteriorating health. In order to avoid any suspicion from Oguaa, Lizzy had one day teased Oguaa that she might be pregnant.

"I am not pregnant", Oguaa had managed to say.

"Then why these signs of early morning sickness and vomitting?"

"I don't know Lizzy. I have not missed my period since I arrived".

"You never can say. Afterall, you have been having fun with Samson," Lizzy chipped in.

"I am an adult. I know when I am pregnant", Oguaa retorted.

"So you think. Don't you know that often times a woman can become pregnant even though she still sees her period."

"That's a biological fallacy. I have to see the doctor."

"No, my dear", interrupted Lizzy. "Orthodox medicine is not the answer. I know a traditional herbalist who will help us. I don't want Samson and his friends to make jest of us. You know they hold us in high esteem."

"Traditional herbalist?" Oguaa querried.

"Yes. There is a popular one who stays at Ogbor hill. We shall pay him a visit without the knowledge of Samson or any of his friends. If we are lucky, he will provide instant cure to your ailment", Lizz concluded.

When Oguaa discovered that she was not making any progress with her health, she heeded Lizzy's advice.

Lizzy was wrong for according to the medicine man, Oguaa was not pregnant. He however prepared some herbal concoction for Oguaa and advised that she should repeat her visit with Lizzy two days later. Lizzy thanked the medicine man and offered him a twenty naira note which he rejected.

"Your friend is sick. We shall discuss my fee as soon as her health improves. Just remember to keep the appointment and report back in two days time."

Oguaa thanked the medicine man and the two ladies left. As they walked towards the major road to pick up a taxi back to Ulasi Road, Lizzy laughed.

"Why are you laughing?" Oguaa asked.

"Look at this area my dear girl. I don't think the inhabitants have even heard anything about the government's campaign on environmental sanitation."

"This place is not bad I assure you. Come to Lagos and

you will see worse places. If you ever pay a visit to Lagos, ask of a place called Badiya or Amukoko and you will hear stories," Oguaa said.

"I can't live in this slum. I pray you get well quick so that our visits to this place will be short lived. I wouldn't want to contact any disease for this area makes me sick."

Lizzy was not laughing at the Ogbor Hill with its highly infested terrain. She was in fact jubilating over her maiden attempt to get Oguaa introduced to her would-be killer. She was even more excited when she realised that the two other men who hid in the adjacent room must have taken in all that happened.

"It was not a bad visit", Lizzy said.

"I think so too", Oguaa replied.

Lizzy did not realise that the sick lady heard her for she thought she was talking to herself.

"I hope your drugs are safe", Lizzy continued.

"They are in my handbag", Oguaa said.

A 504 Peugeot Salon Car drove past the two ladies. Lizzy did not bother to flag down the vehicle or ask for a lift. She knew who the occupants were so she let the car zoom past.

Samson was not in when the two ladies got back to the house. Oguaa took her drugs as directed by the medicine man. She was fast asleep when Kanu and Umeadi came into the house.

"That was smart my girl." Kanu exclaimed as he congratulated Lizzy for a job well done.

"We overheard all your conversation", added Umeadi.

Lizzy simply smiled.

"This is just the beginning. By the time you pay a third visit to the man, we will know what next to do. Where is

Samson?"

"He was not in when we arrived," Lizzy said.

"Just make sure that the girl takes her medicines as prescribed. And don't forget your next appointment", concluded Umeadi.

Kanu dipped his left hand into his pocket and counted out five hundred naira which he gave to Lizzy.

"This is for your effort. Keep up the good job and very soon you will become one of the richest madams in town."

Lizzy thanked Kanu and bade farewell as the two men quickly left the guest house.

Oguaa felt better the next day. At least she had stopped vomitting but the fever was still tormenting her. She anxiously looked forward to their second visit to Ogbor Hill.

* * * * * * *

Biola was becoming a thorn in the flesh of the young executive. She hardly passed Eno's office without making one complimentary remark or the other.

"Aunty Eno. I heard that fine man who comes to see you in the office wants to marry you."

"Who is telling you all these stories Biola?"

"Aunty. You know say this na Lagos. I been don hear the news since last week from my friend Laide".

Eno was getting interested in Biola's rantings so she took her fingers off the computer machine and asked:

"Who is Laide?"

"I'm surprised at you aunty. So you don't know that my friend who is a cleaner at that hotel in Yaba".

"Which hotel are you talking about?"

"How are you behaving as if you are the most ignorant person in the neighbourhood?"

"I know you are madam know-all".

"Which hotel do you think I'm talking about? It's the one and only Garden Park Hotel".

"Oh I remember. So that's where your Laide works?"

"Yes aunty. Laide says that man who visits you is a good stuff. He will like you to marry him since the man has a lot of money".

"How come Laide knows this man so well?" Eno queried.

"That man is her boss. Laide says that he is the owner of the hotel."

"You mean Garden park Hotel?"

"Yes, that's what Laide says but I have heard that he is not the owner but his father's own. Anyway it doesn't matter. Whether it is his own or his father's own, the man has money."

Dotun had been paying regular visits to Eno since he was discharged from hospital. On few occasions, Eno had obliged when Dotun insisited that both of them go out for lunch. Surprisingly they had never gone to Garden Park Hotel to have any meal. More still, Dotun had never mentioned the fact that he either knew, managed or owned the hotel.

Biola's story fascinated Eno but the pretty executive pretended not to be interested in office gossip. With time she would discover the truth. She had never contemplated marriage with Dotun.

In fact she saw the relationship purely from a platonic point of view. Dotun was simply trying to express his gratitude for the assistance and moral support which she offered him during his accident. The love at first sight syndrome was borne out of sheer sympathy. It was now a thing of the past.

But poor Eno had been mistaken. Right from the moment Dotun saw her, he had fallen in love and daily nursed the idea of seeking her hand in marriage. He had foreseen a major obstacle for while he is Yoruba by tribe, Eno came from the South Eastern part of the country. He would not have problems with his parents since the Makanjuolas never liked his former girl-friend Kemi. As free thinkers they would no doubt give their consent provided he did his homework well before intimating them with his intentions. But what about Eno and her parents.?

*   *   *   *   *   *   *

It was about eleven o'clock to midnight. Lagos was still bubbling with activities. Business was still on as the street lights dazzled the entire city and provided the much needed atmosphere for human beings to be functional despite the late hour.

There was a lot to be done the next day. His long absence from duty due to his accident had piled up arrears of work for him. He had to reconcile the hotel account which had been dormant since his absence. The store was almost empty so he will have to travel to Otta the next day to purchase some chickens and eggs from the farm.

As he glanced through his records, his office door slowly gave way and somebody walked in. He had not remembered to lock the door.

Dotun was not surprised to see Jim. The latter usually paid unscheduled visits to the hotel anytime his job afforded him the opportunity to do so. But his visit did not seem a casual one, for Jim was not in his usual high spirit mood. As they greeted and Jim sat down, Dotun noticed that his friend looked worried.

"What is the matter? You don't look your normal self. Any problem in the office?" Dotun asked.

Dotun knew that Jim's job as a custom officer was a bundle of risks as well as a package of joy. He had heard some woeful tales from Jim about custom men who have lost their jobs or even their lives while on active service. He had equally learnt that fortune did often smile on many and within months they usually grow from rags to riches and become instant millionaires. Jim's silence was creating more anxious moments for Dotun who again asked.

"I hope all is well Jim? Do you care for a drink?"

"Don't bother. I have just received my brother's letter."

"Which of your brothers?"

"The one whose daughter spent her last vacation with me."

"You mean Oguaa?"

"Yes".

"So what is the matter?"

"According to my brother, Oguaa left for Lagos two weeks ago. She was supposed to stay with me. I have not seen her."

Dotun stood up from his chair and paced around the room. He was studying the situation and trying to ascertain the credibility of the news. If Oguaa intended coming to Lagos, she should have arrived long before now. But why should she come when the schools have just resumed?

"Did she have any misunderstanding with her parents?" Dotun chipped in after some time.

Jim did not want to disclose the entire contents of the letter for he believed that would be washing the family's dirty linens outside.

"My uncle sent Oguaa on a purpose. He needed some financial assistance," Jim lied.

"So what are you saying?"

"Just what you have heard. My niece left for Lagos about two weeks ago and has since not arrived. That is the story Dotun."

Dotun picked up the hand set and dialed a number. He listened and there was no reply so he dropped the receiver.

"Who were you trying to speak with?"

"Majek is not at home. I wanted to speak with him"

"Thanks. I thought you were trying to get in touch with the Police. Dotun, I hope that girl is safe."

"I hope so too. Now what do we do?"

"I am confused. I don't know where to start."

"Jim. You have to take it easy. First, get in touch with her father. He may have cancelled the proposed trip after posting your mail."

"That's a possibility. I am sorry to have inconvenienced you at this time of the night. All the same take it easy. Remember you still have to rest and get well properly. I shall leave now and see you later tomorrow.

As Jim left the office, Dotun sat down. He like Jim was confused. His thoughts wandered far and wide. He thought about Oguaa. He thought of Kemi and Eno. He thought about Lagos with its mystery of strange disappearances, ritual murders….. He tried to think of something else but he could not. He quickly gathered his files. He would continue tomorrow for he needed some sleep.

On getting into his hotel apartment, he exclaimed, "women and their ways. I hope that girl is alive."

18

She could not understand why some people giggled. The whole story was not funny so did not call for any laughter. For her, it was a sad session. She was even more irritated when she discovered that most of the ovations and applauses came from a particularly naughty group that sat some three rows behind her. She could not identify any member of the group for the entire auditorium was engulfed in darkness.

Doyin was a film addict. It was her past time on campus. But not when it was a horror movie. When she saw the advert at the campus cafetaria, she had felt reluctant to go. The examinations were fast approaching and she would be more useful to herself if she retired to the library to take care of her books. She knew she was generally weak in Statistics, but this time she was determined to pass the course.

In order to pave way for success, Doyin had courted the friendship of one of her course mates who was an expert in the subject. Inwardly she did not like Muyiwa for he was rather the vain type. But her fate hung on a balance so she had to play the ball game and bid for time.

Muyiwa had been surprised over Doyin's recent intimate advances but his naivety prevented him from seeing through this sudden and strange development.

While they were enjoying their lunch at the cafeteria, Muyiwa had hinted on the film that would be screened at the auditorium at 8.30 in the evening.

"The Curse of the Werewolf" must be quite exciting.

"Look Doyin, I would be pleased if you could accompany me to watch this movie."

Doyin's immediate reaction was to decline the offer for the obvious reasons that it was a horror movie and more still the examinations called for more intensive revision. She however conceded, at least to humour Muyiwa and express her appreciation for the assistance she had so far received from him in "Statistics".

All through the film, she clung nervously on to Muyiwa as the horrifying scenes unfolded one after the other. Muyiwa was pleased as he relished in the warmth which the feminine touch added to his body.

As soon as the film came to an end, the visibly-shaken girl was escorted back to the hostel by Muyiwa. In her room Doyin realized that her two mate were already fast asleep. She needed a bath before retiring to bed but the harrowing experience which the movie had generated prevented her from going to the bathroom. She quietly changed into her night gown and was soon fast asleep.

She woke up the following morning to see a letter on

her desk. One of her room mates later explained that she picked the mail from the porter's lodge downstairs the previous night when Doyin was at the auditorium.

Doyin thanked her, picked up the mail and tore open the envelope. As she finished reading the letter, she sat down on her bed and heaved a sigh.

"What's the matter Doyin?" asked Halima.

"Nothing", Doyin replied.

"I don't believe you. You look worried."

"Halima. It is my senior brother. He was involved in an accident."

"Was it fatal?"

"He is alive but the car is a write-off."

"I am very sorry", Halima said.

I wonder why it took such a long time for the letter to get to me."

"That's the efficient system within which our postal agency works."

Doyin did not know what to do. The thought of travelling crossed her mind but she still had to get through with her examinations.

When she eventually rang her parents, Pa Makanjuola assured her that Dotun was fine and advised that she should not let the thoughts disturb her but rather concentrate on her examinations. At least that was a relief.

Doyin quickly took her bath and picked up her books. She was soon on her way to the lecture theatre to join the other students.

*   *   *   *   *   *   *

"You shouldn't have fought that man."

"It was inevitable, Nneji. I couldn't let him drag and toss me around like a ping pong ball."

"Udoka, you know Dozie is a bully. He is older and bigger than you. He could have beaten you to pulp for calling him names."

"At least any time he sees that bite I gave him, he will realise that it is never good to underestimate anybody."

"You are really brave my brother. The cut on your face is not very deep. When we get home, make sure you don't tell mama or anybody else what really happened."

Udoka did not reply to this advice which came from his elder brother. He was sitting on the saddle of the bicycle which Nneji has newly acquired.

Udoka and Nneji were Martina's younger brothers. When the entire family returned after the civil war, Nwayieze had adopted the two orphans and brought them up single-handedly. They were very small when their mother Eringa died. Udoka hardly remembered the circumstance surrounding his mother's death but Nneji who is older knew that their mother was a victim of the cannon fires and their father Pa Anselem had died while they were camped in a refugee centre, during the civil war. However, Nwayieze had taken so much good care of them that the shadow of their late mother had long faded from their eyes.

Udoka proved to be very brilliant while they were attending primary school. He soon caught up with his elder brother Nneji who was not so bright in academics. The two brothers finished their primary school education the same year. Udoka had wished to continue his education to the secondary level but since the funds were not readily available, the two brothers had to seek for jobs as means of sustenance. Three years later Nneji became an accomplished mason while his brother Udoka still served under his master as an apprentice motor mechanic.

Everyday the two brothers left their home for Owerri in search of their daily means of livelihood. They worked hard in order to support their step-mother Nwayieze.

*   *   *   *   *   *   *

There is hardly anybody in the mechanic village that does not know Dozie. He is a friend to the motor park touts who respect him for his physical prowess. He is also the favourite of most car owners who regularly brought their vehicles to the mechanic village either for maintenance or repairs.

Udoka had heard a lot of stories about Dozie before he came to work in the mechanic village.

Success had been his watchword and he was determined to achieve it no matter what it caused him. He had closely observed Dozie and had seen him an avenue towards his ambition.

Dozie had not liked the little fragile looking youngman who wanted to be an apprentice. He felt that the weakling would not survive the arduous tasks of lifting heavy motor machinery. But after the first year, he discovered Udoka's relentless qualities and courage hence he was determined to help the boy achieve his goals.

Within two years, Udoka had learnt much to Dozie's amazement. He could effectively repair any brand of vehicle ranging from the Volkswagen Beetle to the heavy duty trucks. He had also learnt how to drive. Soon people began to marvel at the friendly relationship which existed between Dozie the bully and Udoka the little boy from Umuayalu.

Dozie had come back from lunch one afternoon to find Udoka relaxing complacently on the bonnet of one of the vehicles that a customer had brought for repairs. He was actually taking a nap on the bonnet. This annoyed the bully, who walked up to the little boy, pulled him by the ear and threw him off the vehicle.

"You stupid boy! How dare you sleep on the bonnet of a customer's vehicle?" Dozie yelled at Udoka.

When Udoka found himself on the floor, he was confused for he was actually sleeping. Dozie had expected an apology but when this was not forthcoming, he further unleashed a heavy knock on Udoka's clean shaven head.

"You are growing wings. Look at you. You can't even buy the spoke of a bicycle wheel yet you have the guts to sleep on top of a Mercedes Benz car."

This was too much for the little boy who reacted.

"Dozie, I know you are a bully but I assure you that you will one day meet your match. That day will definitely spell doom for you."

As Udoka dusted his entire body which was covered with dirt, his left palm glided over his face and he felt some blood stains. He had sustained some injuries. Dozie noticed the red patches on the little boy's face and froze. He never intended to hurt his little friend. He only wanted to teach him that as a senior, he deserved some respect. Unfortunately, he had overreacted and his action had left the little boy with bruises all over his face.

With the help of some mechanics, Dozie took his little

friend to a nearby chemist shop where the latter was promptly attended to. As Udoka groaned over the pain he had sustained, Dozie winced. He had really over-reacted and sworn never to hurt his little friend again no matter the circumstances.

When they arrived at the village, Nwayieze was shocked when she saw that Udoka's face had patches of plasters here and there. Nneji however explained that his brother fell at his place of work. Nwayieze believed the lie and warned Udoka. She wanted to remove the plasters and apply hot water on the bruses but Nneji assured her that Udoka had already received adequate medical attention. However, Nneji who later heard the true story at the mechanic village never forgave Dozie the bully.

* * * * * * *

It was their third visit to the medicine man's house at Ogbor Hill. Oguaa had complained that the vomiting which subsided after their first visit had started her second course of medication. Lizzy who accompanied her confirmed the story so the medicine man decided that Oguaa would have to spend some hours in his house in order to undergo some observations. She was again given some herbal portion to drink after which she fell into a deep sleep.

This move by the medicine man was quite intentional and in tune with the plan of action. On their second visit, Oguaa had slept for about two hours at Ogbor Hill under the watchful eyes of Lizzy.

The third visit was not to be for as soon as Oguaa fell asleep, Lizzy left Ogbor Hill and returned home leaving Oguaa to enjoy her sleep. She knew that very soon the unfortunate lady's ordeal would commence. She did not want to witness the beginning of the tortuous moments.

As soon as the medicine man was satisfied that Oguaa was fast asleep, he uttered a guttural sound which summoned Umeadi who was waiting in the next room. With the help of Umeadi, Oguaa's hands and feet were tied and she was carried to bed which was already made for her in the room where Umeadi hid. Satisfied with a job well done, Umeadi also took leave of Oguaa and the medicine man.

The old wall clock which hung feebly on the wall of the room struck seven o'clock. It was already past twilight. Soon the medicine man fell asleep on the mat. He was indeed exhausted after concluding a long ritual. However he entertained no fear for Oguaa would not wake up until the early morning of the next day.

19

Doyin was surprised to see Majek and Dotun in Jim's house. As soon as she was through with her last paper, she had left for home. On visiting the Supermarket and Restaurant, she did not see any of her brothers. By sheer intuition, she left for Jim's house.

When she saw Jim arranging his belongings, she thought Jim was about embarking on one of his usual emergency trips.

However, she became curious when she noticed that Jim's luggage included some food stuff which ranged from onions, pepper, two bags of imported rice and assorted types of beverages.

Jim was not a heavy feeder so Doyin wondered why he had to carry such a large consignment with him on an official trip.

"Where is brother Jim taking these to?" Doyin whispered into Dotun's ear.

The unusual situation which she met had made her forget to ask Dotun about his health.

"He is travelling home", replied Majek who over-heard Doyin's question.

Before Doyin could ask another question, Jim emerged from his bedroom carrying two cartons of assorted wines and spirits.

"Ah brother Jim. I am surprised you never told me of the development. At least as a friend of the family, I think I deserve to know".

"Know what?" Dotun demanded.

"I am not blind dear brother. I know the marriage customs especially when the bride concerned is from the Eastern part of the country. I am happy that brother Jim has listened to my advice and has at last decided to settle down".

"You are embarrassing Jim", Dotun told Doyin.

Doyin did not see her actions as any cause for embarrassment so she said to her brothers.

"I hope you Majek will take a cue from brother Jim. I would like to have a sister-in-law and become an aunty as soon as possible."

As Doyin ranted, Jim realised that she was not aware of what had happened. His journey was neither for pleasure nor was it an official one. But he would rather not break the news to Doyin. He continued arranging his luggage as Doyin resumed her running commentary.

"I understand that marriage ceremonies are very expensive in your area. I hope you purchased enough kolanuts for they are cheaper and more abundant here in Lagos than in the East. And brother Jim, I have not seen the heads of tobacco which your people demand during your traditional weddings".

The two brothers did not expect Jim to reply so they were surprised when Jim spoke to Doyin.

"You are right. But during the first stage of marriages in my area, tobacco is not one of the requirements."

"Pardon me for my mistake", Doyin apologised.

Doyin's rantings were beginning to irritate Majek and he soon reacted.

"I would advise you to return to the house instead of staying here and causing more embarrassment to Jim".

Doyin let out a loud laugh.

"Marriage should not be made a secret affair: It is an achievement and not a shameful act. So it does not call for any embarrassment.

She however continued her inquiry for she was bent on satisfying her curiosity as well as enriching her knowledge.

"Brother Jim, are you happy to be getting married? Have your people forced a virgin bride on you?"

Jim managed to laugh. Afterall what else could he have done in order to appease the naïve lady.

"I am set", Jim finally said.

Doyin watched as Dotun and Majek helped Jim in packing the luggage into the boot of Jim's 505 Peugeot Saloon Car. As soon as everything was safely tucked into the car, Jim locked his door, bade his friends goodbye and drove off into the busy highway.

Majek and Dotun had come to see Jim in Majek's car. Doyin too joined them. As the company drove towards Dotun's hotel, Doyin then remembered to inquire about Dotun's health.

"As you can see dear sister, I am well again. The accident cost me my car but I thank God that I survived," Dotun replied.

"But why did it take you such a long time to inform me of your admission and subsequent discharge?"

"You had your exams to face. We did not want to get you worried," Majek said.

"That was very thoughtful of the family. Afterall, if brother Dotun had died, no one would have informed me until after the burial and possibly funeral."

"No sister."

"Yes", replied Doyin. "At least you would not have wanted to get me worried since I had my exams to face."

"You are getting the whole issue wrong my dear sister," Dotun said.

"I expected that reply anyway, I only wish to get over soon with this whole course and get married so that I will no longer be a pest to the family. I am tired of always being regarded as the family's pet."

The brothers were beginning to see that Doyin was getting highly agitated, so they never discussed any issue until they took Dotun to the hotel and drove towards the supermarket.

Majek knew that with Dotun out of the way, Doyin would now direct all the accusations at him. He tried to maintain the code of silence that had prevailed, but Doyin was soon to break it as they entered Majek's apartment.

Majek had completely renovated his room. The door and window blinds had been replaced with new ones and everywhere looked radiant and beautiful. Doyin did not compliment the new set up. She sat down and suddenly broke into tears. Majek sat beside her on the bed. He could understand how his sister felt bad but all that the family did had been in her own interest.

"Doyin. Don't be upset. We did not neglect you. As I said, there was no need to inform you since the family knew you would soon come back on holiday. I still don't know how the news got to you."

"Somebody who cared wrote me," replied Doyin.

"And if I may ask who is this somebody?"

"Who else but Kemi, Dotun's girl friend."

"Oh! that busy body. I am not surprised. The stupid girl is staging a comeback. She will never give up."

"Majek. I know Kemi is the wild type. But no girl is a saint. At least not in this area. If Dotun can tame her, I don't see why both of them should not get married."

"Doyin!"

"Yes, Majek".

"Dotun should settle down with one woman. The mere thought of the rate at which that big brother of mine changes his girl friends make me shudder. He is making himself very vulnerable".

"How, Doyin?"

"You should understand Majek. It is all part of sex education. I don't blame brother Jim for taking the safest way out by getting married."

"Who told you that Jim is getting married?"

"Don't be ridiculous Majek! Or are you jealous?"

"Doyin. Jim's journey home is not a pleasant one. He received some urgent news two days ago."

"What news?"

"Her niece who came to spend her last holiday with us here in Lagos left home for Lagos about two weeks ago. We are yet to see or hear from her".

"Who are you talking about?" Doyin asked.

"I mean your friend, Oguaa. Her father wrote Jim asking if she had arrived. Since we have not seen her, Jim had to make that emergency visit home to confirm the situation."

Doyin was dumbfounded. She felt lost and lonely. So many thoughts fleeted past her. What is happening? Why had she made a fool of herself in front of Jim? Will Jim understand and forgive her ignorance? Where is Oguaa? What is happening? The questions were endless, and the answers were not forthcoming.

After a long silence, Doyin slowly got up and looked at her brother. It was not a friendly look. She walked up to the door and opened it. As she stepped out, she once more turned and looked at her brother.

"Majek, if anything happens to that girl you will bear the consequences."

With those parting words highly ridden with guilt, fear, suspicion and accusations, Doyin banged the door noisily and made her way out of the building.

*   *   *   *   *   *   *

She was moving rather blindly towards a destination unknown to her. The whole episode could be aptly described as a nightmare.

Far away from where she lay, she could see little shining spots littered here and there. Instinctively, she felt that those spots could be habitable places. If only she could muster enough strength to get to one of those spots.

She had been feeling dizzy since she escaped from the

medicine man's apartment. Her feet and hands were sore. The cool breeze was intense and she was shivering. What was happening to her? She could not answer her own question since she could hardly remember anything. She continued to totter towards the spots that lay ahead. It was still dark.

Back at Ogbor Hill, the medicine man was fast asleep. He snored peacefully. His senses were lost to the world. His subsconscious mind was even non-functional.

He will certainly wake up more refreshed and ready to perform the final stage of his ritual. It will soon be dawn.

The Long awaited dawn came and the medicine man woke up with a start. He felt worried and was sweating profusely. This sensational atmosphere had never visited him over his many years of practice as a herbal doctor and traditional healer. He felt very uncomfortable as he tried to rise from his mat and gain some sitting balance on a nearby kitchen stool. This hitherto simple act was now proving difficult for the cripple.

When he was finally seated on a chair, he cursed humanity for being responsible for his present plight. His deformity had never been a source of concern to him until now. But come what may, he must survive. A long day awaited him for his patient would soon wake up.

He stretched his hand to switch on the light in the room. "Oh dear! These people have struck again", he cursed. There was no light.

It then dawned on him that he must make haste. He quickly lit up his old hurricane lantern and wobbled with the aid of the light until he reached the room where Oguaa was lying.

You could imagine the shock when he discovered that the room was empty and its window open. He searched the corners of the room and under the bed but he could not find his patient. "Something is wrong. That girl thinks she is smart but she is in for a surprise", he muttered.

Meanwhile Oguaa had finally reached one of the spots where she saw the illumination.

*   *   *   *   *   *   *

It was early morning and from a vantage point, Oguaa watched people hurrying past in pursuit of their various activities. The school children were hurrying to school. The civil servants and business men were equally hurrying to work. Cars, buses and trucks fleeted past her. To a normal human being, this scene was nothing strange. But to Oguaa, it was a funny sight. She mused at the stupidity of the human species and suddenly burst out laughing. This action alerted some commuters who merely turned to identify the source of this unusual early morning excitement. They were not surprised. Some took a quick glance at her and resumed their journey.

However, for the school children, it was a recent development as they stopped to watch the beautiful lady who sat outside the uncompleted building situated beside the Aba Town Hall.

As Oguaa laughed at intervals, the children chorused her laughter. The crowd grew as more children joined their peers. Soon an adult passer-by stopped and on seeing Oguaa, she shook her head sadly.

"Oh God! What is happening?" she lamented.

"Nothing my sister", echoed another woman. It is only a mad woman."

"But I have never seen this one before."

20

Madam Ezechi needed the rest. It has been a three-day hectic session for her. When she received the letter about the National Educational Planning Convention scheduled to hold at Port-Harcourt, she had under-estimated the rigours that would be attendant to the convention. No doubt, she was required to present a paper on behalf of her zone. This to her was no problem for an experienced principal. It would take her only two days of serious research and she would finally emerge with a thought-provoking paper. This she did and was delighted when she received loud ovations and subsequent verbal congratulatory messages from members of other zonal headquarters who had attended the convention.

She was happy with her achievement although the entire exercise had ended up making her feel exhausted and worn out.

She was trying to take a nap as she relaxed at the back

seat of the official vehicle which had conveyed her from Owerri to Port-Harcourt for the convention. She and her driver were going back to Owerri.

The noisy atmosphere that woke her up from sleep made her realise that they had reached the commercial town of Aba. The traffic had gradually slowed down but she was not feeling uncomfortable for the air-conditioning unit in the vehicle provided a cooling effect which waded off the excruciating heat that characterized the entire sunny atmosphere.

"Matthew. It seems we are caught in a traffic jam", her driver answered.

The traffic situation was chaotic although the vehicles were moving at a snail pace.

At the Aba Town Hall, Matthew took a quick glance off the major road to observe a scene. He saw what appeared to be a struggle between two women. Such scenes were common place events at Aba, so the driver quickly adjusted his seat and continued his journey. The traffic situation had eased out so the road was now free for a smooth ride. They were on their way to Owerri.

*   *   *   *   *   *   *

On her return from the trip, Nnenna decided to rest for a day. She was not in a hurry to see her customers whom she believed would be interested in buying some of the wares which she brought along with her on the trip.

She had learnt from her assistant that Oguaa had left for Lagos. The news brought no joy to her for she had bought her niece some wears too. She however regretted Oguaa's stubbornness and impatience to wait for her arrival before taking any decision. Since her brother Anyamba was aware of the development, she decided to think less of the matter. The next day after her return, she was boarding a taxi to Umungasi where she hoped to attend to some of her customers.

As they approached the town hall, Nnenna saw a large crowd gathered in front of a nearby uncompleted building. As a business woman, time for her meant money so she urged the driver to neglect the crowd and move on. While the driver proceeded, Nnenna looked out from the vehicle and a face greeted her sight. She became apprehensive for the face was indeed familiar.

Impulsively, she asked the driver to stop.

"Madam, na here you want drop?"

"No, I just want to know what is happening".

"Make you take am jeje! I hear say that mad woman strong well well", the driver warned.

One can imagine the shock that registered on Nnenna's face when she realised that the mad woman was non other than her niece, Oguaa. She forced her way through the surging crowd and eventually stood face to face with Oguaa. The latter took a long belligerent look at Nnenna then turned her face towards another direction. Nnenna stood still. She looked at Oguaa. She was apparently confused and even wondered whether her eyes were not deceiving her. Oguaa was supposed to be in Lagos. Certainly it was not Oguaa. As Nnenna made to go, she turned again and looked at the "lunatic."

"Oguaa!" she called.

Her action only met with a frozen look from the lunatic.

"Oguaa!" Nnenna repeated.

Most of the on-lookers had turned their attention towards Nnenna.

"Abi you know am?" one of the men questioned.

Nnenna did not answer. She quickly moved towards the lunatic and held her by her hand.

"Oguaa! What are you doing here? What is happening to you?"

For a reply, Oguaa wrestled her hand from Nnenna's grip.

"Make you leave am o", another on-looker warned.

"I can't leave her. Please help me! She is my sister. She is my niece. Please help me!" Nnenna pleaded and cried.

A young man of about twenty moved out of the crowd to come to Nnenna's rescue. A young girl obviously his companion pulled him back and whispered into his ear.

"What are you trying to do? How are you sure that the woman is the sister. Look, I have warned you. You are new in this town. What do you think will happen if the police meets us here?"

"But can't you see that the woman needs help?" the young man questioned.

"Are you the only young man around? Why don't the others help her? Please come and let's go. I will not allow you to put me in trouble."

When the young pair left the scene, the girl called her companion and treated him to a long lecture on the goings-on at Aba. She explained to him that Aba is a town that is full of mysteries. It is a town where sympathy is not sacrificed on the alter of sentiments. She hinted him that the older lady's actions may not be of good intentions. Some of these sophisticated ladies parade the town looking for their victims which range from lunatics to virile young men and attractive teenage girls. Those who are lucky succeed in luring their victims to their untimely deaths. The unlucky ones get caught in the police net and spend the rest of their lives behind bars.

The young man could not understand what her sister was saying. Her arguments baffled him for he saw nothing wrong in playing the good Samaritan. At least the holy book advocates such acts.

"Forget your religious doctrine. That was why I was not happy when Papa agreed that you should go to the seminary. There is another world. A world that is more of a closed system. You don't know what is happening outside", the sister concluded.

The young man smiled over his sister's misguided notion. He knew she was very wrong in her assertions but he dared not argue further.

As they moved away from the crowd, they could hear the sound of a police siren approaching.

"Do you hear that?" the lady continued.

"If the crowd is still there, the police will definitely arrest all those who are involved in the side attraction. Thank God we are lucky to have left the scene on time."

The young man could not understand the whole issue. It however dawned on him that the world was turning into a place where to do good or show mercy is often misinterpreted as an evil design. He was not happy for not doing some service to humanity. He could do nothing but trail behind his sister.

When he eventually looked back, he tried to strain his eyes in order to assess the situation of things near the town hall. The place looked deserted. Everybody seemed to have fled as soon as the police arrived. He could only make out some few figures from his distance. He could hear dismal voices. He looked up, and it was all mystery.

*　　*　　*　　*　　*　　*　　*

Jim arrived Umuayalu at about nine o'clock in the evening. This late arrival was not due to the traffic jam which usually characterized the short stretch from the bridge at the Asaba end of the famous River Niger on to the outskirts of the town of Onitsha enroute Owerri.

Rather, Jim was unlucky with his car. Despite his having serviced his vehicle before leaving Lagos, he had been faced with the task of draining his tank to replace the fuel which he bought on his way. He suspected that, that fuel had been adulterated and had greatly affected the performance of the engine. He also had to contend with the ordeal of changing two of his tyres which had been punctured in the course of his journey.

The village was as quiet as a graveyard when Jim finally arrived. The entire inhabitants who were not accustomed to night life had long retired to bed.

On arrival Jim had packed his car and gone straight to his brother's house. Anyamba heard the reverberation of the engine hence was not surprised when he heard a knock on his door.

"Who is there?" Anyamba asked.

"It's me brother", was the answer

"Who are you?"

"I am Jim, brother Anyamba. I am just coming from Lagos."

Anyamba jumped out of bed and hurriedly opened the

door to see Jim standing in front of him.

"Jim! What happened? Why did you have to come in so late?" Anyamba queried.

"I left Lagos early but had a lot of problems with my car!"

The discussion had awakened Mary who came out to welcome her brother-in-law. As soon as Jim was seated, Mary asked. "How is my daughter?"

"She is fine," Jim lied.

Jim did not want to cause any uproar within the household especially at such an unholy hour of the midnight.

Mary who was excited over the good news had immediately left for the kitchen to prepare some hot water for Jim to have his bath and probably nibble at a scanty meal despite Jim's protest that he was not feeling hungry.

While the two brothers discussed, Anyamba noticed that the answers he received from his junior brother were monosyllabic. He observed Jim for sometime, saw it all before he finally asked about Oguaa.

"That's why I have come brother Anyamba. The contents of your letter scared me for Oguaa is not in Lagos. I wanted to come and confirm the situation before informing the police."

Anyamba did not utter a word. Rather he advised that Jim should take his bath and eat before they could discuss further. For him it was the dawn of a new day. Their discussion did not end until the first cock crow in the morning.

*   *   *   *   *   *   *

Since Munachi arrived home after his visit to Umuayalu, he had not found peace within himself. He had his fears but prayed that they would not be true. He was listening to his grandfather's tale. The story sounded weird.

"Yes, my son. As I was saying Nwaonuma never recovered from his sickness. His limbs continued to grow thinner until he could hardly walk."

"But it is quite unfair for the whole village to disown him", Munachi added.

"You young men are luckier today. During my youthful days, there was hardly any crime that escaped punishment."

"What crime did Nwaonuma commit?"

"Your question is a bit difficult to answer my son. One may not rightly say that the boy committed any crime. The logic actually lies in your biblical doctrine that the sins of the parents are often visited on their children. Nwaonuma was a posthumous child. He was born at the time his mother was still mourning the death of her husband. As a little boy then, stories had it that Nwaonuma was not really the true son of his father. His mother had committed adultery during her period of mourning. In fact the circumstances surrounding his birth earned him the name Nwaonuma which literally means "A Child of Sorrow".

Unfortunately, this child of sorrow was unable to walk after four years. All efforts by his mother to get her child cured proved abortive. Tongues started wagging all over our village. Nwaonuma's mother could no longer bear the cynical remarks which accompanied her wherever she went. She could no longer bear the gossip. When her child was barely five, the woman left the village with her invalid child. No one has heard about mother and child until this day."

Munachi had never been in doubt about his grandfather's wisdom. To him the old man was a sage and his story has further increased Munachi's anxiety. He must travel back to Umuayalu to see his in-law in connection with Oguaa's story.

'Any reader could easily see the naivety that characterized the Stone Age traditional wisdom. Nwaonuma's predicament shouldn't have been attributed to the vengeance of any god. The invalid met his unfortunate fate because villagers were ignorant of modern child survival remedies. Nwaonuma was indeed a victim of poliomyelitis or infantile paralysis. This affliction constitutes one of the six child-killer diseases which till this day is responsible for the high rate of infant mortality.'

* * * * * * *

The scene that had been enacted near the Aba Town Hall was better seen than described. As the youngman and his sister left, the police had actually arrived and the teaming crowd had quickly taken to its heels, leaving Nnenna and Oguaa.

The former was crying as a result of the bite which Oguaa had inflicted on her during the struggle. But despite this ugly and unfortunate incident, Nnenna still pleaded with the police to help her for the supposedly mad lady was indeed her niece. Her assertion was doubtful but the police had to do something.

"Madam! How do you want us to believe your story?" one of the policemen asked Nnenna.

"She is my niece, officer. I left her in my house before I travelled. I only came back to hear that she had left for Lagos", Nnenna lamented.

"But this is not Lagos?" the other police officer interrupted.

"That is the mystery, sir. I don't know what is happening to her. Look at my body; she has not only torn my blouse but has bitten me on my left arm. Please help me get hold of her."

The three policemen discussed briefly and eventually decided to help the wounded lady. Oguaa was over-powered and the two women were put into the police van and whisked off to the Central Police Station.

Oguaa created a stir at the Station. She raved, rented and cursed Nnenna. The latter who had received some first aid treatment as a result of the bite simply stared at her young niece. Despite the handcuffs that had been put on her hands, Oguaa was still screaming and constituting a nuisance within the station environment.

Nnenna was led into a room where he was asked to write a statement in connection with the circumstances that led to her being at the Central Police Station. She narrated her ordeal.

After making her statement, Nnenna was informed that the DPO in-charge of the station wanted to see her.

She promptly stood up and followed her informant who led her to the office of the DPO. She knocked and a familiar voice asked her to come in.

The DPO continued to write with his head bent down as he signalled Nnenna to sit on one of the settees in the moderately furnished office. Soon the officer raised his head and looked at Nnenna.

"Yes, what can we do for you Madam?" the police boss asked.

As Nnenna narrated her story. The boss listened. But

he was no longer looking at the lady who sat opposite him. No one would dare suspect that the officer was in a pensive mood.

"Madam Celina! What are you doing at Aba?"

Nnenna was shocked as soon as she heard herself being referred to as Celina. She just gazed at the police boss.

"You may not recognize me, madam. I would like you to cast your mind back to some years ago. To be precise, madam, do you remember the civil war period when you ran a food canteen at the Ojuelegba junction in Lagos Mainland?"

Nnenna paused for a while then exclaimed:

"Don't tell me you are Yusuf?"

The officer did not answer.

21

The three men were engaged in a very thought-provoking discussion. Fate had brought them together for non expected to see each other talkless of waiting together on that fateful afternoon.

The main issue of their discussion was Oguaa, Anyamba's daughter whom they were now convinced was missing. As they discussed each brought out his major trend of thought and they all pondered over it.

"The first step is to report the matter to the Police," Jim said.

"You are right. But I have the feeling that since Oguaa's whereabout could not be traced in Lagos, there might be the possibility that she is still at Aba," said Munachi.

"She might have been involved in a road mishap on her way to Lagos", Anyamba suggested.

These were all possible alternative which the men offered.

Any of them could be right. But all might as well be wrong.

Munachi's thought further expressed the possibility that Oguaa may have fallen victim to some ritualistic motives. He believed strongly in tradition and the influence his grandfather had over him had not diminished one bit.

Grandfather's influence has been responsible for Munachi's lukewarm attitude towards the issue of his wife Agnes. His grandfather had assured him that Agnes was not a barren woman. All that was needed was patience for with time Agnes would definitely conceive.

His grandfather was not the boastful type. He had stood by his grandson's side when the entire members of the family advised that Munachi should take another wife, rather than remain tied to the apron strings of a log of wood as Agnes was often referred to. To allay his fears and strengthen his conviction, Munachi's grandfather had assured his grandson that he would rather die and reincarnate in order to ensure that Agnes had a child for her husband.

While grandfather was still alive, Agnes had hoped that one day she would enjoy the good fortune of having a child to suck her firm and succulent breasts.

Mary had learnt the bitter truth in the morning. She did not cry or express any misgivings about the news. Her face was expressionless as she quietly withdrew into one of the rooms. She was there when Nnenna arrived.

Mary did not come to greet her sister-in-law as she usually did. Nnenna had told the gathering about her experience at Aba. Her story brought some momentary relief to the three men who were discussing. Anyamba was happy that at least her daughter was alive despite the deplorable condition which Nnenna had told them Oguaa was. Jim was furious and urged that they go straight into action and punish whoever was responsible.

Munachi took in the whole story and was already scheming some other ways of tracking the perpetrators without resorting to any help from the police.

* * * * * * *

"My wife. You have refused to say something since I came in. I have told you all and even assured you that despite the state of affairs, your daughter will not die. We will all try our best to make sure that whatever or whoever is responsible for Oguaa's predicament does not go unpunished. Do you doubt me? Are you not yet convinced?"

Mary was not listening to Nnenna as she narrated her findings at Aba. Her mind was filled with monstrous thoughts. She had been a faithful and loyal wife to Anyamba. Her diligence and submissive nature were responsible for whatever was happening to her daughter. She recollected every moment of her life right from the birth of Oguaa to the present. She was a wounded lioness searching for a prey.

Nnenna's entry into the room where she had quietly retired to seemed to have given Mary the long awaited opportunity to explode. She would not let her prey escape for to her, Nnenna was the virus that had ruined her family. As soon as she sensed that her sister-in-law had paused during her speech, Mary reacted.

"Nnenna. I may be poor but I am not starving. Since the birth of Oguaa my daughter, I had patiently allowed you and your brother to dictate the tune because I wanted peace to reign. What both of you forgot is that there is always a limit to one's endurance. Let me tell you the truth Nnenna. You and your brother Jim are responsible for what is happening to my daughter."

Nnenna had never heard Mary talk to her in such a disrespectful manner. She could not believe that what she was hearing were proceeding from the mouth of her loving sister-in-law. She was dumbfounded but Mary couldn't be bothered.

"The life of a prostitute is a precarious one. That was why I vehemently opposed the idea that Oguaa should visit you at Port Harcourt. I did not want her to taste the bitter pill which is attendant with the travails of your profession. I was not wrong. Oguaa learnt fast. You had within her short period of stay drilled her and she even perfected in the game. I was not happy but as I told you, I wanted peace to prevail.

Nnenna! What do you gain by living this kind of life? It has earned you nothing but great wealth and abundant vices. Why didn't you allow the vices to trail you and you alone?

Why did you lead my daughter into this dishonourable profession? I know you have to survive as a widow. I know you understand all the grimmicks that go with the life of a prostitute in the city. Why did you have to use my daughter as your victim?"

"Shut up you ingrate?" It was Nnenna's voice and she was really shouting at the top of her voice.

"Who are you to address me in such a rude manner?

You have the guts to accuse me of being a prostitute yet you have all the while accepted all the gifts which your prostitute showered on you each time she paid a visit. Listen Mary. You claim to be a mother but you know nothing about motherhood. If you claim you do, your daughter would not have found herself in this position. As a mother you should have educated her on the process of growing up as soon as you noticed she had reached the age of puberty. To be candid, I was surprised when I realised that Oguaa was a greenhorn when she paid me that visit at Port-Harcourt some years ago. I sympathized with her plight and took all the pains to intimate her on what to expect as a young girl who had attained maturity. Mary! You never taught your girl any morals. You probably felt that sex education was dirty and as such should not be discussed. I pity you and regret having you as a sister-in-law".

Mary wanted to talk but Nnenna would not give her that opportunity as she continued.

"Listen Mary and listen very carefully. Your second daughter Chinwe is growing up. I would advise that you sit her down and explain to her the basic facts of life. Otherwise you will end up being a laughing stock of the village and a disgrace to womanhood. Talking about prostitution, who is a prostitute? You do not know, so I may help you. A prostitute is a woman of loose virtues who sells her body to any man in order to make money. That is what you have called me. I wonder how you got your information. Certainly Anyamba could not have fed you with such rubbish about me. We are a decent family, hardworking and progressive. Jim my brother is a case in point. Oguaa's waywardness surely stems from your own family stock. Your carelessness and extreme ignorance exposed your daughter to many anti-social behaviour one of which led to her being suspended from school.

Mary! What did you do when your daughter was sent packing from school? Nothing! You did nothing until your prostitute came to your rescue. I, Nnenna, spoke with Oguaa's

Principal Madam Ezechi when I last visited home and subsequently arranged for your daughter to receive prompt medical attention. What was my reward, Mary! Nothing but what I am now receiving from you. A prostitute indeed!

You have to grow up Mary else you will become a village idiot who knows nothing other than being a baby factory. You already have four children. The number of children does not matter. What matters is how many have been prepared and nurtured to be a source of pride to the family in future. Education is not all that it takes. Udoka and Nneji did not attend any secondary school. The same goes for Agnes and Martina. I don't need to talk more Mary, but you will certainly regret the day you called me a prostitute".

This scene was still raging as the three men discussed in Anyamba's sitting room. Nnenna had arrived and after narrating her tale had inquired of Mary. Under Anyamba's directives, Nnenna had gone into the room where she met her sister-in-law in a depressive mood. Her efforts to console Mary had generated the unpleasant situation which had earlier prevailed. The situation had degenerated to exchange of insults and abuses which was terminated by Jim's dramatic entry.

"What is happening here", Jim asked.

"That's your sister-in-law. Look at Mary, Jim. She called me a prostitute".

"Why? What for?" Jim further demanded.

Nnenna was not ready to go into details. She had spoken a lot and the only reply she could further give was to burst into tears.

"Mary! What is going on between you and aunty Nnenna?" Jim again asked.

Mary ignored Jim's question. She sat quietly on the bed. She was neither prepared to give any reply nor offer any explanation.

Jim went up to Nnenna and tried to console her.

"She called me a prostitute," Nnenna repeated.

"Don't mind her aunty. Try to understand. The news has greatly upset her so I would advise that you forgive and forget whatever she said or called you. This is not the time for quarrels."

"Of course, what else would you say? You are both partners in the game. Both of you have successfully schemed and now my daughter's life is in danger, you pretend to be on the sympathetic side."

"Mary! What has come over you?"

"Nothing. I am still with my senses. Oguaa may have gone mad. She may be dead by now but I am not mad neither do I wish to die presently. Listen Jim. Oguaa's visit to Port-Harcourt changed the life of my daughter. Her visit to Lagos finally ruined her. I am yet to be convinced that both of you did not conspire to bring shame and disgrace to my husband and me. I still wonder what both of you stand to gain by your actions."

Jim knew that he had to be very careful in dealing with this unprecedented situation. He could not understand why this state of turmoil should arise at a time when reason and cordiality should reign. Like a dumb waiter, he led the weeping Nnenna out of the room.

Mary did not look up as the two figures disappeared. For her there were no regrets or any feelings of remorse. She had expressed her innermost feelings. She had thoroughly bared her mind and ridden herself of the burden which had weighed her down for almost three years.

*   *   *   *   *   *   *

At the Ogbor Hill residence, the medicine man was engaged in midnight vigil. His patient had fled but he strongly believed that she would wander back into his den no matter how hard she tried to escape. Her mind was already diseased and the hypnotic effect he had imposed on her would surely lead her back to his house.

He had assumed the yoga position since nine o' clock in the evening. With his eyes dimly shut, he chanted and made invocative utterances in order to accomplish his task.

Things did not seem to go right. The signs which he received were not encouraging. He laughed for he felt the spirits were trying to put him to test. He usually enjoyed such trials but not with the present case. He felt he had meditated enough. It was now time to look through his magic mirror before taking on the next step.

When he opened his eyes he noticed that the light from the hurricane lantern was fast dying out. He did not want to switch on the electrical bulb for the ritual did not call for a very bright atmosphere. There was still some little kerosene in the bottle so he decided to refill the lamp before consulting his mirror.

There was no need extinguishing the light from the lantern since the flame was very faint. He would refill the lantern while the light was still burning and later adjust the wick to get the room once more brighter. That was easy.

Despite his physical disability, he picked up the lantern

and limped towards the side of the room which served as his sanctuary. He suddenly felt all his body growing stiff. He had experienced such feelings before but that was about a year ago. He tried to take a second limp but he could hardly move. Dizzy spells succeeded and soon the cripple slumped on the floor still holding the burning lantern. The globe which shielded the light in the lamp broke with the fall.

The room grew brighter as the kerosene flowed freely covering the entire floor. He was not aware of the goings-on for his body shook with spasms. He was undergoing another bout of his perennial ailment. He was an epileptic.

* * * * * * *

Superintenent Yusuf Meriga was a sergeant in the army during the civil war. He was part of the amphibious brigade that had a fierce and blody encounter with the rebel forces at the reverine town of Oguta.

On one of his visits to Lagos, he had come across a very beautiful lady. On further inquiry, Yusuf had been informed that the lady who hails from Itshekiri land was one of the workers who served at a popular restaurant situated at the Ojuelegba junction in Lagos. Yusuf had trailed the beauty to the restaurant where he met Celina.

The sergeant was particularly impressed by the way Celina attended to her customers. The food was highly appetizing and despite the fact that the customers were numerous, Celina and her assistants tried to make everybody feel important.

Yusuf continued paying regular visits to the restaurant with the intention of seeing her Itshekiri heart-throb and her benevolent employee.

But he had to go back to the war zone where he stayed until the war came to an end. On getting back to Lagos, Yusuf learnt that both Celina and her restaurant no longer existed. He soon retired from the army and joined the police force as an Inspector. He later attended the course at the Police College in Kuru near Jos where he graduated as an Assistant Superintendent of Police. His first transfer took him to Kano. By the time he finally came to Aba to assume the post of a Divisional Police Officer, he was a Superintendent of Police.

As the memories of his war days flashed across his mind, he could hear the cacophony that emanated from the Police Cells. He marvelled at this strange meeting with Celina who had explained how she came to be known as Nnenna. He never suspected that the lady gave out any clue to suspect that she came from Eastern part of the country.

The meeting brought back pleasant memories but Nnenna's visit to the station saddened the young police officer. He had assured her that he would do all in his best to see that her niece was well taken care of before Nnenna left for Umuayalu. The police doctors had attended to Oguaa but the girl had been very uncompromising and had refused to yield to any medical attention.

"Your niece is in a very bad shape. We have tried our best but she has refused to cooperate. The doctors have hinted that her case will need some psychiatric attention and that we can't give her. I would advise that she be taken to a mental home", the DPO said.

Nnenna, Anyamba, Munachi and Jim had listened to the DPO as he explained Oguaa's condition. They had arrived Aba but could not see the DPO until four o'clock in the evening since the officer was not on seat. It was not their fault. The delay at the mechanic village was responsible for their late arrival.

Anyamba who had been introduced as the girl's father signed all the necessary papers before Oguaa was handed over to them with caution from the DPO. To ensure that his orders were carried out to the last letter. The DPO instructed one of his assistants to accompany them to the mental home.

*   *   *   *   *   *   *

Before Jim left Umuayalu for Aba, he felt he needed to service his car in order to prevent any breakdown. He was happy that neither Anyamba nor Munachi was aware of the bitter encounter that took place between Mary and Nnenna. In order to avoid any further development, Jim had appealed with the reluctant Nnenna to accompany him to the mechanic village. After effecting repairs, they would come back to pick Munachi and Anyamba for the trip. Nnenna had consented.

There were a few people at the mechanic village when Jim and Nnenna drove in. They needed immediate attention hence they drove straight to Dozie's shed where they hoped to see their little nephew Udoka.

Udoka was not around when they arrived but they saw Dozie who was engaged in a fierce argument with two customers who had obviously brought their vehicles for repairs. The two customers were abusing Dozie while the latter was making frantic efforts to pacify them. Nnenna intervened.

"Madam Ezechi! What is the matter?"

"Ah, Nnenna, replied the elderly lady. I didn't know you are the one. How are you?"

"We are fine. What is the problem?"

"My vehicle developed a fault as I was returning from Port-Harcourt. This mechanic promised I should come back this morning and collect it. As you can see, he has not even started working on it," Madam Ezechi explained.

You brought your vehicle only yesterday. My Mercedez Benz Car has been here for more than a week. I have made several trips but each has ended with one excuse or the other", the other gentleman retorted.

"Your car has a major engine problem, sir. We are doing our best to get it back on the road. I have been pleading that you exercise patience", Dozie explained.

"What type of patience do you want me to exercise? You are still working on the engine. The dent has not been mended and you still have to give the car a new coat of paint".

"The spraying is no problem sir. We have bought the red paint which you demanded should be used to cover the original white colour of your car. Just exercise some patience. We are trying to be careful. I assure you that before the end of tomorrow, your car should be ready."

"These mechanics are all the same. Don't ever believe them", Madam Ezechi chipped in.

"But Nnenna, what is wrong with your car?"

"My sister, we are on our way to Aba. We only wanted to check our tyres and do the wheel alignment."

"Don't worry Madam. Udoka will attend to you as soon as he comes back", Dozie said.

As Jim and Nnenna waited, Jim took time to admire the Mercedes Benz Car. It was the 200E model. He wondered why the owner wanted the whole car to be completely resprayed. The dent was very minor and he mused at the way some men take delight in wasting their hard earned money.

Nnenna had moved over to chat briefly with Madam Ezechi. The latter who could no longer wait soon left with a threat that Dozie would be in trouble if her car was not ready by the next day.

For Nnenna, Madam Ezechi's exit was good riddance. She did not introduce the elderly woman to Jim for fear that her identity might generate some ill-feelings from Jim.

By the time Udoka came and worked on Jim's car, it was almost past noon. As they drove back to Umuayalu to pick Anyamba and Munachi. Jim asked Nnenna.

"Who was that woman we met at the mechanic village?" Nnenna's fears were confirmed but she had a ready answer.

"Oh my brother. Sorry I did not introduce you. She is just a friend."

22

Nobody spoke as Jim drove his car out of the Police premises. The presence of Anyamba must have quietened Oguaa who sat in between her father and the Police Officer at the back seat. Munachi shared the front seat with Jim and Nnenna. They were on their way to the mental and nervous diseases hospital at Aba.

As he drove, Jim tried to enliven the rather unusual quiet atmosphere by making some humorous remarks about the women of Aba and their mode of dressing. His jokes met with no laughter for everybody was in a pensive mood.

"Why don't you go by Jubilee Road? It's faster", Nnenna managed to say. Jim was not familiar with the town so he obeyed and turned towards Jubilee Road. Just as the car made for the road, Oguaa who had been silent suddenly let out a wild cry.

"That's her! That's her!" she shouted. She was pointing at a female figure who stood by the road side apparently waiting for a taxi. The figure was dressed in black jean trousers and a red shirt.

"Who is that?" Anyamba asked.

"That's her! My friend!" Oguaa cried louder.

Jim wanted to stop but on second thought, he stepped harder on the accelerator and the car moved on faster.

When Oguaa refused to stop her yellings, the policeman ordered Jim to stop. He wanted to satisfy his curiosity before they could proceed further.

Jim made a reverse turn and drove to the spot where the lady stood. As soon as Oguaa saw the lady, she resumed her screaming. The police officer stepped out of the car and walked towards the lady.

Meanwhile the lady walked past the officer and on getting to the waiting vehicle peered inside only to see Oguaa seated at the back. She immediately took to her heels.

It was a futile race for she could not go far before the policeman caught up with her and dragged her back to the vehicle.

"Do you know this lady?" the police officer pointed at Oguaa.

"I have never met her in my life," the lady in jeans replied.

"Lizzy! Please please help me! They want to kill me! Please don't let them take me away!" Oguaa pleaded.

Lizzy surveyed the gory spectacle in handcuffs. She could not believe that the apparition was her classmate and bosom friend Oguaa. She did not even hear the questions which were directed at her by the police officer. A crowd had gathered and everybody in the car had alighted. Only Oguaa and her father stayed in the car. Jim, Nnenna and Munachi stood and watched as the policeman quizzed the young lady.

"I have told you that I don't know her", Lizzy said.
"But how come she knows you?"
The Officer did not believe the lady's story.
"Now young lady what is your name?"
"My name is Elizabeth."
The officer needed no more answer. He explained to Jim and his group that circumstance demands that the strange lady be taken to the police station for serious interrogation. She could be a suspect but would be released if his suspicions were not confirmed. He however demanded that one of them should accompany him to the station for he needed a witness. Munachi volunteered to go with him.

As the officer boadred a taxi and left for the station in company of the lady and Munachi, Jim drove off towards the hospital with Nnenna and Anyamba. Oguaa was still shouting and calling on Lizzy to come to her rescue.

*   *   *   *   *   *   *

When Jim and others left Umuayalu for Aba, Mary emerged from the room and asked her second daughter Chinwe to call Nwayieze for her. No doubt she had told Nnenna the bitter truth. But she still felt that somehow her sister-in-law was right in apportioning some parts of the blame to her.

What is the secret of bringing up children to be responsible individuals? She had called Nnenna a prostitute. What will happen if her husband Anyamba got to hear the news?

No doubt her marriage would be threatened for she knew her husband and had always dreaded his militant approach to issues.

Her encounter with Nnenna would certainly get into her

husband's ears. If Jim does not mention it, she was convinced that her sister-in-law would tell her brother. She had to prepare herself for any eventuality whenever the party returned from Aba. Part of the preparation was the reason why she dared to send for Nwayieze.

Nwayieze was surprised when she received the call. Mary had never sent for her. She always came to her house whenever she wanted to talk things over with her. She knew that Mary had been feeling bad in recent times and feared that she might have fallen ill as a result of the early morning news which Jim told the entire family gathering.

When she entered Anyamba's house, she saw Adaugo and Mary. None seemed to be talking. They were apparently waiting for her to arrive.

She was right for no sooner had she arrived than Adaugo heaved a sigh of relief. Nwayieze sat down and inquired what was amiss.

"Mary had a disagreement with Sisi Potacot before she left for Aba", Adaugo said.

"What type of disagreement?" Nwayieze inquired.

"Sisi Potacot accused Mary of being responsible for Oguaa's fate. Mary was not happy with the accusation hence replied rudely to Sisi's insinuations."

"What did Mary say to Sisi Potacot?" Nwayieze further demand.

Adaugo looked at Mary and back at Nwayieze. She expected Mary to answer the question but the latter simply kept mute. Nwayieze could not understand what was happening but she had to satisfy her curiosity. When she repeated her question, Adaugo paused before answering.

"She called Sisi Potacot a prostitute".

Nwayieze could not believe what she had just heard. She moved closer to Mary who was sitting on the bed.

"Mary! Is Adaugo right? Did you call your sister-in-law a prostitute?"

Adaugo wanted to reply to the question but Nwayieze ordered her to shut her mouth and let Mary speak for herself.

Mary then narrated the incident that took place between her and her sister-in-law. She deliberately omitted some aspects of the encounter which she felt would further discredit her in the presence of the two older women. When she ended her story, Nwayieze spoke:

"You were very wrong my child. I understand how you feel about your daughter but you went too far in your attitude towards your sister-in-law. Your calling Sisi Potacot names would not solve the problem. Rather you have made the situation worse and created a rather bad image of yourself."

"I don't agree, Ma, Nwayieze. She and her brother Jim ruined my daughter's life".

The old woman sensed that Mary was not prepared to accept her faults. She wanted to help but did not know how. She would think over it but before she left she spoke to Mary.

"The matter is a serious one. I don't know how your husband would take it. I will see what I can do to help. But whatever happens Mary, know it that today marks the beginning of enmity between you and your sister-in-law. You have called for the tune so you must be ready to dance."

With those parting words, Nwayieze left Anyamba's house.

* * * * * * *

Under serious cross-examination, Lizzy was able to divulge some vital information to the police. Her story sounded incredible but Superintendent Yusuf was bent on investigating every aspect of what the lady in jean trousers had said.

Lizzy's story exposed the hideout at Ulasi Road. For Yusuf this was a starting point. Some people were really instrumental to Oguaa's predicament and if the culprits had to be arrested, any further delay could be dangerous.

Lizzy's story about the medicine man at Ogbor Hill was another vital information which should be attended to. Lizzy did not mention Samson's name in the course of her interrogation. She rather told the police that one Mister Kanu owned the house and rode a white Mercedes Benz Car.

Yusuf had heard enough. He immediately swung into action as he despatched two different police squads to the Ulasi Road residence and the medicine man's house at Ogbor Hill. Soon the two squad's returned having made little or no success in their assignments.

The Bungalow at Ulasi Road was deserted when the anti-crime police squad arrived in company of Lizzy. There was nobody around so the police moved over to neighbouring house to see if they could obtain any useful information about the occupants of the deserted house.

The neighbour whom the police accosted was an old woman with three little boys who were between the ages of four and nine years. The woman was afraid on seeing the police at her door steps. She had not committed any crime so what could the police be looking for at her apartment.

The squad was the understanding type and patiently

explained their mission before asking about the occupants of the deserted house.

The old lady explained that she had only arrived some two days ago. The three children were her grand-sons whose parents had travelled abroad leaving her to take care of their children until they return in about a month's time. She had no idea who lived in the neighbourhood and apologised over her inability to be of any use to them.

For Lizzy it was the beginning of a nightmare. She had withheld some facts from the police. Samson's disappearance did not bother her for she knew that he was safe. She was determined not to expose the good samaritan who saved her from the hoodlums at the Aba Motor Park on that fateful evening and further took her into his house and treated her like a sister.

For the police, the name Kanu lingered. His white Mercedez Benz Car was an invaluable clue towards locating his whereabouts. But they had to return to the police station to report their findings and wait for further instructions.

Munachi accompanied the second police squad to Ogbor Hill. When Lizzy was being cross-examined, the police had asked for the name of the medicine man. Lizzy had told them the name was Nwaonuma. Munachi remembered his grandfather's tale about the cripple who with his mother left Item many years ago. Could the herbalist be the five year invalid his grandfather talked about? He did not know so he kept his thoughts to himself as the police van moved towards Ogbor Hill.

It may be wrong to say that the police eventually got to the house of the medicine man since there was really no house to enter. The site as Lizzy had described was nothing but the remains of a rather ramshackled apartment that was almost destroyed by fire. A large crowd had assembled there when the squad arrived. Their findings revealed that a medicine man once lived there but had met an untimely death as a result of fire accident that gutted the apartment. There, lying in the heap of some ashy debris were the remains of a man who had been burnt beyond recognition.

The corpse was indeed that of Nwaonuma as most people in the crowd affirmed. Some of the herbal kits which made up the deadly arsenal had escaped the inferno. The police had no clue as to verbal statements from the crowd. They picked up a few exhibits from the site and sent a radio message for an ambulance to remove the corpse. Perhaps an autopsy might help.

For Munachi, it was a sad adventure. He had hoped to see the medicine man and probably confirm his grandfather's tale. If the corpse was really that of Nwaonuma, he had lost the opportunity of meeting the devil incarnate of a kinsman whom fate had deprived him the privilege of knowing.

The squad soon returned to the police station to report their findings and await further instructions.

Meanwhile Superintendent Yusuf had sent out signals to all police stations informing them to be on the look-out for a white Mercedes Benz Car which Lizzy said belonged to one Mister Kanu.

At the police station Munachi peeped along the dark corridors which led to the cells. His eyes could discern the cell where Oguaa stayed when they first arrived to see the District Police Officer. There was a new inmate. No doubt the female figure was Lizzy. Munachi left the station to join the others at the mental hospital.

*   *   *   *   *   *   *

Lizzy's strategic position along Jubilee Road was intentional. She was acting on the instruction of Samson who had advised that she wait for him at that spot. But where was Samson before Lizzy met her fate in the hands of the police?

"For how long do we have to remain here?"

"I don't think it would be longer than today".

Samson and Umeadi had arrived Calabar two days ago. Their trip was prompted by their discovery that Oguaa had escaped from the house of the medicine man. Samson had vacated his Ulasi Road residence after asking Kanu to leave for Owerri and if possible effect a change of colour on the Mercedes Benz car. This he believed would conceal Kanu's identity since Oguaa's escape if not salvaged, would expose them as endangered species. Kanu was never to return to Aba but should move up to North and attempt an escape through the borders into any of the neighbouring Francophone countries.

It was their second day in Calabar and if the information and their arrangements work out, Umeadi would by midnight board one of those engine boats that transported contraband goods into the neighbouring country of Cameroun.

As they waited in the hotel apartment which acted as a hideout, Umeadi peeped to ensure that his master's white Mercedes Benz was quite safe.

Their plan soon worked for at about ten minutes to midnight their informant knocked and immediately Umeadi left. He would board the river vessel and make his escape from the evil hands of the law. He was happy as he considered the free life he would live at Nkobu, where no one would know him. He had enough money to play around with before settling down to invest if the need arose.

He was filled with pity for his boss Samson, whose fate hung on a balance. Samson would travel back to Aba to pick up Lizzy before the duo leaves for the Port-Harcourt International Airport on their way to the United States. The risk was inevitable for if Lizzy was caught, the whole plot would blow up.

Samson did not leave Calabar on time. He had changed the plate number of his car and subsequently obtained a fake registration certificate in order to beat any interrogation at the check-points. It was past mid-day by the time Samson left Calabar for Aba.

He had a smooth and uneventful drive to Aba and headed for Jubilee Road to pick up Lizzy as arranged. But Lizzy was no where to be found.

Time was not on his side so he quickly drove away. As he rode towards the garden city of Port-Harcourt, he wondered what he would do with Lizzy's International Passport which was locked up in his brief case.

*   *   *   *   *   *   *

"You will not be allowed to see her today", the nurse said.

"Why?"

"It's just a matter of protocol. She has to undergo some observations as a new patient. We cannot prescribe until all the necessary tests have been carried out."

"Are you sure she is alive?" Anyamba asked.

"She is. But you know she is sick."

"Yes. That was why we brought her here." Nnenna replied.

"That's the doctor's instruction. I will advise that you go home and return tomorrow. The doctor may then be in a better position to talk to you."

"She is my niece. The others can go while I remain till tomorrow. I hope the authorities don't mind. I can make myself comfortable on one of the chairs here", Nnenna again said.

"Sorry madam. We don't allow visitors spend the night here. You know that this is a mental hospital. We also deal with a lot of diverse nervous disorders. Most of the cases are handled with utmost secrecy especially when the relations of the patient insist on that. That is why we do not allow visitors to spend nights within the hospital premises."

Jim understood the nurses sense of reasoning. It was a female ward in the first place so male visitors will definitely be prohibited. He had thought that Nnenna would have succeeded but since she too must leave, there was no need arguing with the nurse. They will all have to go for it was getting late.

Munachi had narrated all that happened. The two incidents at the deserted house at Ulasi Road and the death of the medicine man at Ogbor Hill created no excitement. No questions were asked for everyone's interest was directed towards ensuring that Oguaa received adequate medical attention that would enable her recover quickly from her ailment.

After some deliberations, it was agreed that Anyamba should go back to the village while Munachi should return to Item and inform his people on what had prevailed. Jim would stay with his sister Nnenna at Aba for obvious reasons. He needed to get in touch with Majek or Dotun and explain the development since he left Lagos. His friends in Lagos also had to help deliver some messages to Jim's office since he might have to stay some days longer than the period he had officially asked for.

Jim had noticed that his brother looked pale, weak and worn out, hence advised that Anyamba should not come to Aba the next day.

With the help of Nnenna, Jim hoped they could effectively handle the situation.

*   *   *   *   *   *   *

The delay in getting the Mercedes Benz Car repaired affected Kanu's plan. Had Dozie and his team succeeded in giving the car a new look, he would have hurriedly gone to see his girl friend at Port-Harcourt before undertaking his journey of no return across the country's borders.

He had arrived at the mechanic village the next day only to discover that the engine had been fixed and the car was in perfect working condition. But the colour was still white.

His long stay in the hotel at Owerri had left him almost bankrupt. He needed some money to enable him undertake his trip but his bank was also situated at Port-Harcourt.

Yes. He would abandon the idea of spraying the car and quickly drive to Port-Harcourt and collect some money and also pay his farewell visit to Tonye.

There was no harm in taking the risk as he quickly paid off Dozie for the job so far done and left in his car for Port-Harcourt. He was not aware that the police were on the alert. They were searching for a youngman called Kanu who owns a white Mercedes Benz.

23

It was indeed a long and hectic day. He had been busy supervising the renovation work within the hotel complex. No wonder he needed that peaceful Saturday night's sleep. Nobody disturbed him.

Eno his girl friend was lying by his side. She had come to spend the weekend on Dotun's request. Their relationship was becoming more intimate. She had met Dotun's parents. Although she had not told her own parents, their action indicated that they were aware of their daughter's relationship with the Makanjuola's. Dotun was madly in love with Eno but Eno was not the type of girl who got easily carried away by romantic sentiments. She knew what she wanted but must be careful how she goes about it. She wanted to make sure she was taking a step towards the right direction.

As Dotun lay snoring, Eno was wide awake thinking about this young millionaire in the making, who professes to love her.

Certain questions still made her uncomfortable. But for

the office gossip Biola, she would not have known about the hotel. "Why did Dotun hide such facts from her until she confronted him with the obvious? Was he trying to be modest?" Probably Dotun had a girl friend whom he did not want her to see or know about hence the delay in inviting her to the hotel. This was her second visit since their affair started.

The noise from the telephone disrupted her thoughts. It was very late and who would be calling at such an ungodly hour. She wanted to take the call but hesitated. What if it is one of Dotun's girl friends? Yes. It certainly must be. She had to find out and the best way was to wake up the lover boy and watch him pant as he answered back to the voice that called.

"Hello! Yes. Where are you calling from? Oh! you don't mean it. Well it's the same problem here. You were lucky to have finally got through."

The caller was Jim. He was speaking from Nnenna's residence at Aba. Their discussion was very brief and only succeeded in making Dotun sad. Eno overheard Dotun's answers hence could not help asking some questions.

"He's a very good family friend. Jim by name. He lives here in Lagos but had to travel as a result of some news he received from home".

"I am sorry about your friend. But what is the position as at now? Who is sick?"

Dotun did not know whether it was right to tell Eno the story of Oguaa, Jim's niece. Women no matter their age and experiences are prone to exaggerate issues so he decided not to.

"It's Jim's brother. He underwent some surgery but Jim says he is getting better. Eno, Jim wants me to inform his boss in the office that he will not be coming back on the day he promised. This is due to his brother's health".

"You will do that early Monday morning," Eno said.

"Yes. I should be at Jim's office by eight thirty in the morning".

"Dotun why don't you continue enjoying your sleep? I don't want you to be late for the early morning service tomorrow".

Dotun could sense the cynicism underlying Eno's statement. He had never been an ardent church goer. Not even a nominal Christian. He understood what Eno meant. He had neglected his heart-throb who looked forward to a happy weekend with him. Come Monday, she would go back to the office and probably swear never to come on such a dreary weekend visit again. The hotel job was sapping his energy leaving him with little or not time for fun and relaxation. A brief holiday might help. He would discuss with Eno so that they can travel out together.

Sleep was no longer in sight. The news about Oguaa had unnerved him. He visualised the pathetic and agonizing moments which Jim must be undergoing as a result of Oguaa's condition. The call was brief and the message was loud and clear. He heaved a sigh and stretched his arm to reach out and cuddle Eno. His hand felt an empty bed. He switched on the light and there was Eno at the extreme of the bed. Her face was turned away from his view. Dotun quickly turned the face only to notice that Eno was crying

"What is the matter?"

"Dotun. I am a woman."

Dotun understood. He had to perform his duty as a

man no matter his mood. He must put away the thoughts of Jim and Oguaa and make Eno feel wanted, happy and satisfied. This he did and Eno was grateful.

When Eno woke up at about seven o'clock in the morning, she realised she had missed the six o'clock early morning communion service. She must have a quick bath and dress up in order not to miss the eight thirty Martins.

As she moved toward the bathroom, Dotun woke up and demanded if anything was wrong.

"Sorry to have disturbed your sleep. I had to switch on the light in order to find my way to the bathroom. I am already late for service."

"Why didn't you wake me up. I would have loved to accompany you", Dotun demanded.

Eno knew that Dotun was merely teasing her so she laughed and went into the bathroom. Dotun switched on the radio for he wanted to listen to the seven thirty news.

There was a knock at the door.

He quickly got dressed and on opening the door his sister Doyin was there standing.

"Come in. How is Majek?", Dotun asked.

"I was just returning from service when I decided to check on you. I was at Majek's place yesterday. He told me you would be busy hence I did not call."

Doyin sensed the presence of a visitor but preferred not to ask.

"Have you heard from Jim since he left Lagos?" Dotun asked.

"In fact that is why I am here. Majek complained that Jim had not called too. I wanted to find out if it was the same with you."

"Jim telephoned last night from Aba".

"I thought he went to the village. What is he doing at Aba?" Doyin inquired.

"He is staying with his senior sister."

"Have they found his niece who was supposed to have visited us.?"

"Yes. Oguaa is at Aba. That was why Jim called."

"That girl must be naughty, Dotun. Why did she have to create so much anxiety for everyone by telling her father that she was visiting Lagos?"

Just then the bathroom door opened and Eno emerged fully dressed. Dotun immediately got up as Eno greeted Doyin.

"You never told me you had a visitor", Eno said.

"She is not a visitor. Doyin, this is Eno a friend and Eno, here is my dear sister Doyin. She has just completed her course at the Polytechnic. Eno works with the Albatros Finance Company here in Lagos."

The two ladies exchanged pleasantries. Doyin could not hide her admiration for Eno was indeed a pretty lady. Their discussion was very brief. Eno was already late for her church service but promised to come back as soon as the service was over.

"Brother Dotun. Another prey has fallen into your trap, so the sowing of wild oats continues."

"You are wrong this time Doyin. I am really serious about that lady. I think we may make the relationship a permanent one this time."

"The same old story. Come into my parlour says the spider to the fly."

"Not the same story. I am sure I have at last made my choice. Papa and Mama have met her and I think they equally approve."

"So I am the last to know?"

"You are not dear sister. You remember the story of Florence Nightingale, the lady with the lamp?"

That's history of civilization", Doyin replied.

"Well, history has changed my life for the better. That lady who left here some minutes ago is my Florence Nightingale. She nursed me during my stay in the hospital and after my discharge from the sick bed."

"I didn't know you were interested in nurses."

"I have never been, Doyin".

"A day, they say begins a story. Eno had made you change your impressions about nurses".

"Eno is not a nurse Doyin. She is a Confidential Secretary. I remember saying that she works with the Albatros Finance Company."

"I see. Well I am only trying to find out if Jim has called. So why don't you tell me about that?"

Since the telephone message was brief, Dotun was also brief in telling his sister the pathetic news about Oguaa, her mental state and how she finally ended up in a psychiatric home.

Doyin was a good listener. The story sounded like a fairy tale but it was real. She wondered how Majek would take the news.

"Maybe it is better if he is kept in the dark".

As she rose to leave, she pleaded that Dotun should not tell Majek Oguaa's story. She did not say why and her big brother did not demand an explanation.

* * * * * * *

The traffic on Sundays was unusually light so it did not take Jim and Nnenna a long time to arrive at the mental Hospital. There was no protocol for the doctor had already informed nurses to allow Nnenna see Oguaa. Jim was not allowed but rather the doctor instructed that he should see him as soon as he arrived.

Oguaa's eyes were shut when her aunt entered. Nnenna asked the nurse if there was any improvement.

The nurse assured her that Oguaa had been of good behaviour. Her hysterical utterances had been reduced to occasional murmuring and a few hallucinations. At least that was a good sign as the doctor said.

She was an experienced nurse having worked in the hospital for over seven years. She had seen many cases and she felt Oguaa's transition overnight was a remarkable medical feat.

Nnenna was excited over the good news. She wanted to ask more questions but she did not want to disturb the sick lady. She would ask her questions later.

As the nurse and Nnenna were leaving the special ward where the patient lay, Oguaa opened her eyes. Nnenna stopped and quitely moved towards her niece. Both aunt and niece stared at each other until Nnenna called Oguaa by name. She asked her how she was feeling. The sick girl just stared. It was too early to draw any conclusions so Nnenna left with the nurse.

Jim had been discussing with the doctor while Nnenna was seeing Oguaa. The doctor had assured Jim that the hospital was capable of handling Oguaa's case. Jim had pleaded that the doctor try all within his reach to ensure that his niece was cured. Finance, he emphasized should never deter him from giving the sick lady the best of medical attention. Jim had even continued by saying that if the situation was a hopeless one, he would be prepared to pay for the sick lady to be flown abroad.

To all these, the doctor affirmed that the situation was within his medical realm and God's mercy.

However, the doctor had invited Jim as a result of the telephone message which came from the police station. The Divisional Police Officer had requested to see Jim or Nnenna.

"What for doctor?" Jim demanded.

"I don't know but there was a note of urgency in his demand to see you."

"Thank you. I shall leave now doctor. Please don't forget our discussion. That sick lady means a lot to the entire family."

Nnenna was sitting by the door which led to the doctor's office when Jim came out.

"What did the doctor say, Jim?"

"There's no time to waste aunty. The DPO wants to see us immediately."

Nnenna hastened to catch up with Jim's giant strides as the latter hurried towards his car.

*   *   *   *   *   *   *

"Are you sure your friend's niece is not on drugs?"

"No, mama. Oguaa would never have done that. I know that girl. She hardly tasted anything alcoholic when she visited us."

"Don't say so my son. No one can trust these modern girls. Their sense of adventure is so absurd that the mere thought of what some of them venture into makes me shrink".

"I don't know what might have been responsible for this unfortunate incident."

"Take it easy my son. I wish I had known about it before now. Perhaps I would have advised that they first trace the source of her ailment before taking her to the hospital."

"What do you mean, Papa?"

"You are too young to understand my son. There are enemies everywhere. The world is full of people who do not like one another. Remember my son, I was a customs officer. I don't need to narrate the terrible experiences I witnessed. Many of them led to untimely deaths. Others left their victims partially or totally paralysed while some victims eventually ended up as lunatics. All these my son are not mere coincidence. They are the handiwork of some evil forces".

Throughout the night Jim had been trying to reach Majek on the phone. In the morning when he eventually got through, there was no reply. He decided to call at the Makanjuola's family house and luck was on his side because Majek answered. Doyin had gone to church. Both parents were at home. They overheard their son's conversation and had inquired what was the matter.

Majek had told them the pathetic story which the caller from Aba had just narrated. Oguaa's story thus became the subject of the family discussion. But that was not long for as soon as Doyin came back from church, the family changed the topic. Nobody especially Majek wanted Doyin to hear the news.

* * * * * * *

When Jim and Nnenna arrived at the Police Station, Superintendent Yusuf was about going out. He however came out of his vehicle when he saw Jim and Nnenna. Jim apologised for the delay in attending to Yusuf's urgent call.

Yusuf accepted the apology but there was no time for long discussion for two police vehicles were already set to move out of the premises.

The Superintendent briefly explained that he was on his way to investigate the information he received the previous night. There has been an accident along the Port-Harcourt-Aba road in which a white Mercedes Benz Car was involved. The driver of the car died on the spot and his corpse had been deposited at the Obigbo General Hospital Mortuary.

Lizzy was in the second police vehicle. If the corpse is identified to be Kanu's then the mystery surrounding Oguaa's ailment was on its way towards being solved.

"I would like to accompany you sir", Jim pleaded.

"That wouldn't be necessary since we have Lizzy to help identify the car and corpse", Yusuf said.

Jim is not a man who easily gives up. He wanted to join the police squad in the trip to Port-Harcourt. The DPO noticed his anxiety and finally obliged him. Nnenna would however stay and take care of Oguaa.

A twenty-five minutes drive took the squad to the Obigbo Police Station where the accident vehicle had been parked. As soon as Lizzy saw the battered Mercedes Benz Car, she knew that the corpse lying in the mortuary was Kanu's. With tears and great pain she hinted the DPO on her observation.

The mortuary was filled with many corpses each glued to the other like a pack of imported frozen fish. The police demanded for the corpse of the accident victim which was brought in early that morning. It was easy for the body was only stiff and not yet frozen.

It was Lizzy who froze. It was not Kanu's but the lifeless body of her benefactor. As she was led out of the mortuary, she continued to bewail and openly cursed the twist of fate that had snatched Samson and handed him over to the cruel hands of death.

Yusuf shook his head. He was disappointed. Who was Samson? The mystery was getting deeper. Lizzy certainly had more skeletons in her cupboard. The DPO was worried. He thought he had all the cards but the mortuary scene had revealed that Lizzy still held on to the joker.

*   *   *   *   *   *   *

Since Anyamba returned from Aba, Mary had been on her guard. She inquired about her daughter but the much she received was a direct reply that Oguaa had been admitted and was receiving treatment at the Mental Hospital. Her husband had asked for some food which he ate to Mary's satisfaction before retiring into his bedroom.

Nothing happened until the next day which was a Sunday.

Chinwe and her junior brothers had gone to church service leaving their parents at home. Mary was surprised that her husband never discussed Oguaa nor did he indicate an intention to revisit Aba. She dared not ask any question for fear of the consequences. Her fears were further confirmed when she realised that Adaugo and Nwayieze had not come back to get the whole details from her husband. Why was everybody being very evasive? Something must be wrong so she too had to be careful.

Chinwe came in at about three o'clock in the afternoon. She greeted her parents and went to the backyard to see if there was any food to eat. Mary followed her.

"Where are your brothers?" She asked Chinwe.

"They refused to come with me when the Sunday School Session was over. Mama I was hungry so I left them to continue playing their game of football."

"And why didn't you wash up the breakfast plates before leaving for service?"

"Mama. I asked Lucky to do the washing. At my age I don't think I should be doing all the household chores while Lucky and Ofor do nothing."

"You are a silly girl. So you now want to compare yourself with the boys?"

"I know you will support them Mama. Now that Sister Oguaa is away; I don't have anybody to be on my side."

"You are just lazy Chinwe. Why do you need someone to support you.?"

"Lucky and Ofor used to do the washing. Since you drove Oguaa away, my brothers have refused to do anything. The whole work now rests on me."

Mary was surprised when her daughter accused her of driving Oguaa away.

"Who told you that I drove your sister away? Were you not the one who informed us that Oguaa had left for Aba?"

"Yes, mother. That was why I said you drove her away.

Why mama? Why did you have to send her to stay with sister Loretta and her parents? Were you ashamed of having her stay with us because her Principal suspended her from school? After all mama….."

Chinwe could not finish that statement for she suddenly held on to her stomach. She felt a slight pain around her groins but managed not to let out any cry of anguish. Her mother was surprised and moved nearer her daughter. Chinwe was equally surprised for part of the dress which covered the mid section of her body was soaked in red.

"Mama. I have hurt myself. There is blood all over my dress."

Mary knew what was happening. She called her daughter and quietly led her into her own room. Nnenna was right. She had failed in her duties as a mother. Here was Chinwe growing into womanhood. Yes. Her daughter was having her first monthly cycle and the little girl did not know.

Yes. Nnenna was right.

24

His bank transaction at Port-Harcourt was swift. He had enough money to see him through his journey. He was happy to see Tonye although his girl friend was sad when he told her he had some business deal to execute in Kano and would not be back till the upper week. He spent a long time with Tonye and did not leave Port-Harcourt until twilight. His car was in perfect condition hence he did not anticipate any fears driving at night.

Kanu did not encounter any check points as he drove through the express road that linked the garden city of Port-Harcourt with the coal city of Enugu.

When he arrived Enugu, he did not know which of the routes would facilitate his journey. He wanted to travel through Jos from where he would go to Markurdi and finally go over to the Republic of Chad.

However he was apprehensive of this route. Chad would not be a safe place to seek asylum since the country had been engaged in a civil war – a war which had led to the influx of many Chadian Nationals into Nigeria - that route would certainly pose some problems so he abandoned the idea of going to Chad.

Cameroun was ruled out since he suspected it would be Umeadi's destination. He would not want to compound the issues of two fugitives staying in the same country. Yes, he would go to the Republic of Niger. He knew the route very well so there would be no need getting to Jos. His trip would take him through Kafanchan, Katangora, Pambegua and Nguru, from where he would escape into the Francophone country of Niger.

As soon as the first cock crew, Kanu left Enugu enroute Kafanchan. He was actually enjoying his journey as he listened to the melodious tunes that came from the cassette player compartment of his car.

At Kafanchan, he bought a lot of fruits by the roadside market. He was not hungry despite the fact it was mid-day. He was indeed too excited to think of food. The fruits would do hence there was no need wasting his precious time for meals at a roadside restaurant or hotel.

At Kagoro, he filled his tank at a petrol station and continued his journey. At about three o' clock in the afternoon, he was on his way to Pambegua. He soon felt tired and uncomfortable.

His tommy was rumbling. Too much fruits he supposed. He felt the urge to answer the call of nature. Pambegua was still some hundred kilometres away, so Kanu carefully packed his car and decided to ease himself in a nearby savannah bush.

*   *   *   *   *   *   *

When the disappointed police returned to Aba, Jim left

for Nnenna's house. Like the Superintendent, Jim was equally worried. Lizzy's utterance had opened the Pandora's box and the discovery of her passport, among the items in the accident vehicle, had convinced the Divisional Police Officer that Lizzy was indeed a hardened criminal. He would leave no stone unturned in order to get the entire story from this pretty lady who was indeed the most deceptive character he had encountered since he joined the police force. Kanu was still at large and probably there were more individuals whom Lizzy had not disclosed to the police. Superintendent Yusuf ordered that Lizzy be sent back to the cell and never to be interrogated until he ordered.

Jim narrated all that took place at the Obigbo Police Station and the Mortuary at the General Hospital. Nnenna was amazed. The incident was more than a case of mistaken identity. It was indeed the hand of providence for in a bid to track down a criminal, another criminal had been found. At least the numerical strength of the syndicate had been reduced by one.

"Aunty", Jim called.

"Yes".

"Do you remember the Mercedes car we saw at the mechanic village when we went to service my car?"

"I do. What about that?" Nnenna inquired.

"I have been doing some thinking. You remember the owner of the car?"

"You mean that gentleman who was quarrelling with Dozie and Madam Ezechi. What about him?"

"Aunty. You remember his insisting that he wanted his car be given a new coat of paint?"

"Look Jim I don't know what you are driving at. Do you

suspect that the man may be the criminal that the police are looking for?"

"I have the feeling, aunty. That car was new and needed no spraying. Why should the owner insist on changing the colour? I am of the opinion that the man was up to something strange."

"Well, it will be wrong for us to start suspecting anybody who owns a Mercedes Benz Car. We are bound to embarrass quite a lot of people and I don't think they will take kindly to it", Nnenna advised.

Nnenna was right but Jim felt there was nothing wrong in trying. Dozie and his cousin Udoka would be of help. If he failed, he would at least have convinced himself that he did try.

There was enough time to drive from Aba to the mechanic village at Owerri. On getting there, he saw Dozie and Udoka. The Mercedes Benz Car was not there. When he inquired about the car, and its owner, Dozie explained that the owner was too impatient and could not wait for the car to be given a new coat of paint. Unfortunately neither Dozie nor Udoka knew the name of the owner nor the vehicle number.

For Jim it was a sad affair. He had his conviction that the owner may not be innocent. He also had his fears that he might have been making some fruitless efforts to embarrass an innocent and law-abiding citizen. He immediately left the workshop for Umuayalu. He had to see his brother Anyamba.

*　　*　　*　　*　　*　　*　　*

The old man and his grandson could not explain the presence of a white Mercedes Benz Car parked by the road side close to the footpath that led to their millet farm. It was early morning and they wondered where the owner of the car was or what he could be doing within the farm-lands. However one thing was certain. The owner was somewhere around.

Their guess was right for no sooner had the old man and his young companion walked into the footpath than they saw a figure lying helplessly in the bush. The little boy was afraid. He wanted to run away but the old man cautioned that he stayed by. As they moved closer to the figure, they realised that the figure was a fine gentle man. He was half naked and beside him lay a pair of trousers and another pair of underwears.

The figure moved as it sensed the presence of some human beings. Yes he was alive. His eyes were open but he could not speak. He seemed to be in great pain for he was pointing at his left leg which he could hardly move.

"What do we do grandpa?"

The old man spoke to the figure but the latter could not reply.

"It seems the man is hurt. He needs some assistance but we cannot help him. I am not strong enough and you are too small my son."

"Shall I go back to the road and get some help grandpa?"

"That's the only thing we can do my son."

While the little boy went in search of help, the old man moved closer and examined the left leg of the stranger. There were lots of blood on the leg which suggested that the man must have been bleeding. Who knows how long?

The old man also noticed a little open wound on the leg from where the blood did flow. He gave a slight nod for he understood. But time was fast running out and he wondered what could be the cause of delay in getting some help.

The little boy saw three uniformed men standing by a

government van. They were busy enjoying the local cereal drink popularly known as "Fura de nunu". When the boy realised that the men did not understand the language he spoke, he beckoned at them to follow him to the bush.

Kanu could not still utter a word as he was lifted from the bush and carried into the government van. However he gave a nod when asked if the Mercedes Benz belonged to him.

The men were indeed immigration officers who were on their way to the border towns on some official assignment. One of them drove Kanu's car while the other two rode with Kanu in the government van.

The old man and his grandson bluntly refused to accompany the men. Since the officers could not communicate effectively with the two villagers, they left them.

As the immigration officers drove away, the old man who had seen Kanu's wound shook his head and sadly exlaimed:

"Kai! Gobe de Nisa". The officers who did not understand the man drove away. Any nearby hospital or clinic would be able to take care of their patient.

*   *   *   *   *   *   *

It was almost midnight. Anyamba had long retired to bed but Mary and Jim still discussed.

"You said Oguaa would be cured?"

"I didn't say so. The doctor did", Jim replied.

"But how was my daughter before you left?"

"She was fine. At least so the doctor said", Jim again replied.

Mary was not satisfied with Jim's answers which bordered on what the doctor said. She would like to travel and see her daughter. At least to know the true situation.

But she had two problems. She was afraid as to how Anyamba would react over such a suggestion. She also dreaded confronting her sister-in-law who was now taking care of Oguaa in the hospital.

As Mary weighed the situations in her mind, Jim was thinking about the white Mercedes Benz car which he saw at the mechanic village. He wondered why the car and its owner were becoming an obsession to him. Try as much as he could, the memory of the scene lingered in his mind.

When Mary called him to ask another question, she discovered that Jim was asleep. She dared not wake him for it would soon be the dawn of another day. She quietly got up and joined her husband in bed. Jim lay snoring on the couch in the sitting room.

*   *   *   *   *   *   *

The hospital authorities in Zonkwa worked all day to save the life of the patient who was brought in by some immigration officers. The patient could hardly speak so it was difficult knowing exactly what was responsible for his deplorable condition. However based on the rather vague information given by the officials, they were able to administer some medication.

The fever soon subsided and the patient slept peacefully until the morning of the next day. When the immigration officials called in the afternoon to find out how the patient was responding to treatment, the doctor told them that the patient died at about nine o' clock in the morning.

Call it nemesis. Call it the law of Karma. Call it retributive justice, fate or destiny, one thing stands out clear. Kanu was bitten by a rare species of snake that resides among the rocky terrains of the Northern Savannah belt.

"Gobe de Nisa", as the old man muttered, literally means "Tomorrow is too far". The old man knew that the patient who was being taken away to the hospital would not live long. The venom which the reptile injects into its victim is so poisonous that death is always the resultant effect.

The police were alerted and soon the news reached Superintendent Yusuf Meriga at the Central Police Station, Aba. Lizzy travelled to Zonkwa and identified the corpse. Kanu's driving licence which was found in the car lent more credence to Lizzy's assertion. But Yusuf was still worried. Was Kanu the last in the list? Only Lizzy knew the answer.

25

The traditional solemnization ceremony between Eno and Dotun took place seven weeks after Jim returned to Lagos from his village. The first two weeks after his journey were traumatic. He could hardly concentrate at work. At night he suffered from nightmares and often woke up with severe headache and general body weakness. These occurrence could be attributed to anxiety for all his trips to see his doctor did not help. Worse still he could not get through to his sister Nnenna at Aba. The telephone lines were obviously faulty. The headache persisted until he received a letter from his brother Anyamba. This letter explained the circumstances under which Kanu, another member of the syndicate had been apprehended as well as Lizzy's verdict that Kanu now deceased, was the last member of the gang. Anyamba's letter also talked about Oguaa's discharge from the hospital. To Anyamba, his daughter's speedy recovery was a feat which was achieved by both medical and divine intervention. When Oguaa was discharged from the Mental hospital, Nnenna had insisted that she stayed at Aba rather than go to the village. Mary had consented since she had now made up with her sister-in-law. Anyamba however disagreed but when Nnenna offered some explanations like the need for thorough medical check up and the provision of a regular balanced diet for Oguaa at least for some time, Anyamba had agreed.

Ironically, Mary did not want Oguaa to stay at Aba. To her, the city held a lot of unpleasant memories. Inwardly, she felt that Nnenna had not forgiven her. However, Oguaa and her mother spent only two weeks at Aba before returning to Umuayalu. The whole family had gathered at the request of Anyamba. Almost everybody heeded the call. Munachi had arrived a day before the august meeting. His wife Agnes had refused to stay at Item as her husband had advised. This act would have turned into a row but for the intervention of Munachi's father.

"Why are you being selfish my son. Let your wife accompany you to see her people. Or are you ashamed to walk with a woman who has slowly lost her virginity?" Munachi's father teased.

"Of course not Papa. It's just that I wouldn't want my Agnes to undertake such a long journey in her state. She can travel later."

"You young men are cowards. Your wife is strong. You are lucky that she did not mess up your room with her spittle and vomit. Most women are very prone to such disgusting occurrences during pregnancy. Go with your wife and thank our ancestors who have admired your patience and eventually terminated your anxiety."

Captain Obioha also came along with his wife Martina and their children. Agne's two elder sisters Ijeoma and Iwemdi also arrived to answer the call. These two daughters of

Nwanyieze had travelled all the way from the north. They rarely came home. In fact, since they got married before the war and left with their husbands for the Northern part of the country, they had only visited home once during one of the annual yam festivals. Anyamba's compound was teeming with men, women and children both young and old.

Nneji, Udoka, Lucky and Ofor were busy trying to organise the compound so that everybody would be comfortably accommodated. As they worked tirelessly, their little nephews and nieces joined them. It was indeed a family reunion. As the sun was setting and the moon began to show its rays, the family sat under the Udala tree and discussed.

Before he left for Aba in company of his uncle's wives Nwayieze and Adaugo, Jim had called his brother and asked the whereabouts of Lizzy.

"Lizzy's case is an enigma, my dear brother. The police authorities are still keeping her in their custody. I cannot tell you her fate but may be Nnenna will know more", Anyamba concluded.

Jim did not ask further. As he drove off with his aunts, they met Oguaa and Loretta. Jim stopped.

"Uncle. Where are you going to? Can we come along?" Oguaa enthused.

"No my dear. Just stay at home. We will soon be back", answered Jim.

"Good afternoon uncle Jim and thank you for everything", Loretta said.

"And thank you too for being a wonderful friend," Jim added.

*   *   *   *   *   *

The party organised at Aba was a huge success. According to Superintendent Yusuf Meriga, Lizzy may be temporarily transferred to the remand home pending court prosecution. She had undergone a series of interrogation but the police boss still felt that some hidden revelations will emanate from this mysterious teenager. Time, Yusuf affirmed would be the only rescue factor towards solving Lizzy's case.

Jim spent a night at Aba after the party and left for Lagos in company of Doyin and Majek who flew into Aba to honour Jim's invitation. Dotun and his new bride Eno were also in attendant. Jim who needed company had pleaded that Majek and his sister accompany him by road. Doyin who was making her first journey to the East convinced her brother for she wanted to take in more of the beautiful green scenery which the eastern sector provided. The journey would also provide her the long awaited opportunity of knowing Jim's village.

*　　*　　*　　*　　*　　*　　*

The large hall was filled with people from all walks of life. For Oguaa, these people seemed to mingle with ghostly figures. She looked to her side. There was her mother Mary beaming with smiles at every joke. She was particularly happy having finally effected a reconciliation with her sister-in-law. Thanks to Jim.

Anyamba sat beside his wife. His mood could aptly be described as joyous. But with it were flighty memories. His daughter was alive. She had been saved from an untimely death by the hands of providence. What other occasion could call for such a celebration. It was like the biblical feast of the Passover. He had fought gallantly and won the duel. He could well be on his way to the promised land.

Umeadi had sworn that he would one day return to his roots. Experience has taught him that life in a strange land can be trying for a fugitive. He did make it as a renowned industrialist. But the fact that he is a fugitive, having fled his father-land on the basis of criminal tendencies still haunted him like a vengeful ghost. Political upheavals, economic depression, world-wide global recession, natural disasters and the fear of possible detection were enough traumatic convulsions that were mind bending and gave him jitters. Yes, he would one day return to see his friends and family. This was however an illusion, for there will be no friendly faces to see.

> *The ground was so quick and swift,*
> *The wind blew,*
> *Then was thunder and lightening,*
> *Came rain in torrents,*
> *So devastating was the flood,*
> *So quick and swept away sands,*
> *Pains and agonies supervened,*
> *My daughter Oguaa, was in it,*
> *Suddenly all of us were involved,*
> *But for Divine Providence.*

Like a sage Anyamba recited as he narrated Oguaa's story to the whole kindred. Most of them especially those who already knew the story listened with the intention of getting more details. To those who were completely in the dark, the whole story sounded like a fairy tale. But it did happen.

Nnenna darted about attending to everybody's needs. No one would suspect that the ageing lady had so much strength in her reserve. Superintendent Yusuf Meriga could not hide his admiration for his ebullient Celina. To him she was a war heroine, a living legend.

Eno was aloof though she observed with suppressed delight the witty banter that transpired between her husband Dotun and her brother-in-law Majek. She could play a better matchmaker than Doyin if given the opportunity. Afterall Oguaa's regal disposition was disarming. But she was not privy to what transpired and had eventually triggered off this festive occasion.

Nwayieze and Adaugo were busy supervising the cooking in the courtyard. For Nwayieze the celebration provided her the singular and rare opportunity to show off her three happily married daughters Iwemdi, Ijeoma and Agnes. Her joy knew no bounds as her grand-children hovered around her. She did not mind.

Munachi fussed over his beloved Agnes who was now heavy with child. Patience is a virtue which Lizzy ignored. Twins are rare gifts which are highly cherished within our traditional set up. Captain Obioha and Martina relished in their harbingers of good luck. Ure never found her lost love in the custody of Amosu. The life of a lunatic is the life of a broken chinaware. The glittering debris can only be appreciated as a once cherished treasure.

Anyamba intoned a tune and then, the entire crowd joined him:

> *My life is built on nothingness,*
> *Than Jesus blood and righteousness,*
> *I dare not trust the sweetest frame,*
> *But wholly lean on Jesus' name*
> *On Christ the solid rock I stand;*
> *All other ground is sinking sand.*
> *All other ground is quick sand.*

Oguaa

Now I know

As I lounge here in this soft sofa and listen distraitly to the twitter of the birds outside, I know the heart of the matter. As I watch with disinterest, the splendour of the morning sun as its gentle rays filter into the silent parlour, a beam of understanding envelopes my ignorance. I watch with wry amusement the crooked contest of two bloated cockroaches as they scratch across the hard bare floor. An adjoining door is opened and shut somewhat brusquely. The floor vibrates and the startled cockroaches scurry for cover. I quietly suppressed the tinkling beginnings of a laughter. I snuggle up myself in the sofa and train my eyes on the soft filtering rays of the sun that scatter patches of light on my face. Indeed, I know now.

The brightest lights promise the darkest hours.

The widest roads lead to the precipice of doom. I now know. The giddiness of the wine of indulgence has left my head. Now I know better. The scales that blinkered my eyes have all vanished. Now I see even beyond the dark clustering clouds. My ears which were clogged with the wool of coquetry now hear even the whisper of leaves.

My father, Anyamba, would hear no better. I think he knows now. I think the truth of that has since overwhelmed him. Even my mother Mary, who as women do, has wide receptive ears to glean all village gossip, is now no match for my ears. With lewd Lizzy, my ears only heard and understood the language of harlotry and pig-headedness. With Majek and that randy crowd of perverted people, one could not have heard anything but the hum and buzz of the fast sleazy life. But thank God, that's all written off as obituaries now.

Obituaries are not particularly animating. Some people who have pretensions to philosophy may want to hand out long-winded lectures on the essence of life, of living, of dying. But I hardly countenance such bigoted stuff. For me, an obituary is nothing but what it is-a corpse that belongs to yesterday.

If my odious attitudes, aspirations and belief systems of yesterday become obituaries of today, I do not want to mull over them. I shut them resolutely into the grave yard of yesterday. I savour my rebirth like a snake slipping out of an old skin. Obituaries like Lizzy, Kanu and that horrid fettish man called Nwaonuma with Samson and his ban of depraved friends do not live in my today.

Now I know better

Yesterday, I walked in the delusive glare of lights. I walked on roads so wide. I thought that narrow roads were an aberration. Yes, I walked in the glare of bright lights and the assurance of wide roads. Before I knew it, the bright lights became dense darkness and the wide roads ended at a precipice.

The life of a lunatic is like that of a broken chinaware. Ask Ogele, the village crank of Umuayalu. You may not elicit any coherent response from him, but his mere presence alone – the weirdness of it – overstates the lucid metaphor of a broken chinaware. In many curious ways, my life yesterday was like that of a lunatic, of a broken chinaware. Yesterday, I was mad. The madness of mad lust. I could not be persuaded or pampered into sanity.

The life of a lust-mad young woman is like a broken chinaware. You could not find the person you thought you had known all your life. A broken chinaware is less than an apology. A total somewhat tipsy stranger crawls out of the debris of a broken chinaware. My shadow as well trailed out of existence. The broken chinaware leaves the original person in splinters. As a broken chinaware, like Ogele the village loony, my being became strange splinters of anonymity.

Because of this, my childhood friend and confidante, Loretta, lost me. Poor soul. She did not know I had become a broken chinaware, like the village wag, Ogele.

Even my father, Anyamba was stunned to encounter a sudden total stranger in me.

Everybody who knew and loved me regarded me as a jig-saw puzzle. First they were surprised. But this later gave way to exasperation and finally revulsion. I repulsed everybody at sight.

I was claimed by the bright city lights of Lagos, Port-Harcourt and Aba - those cities where male wolves devoured bland-eyed innocent village girls. Cities that pulsated with sex, money and power. The cities devoured me consummately. They ravished me. Devastated me. Nothing remained of me. Even my very shadow abdicated. I lost my essence and chastity to the lure of bright city lights and the human hounds who go by the name men. To these hounds, I became a sweet orange to be mercilessly sucked and then thrown contemptuously into the nearest trash heap. I became only a crust, a crest-fallen shell.

The very sand I had hoped would prop up my feet began to sink before my eyes. It was the kind of sand I thought had been propping up Lizzy in her lustful escapades. I was so sure of those sands that I rebelled against everything that was chaste and sublime. But I was almost swept away by the huge swirling waves of reality. I was painfully bogged down in the quick sands of blithering idiocy.

But suddenly, mercifully, the mist cleared. And I struggled violently against the quick sands that have been holding my limbs hostage. I struggled with a superhuman effort and God saved me. With one mighty leap, I jumped free of the quick sands. I was no longer a prisoner of that mad, unbridled lust. *I am free. I am free,* I practically yelled with glee, and looked back ruefully. I had almost snuffed out my life. The mist cleared. The city light I thought looked so bright had suddenly become drenched in darkness. The wide smooth roads that beckoned to me so reassuringly have suddenly become cobbled with brambles and broken bottles.

But I know better now. I see clearly now. I hear every sound now, even the quiet whisper of the leaves. My father's admonishing voice in the distance now pierces my ears like the blast of a bugle. The voice of my mother is now a symphony of insistent sirens. Only a lunatic ignores the blast of a bugle and the shrill song of sirens. Ogele, the Umuayalu Village wag would promptly ignore it. But I am not Ogele. I am Oguaa. Ogele's life is still like a broken chinaware. But my broken chinaware is now an obituary. I am no longer a being dissipated in splinters.

My anonimity has been annulled. I am now an animated snake slipping out of its old shrivelled skin. I am Oguaa. The Oguaa of Loretta's dreams.

I am now the knowing Oguaa.

I survived the treachery of the quick sands. I now stand sturdily on faithful sands. The quick sands can no longer conspire with the bright city lights and beckoning wide roads to egg me on to destruction. I can now plant fresh seeds in the ravaged soils of my life, seed that will bloom to the fulfilment of flowers.

Anyamba my father has drunk this truth to the dregs. My mother Mary is drunk with this truth. Loretta has savoured the sweetness of this truth. The Umuayalu's caught in the throes of this truth, all confer in quiet startled tones in the recesses of their dim-lit huts over frothing kegs of amazing palmwine.

The ecstatic bird that flew with lustful wildness unto the amorous arms of the wind has returned penitent without the wind and straightened by its solitude and convictions. I am now Oguaa. I am that bird.

They all know.